Praise for *Familia*

"A masterfully woven tale [...] reconciliation, and fami... love."
—**Abby Jimenez**, *New York Times* **bestselling author of** *Yours Truly*

"Lauren Rico's *Familia* has it all: An old crime, unsuspecting victims, a genetic mystery that will explode a family, the enormous tenderness of desperate parents. By page 30, I would have walked on coals to finish reading this story."
—**Jacquelyn Mitchard**, *New York Times* **bestselling author of** *The Deep End of the Ocean*

"*Familia* is an absolute delight. I couldn't stop turning the pages—I needed to know what both the past and the future held for these sisters and how they would put together the pieces of the events that separated them to make their family whole again."
—**KJ Dell'Antonia**, *New York Times* **bestselling author of** *The Chicken Sisters*

"A moving story about the bonds of sisterhood and unraveling the mysteries of your past. I truly enjoyed going on this journey with Isabella and Gabby. A wonderful debut!"
—**Annette Chavez Macias**, **bestselling author of** *Big Chicas Don't Cry*

"A page-turning story of family lost and found, wrapped in the tangled threads of an engaging mystery, and sprinkled with just a bit of Sazón, I loved everything about this modern yet timeless book."
—**Ann Dávila Cardinal, author of** *The Storyteller's Death*

"*Familia* is a compelling and emotional narrative that explores a past wrapped in secrets, the bonds of sisterhood, and what it means to be family. With twists that unfold in every chapter, Lauren E. Rico crafts a compulsive story with engaging characters that hooked me from the start. Gabby and Isabella will stay with you long after you finish the last page. This is a must-read!"
—Kerry Lonsdale, *Wall Street Journal*
and *Washington Post* bestselling author

"*Familia* is a novel of robust joy. The story spills off the page in a rush of emotion that makes you feel like you've been on the journey of a lifetime. Simply marvelous!"
—Amy T. Matthews, author of *Someone Else's Bucket List*

"Rico dazzles with a surprising story of the pleasures and pitfalls of amateur genealogy. . . . Rico perfectly portrays the possible sisters' fraught relationship through a series of surprising twists and turns. This skillful tale enchants."
—*Publishers Weekly* on *Familia*

Dear Reader,

If you're anything like me, you enjoy tucking into a good true crime series. I'm fascinated by the way law enforcement use a combination of forensic science and good old "gum shoe" detective work to reverse-engineer their way to suspects, evidence, and motives. Of special interest to me are the cases where people simply disappear, never to be heard from again. I think what I find so compelling about these stories are the loved ones who are left behind—the ones who are doomed to spend the rest of their days living in that hellish space of "not knowing."

Still, so many never stop looking, hoping, loving. They never give up even as the years go by. Even as the world keeps on spinning.

It was in this concept that I found the inspiration for *After the Ocean*.

When Paul, Emilia's husband of two days, goes missing she has so no idea what's happened—nor does she have the luxury of sticking around to find out. Later, as the decades pass, even while she builds a new life, he has been enshrined in her heart—a perfectly preserved specter of the sweet twenty-two-year-old cellist she can't bring herself to stop loving.

Not that her daughters know this about her. As far as they're concerned, she's just a piano-teaching, cookie-baking PTA mom who couldn't possibly understand what it is to be a woman in the modern world. But isn't that the way it is with parents and children? I think daughters have an especially difficult time appreciating their mothers' perspectives until much later when the black-and-white thinking of youth has been tempered by time and life experience. And by then it may—or may not—be too late.

Perhaps it's regret over my own youthful—and not so youthful—transgressions, but I think everyone deserves a chance to go back and "make it right." So much so that it's a common theme in all my stories. Because, once again, our lives are not black-and-white. Nor are the people who populate them. If we're lucky we change and grow. And if we're strong we can find a way past stubborn pride to right the wrongs of the past. Especially when those wrongs are of our own making.

I hope you enjoy *After the Ocean*, a story of love and redemption that's threaded with a little magic and a lot of music.

With all my very best wishes,
Lauren

Also by Lauren E. Rico

Familia

After the Ocean

Lauren E. Rico

KENSINGTON
PUBLISHING CORP.

kensingtonbooks.com

Content warning: Discussions of sexual assault, molestation, and grooming. Depictions of violence, incarceration, traumatic brain injury, and gaslighting.

KENSINGTON BOOKS are published by
Kensington Publishing Corp.
900 Third Avenue
New York, NY 10022

Copyright © 2025 by Lauren E. Rico

All rights reserved. No part of this book may be reproduced in any form or by any means without the prior written consent of the Publisher, excepting brief quotes used in reviews.

All Kensington titles, imprints, and distributed lines are available at special quantity discounts for bulk purchases for sales promotion, premiums, fund-raising, educational, or institutional use.

This book is a work of fiction. Names, characters, businesses, organizations, places, events, and incidents either are the product of the author's imagination or are used fictitiously. Any resemblance to actual persons, living or dead, events, or locales is entirely coincidental.

To the extent that the image or images on the cover of this book depict a person or persons, such person or persons are merely models, and are not intended to portray any character or characters featured in the book.

Special book excerpts or customized printings can also be created to fit specific needs. For details, write or phone the office of the Kensington Sales Manager: Kensington Publishing Corp., 900 Third Avenue, New York, NY 10022. Attn. Sales Department. Phone: 1-800-221-2647.

Kensington and the K logo Reg. U.S. Pat. & TM Off.

ISBN: 978-1-4967-4467-8 (ebook)

ISBN: 978-1-4967-4466-1

First Kensington Trade Paperback Printing: January 2025

10 9 8 7 6 5 4 3 2 1

Printed in the United States of America

For Nika . . . and Lisa.
I'm so grateful for you both.

After the Ocean

PROLOGUE

PAUL

Thirty Years Ago

Paul was falling, the rush of warm, moist air causing his untucked shirt to billow out around him. His hair whipped around his head, delivering tiny, stinging slaps across his eyes, nose, and mouth. By far, the worst was the sound—equal parts whistle, wail, and roar—so loud that he wished he could move his hands to cover his ears. But his limbs were useless, pinned heavily against his body as he tumbled.

They say when death is imminent, your life flashes before your eyes—a torrent of images that span from cradle to grave, streaming across your mind's eye like a video stuck on fast forward. But the only picture filling Paul's field of vision was her face—every arch and plane, curve and dip memorized long ago. It had—*she*—had taken his breath away four years ago when she'd walked into their freshman Music Theory class at the conservatory. He had known even then that he'd marry her. And he had. Not forty-eight hours ago, they'd stood, hand in hand, on a white, sandy beach, where he vowed to love her for the rest of his life. A life which, apparently, was to be much shorter than either of them had anticipated.

Bits and pieces of it floated around in his mind like individual puzzle pieces that he couldn't quite click into place, no matter how hard he tried. They were out of order, out of time, out of place. The boat. The island. Drinks. Friendly faces and laughter. She was there . . . then she wasn't. He was standing . . . then he wasn't. It was dark. He was suffocating. He was on solid ground. He was in freefall.

All at once, the cacophony around him ceased, and he had the distinct feeling he'd entered a tunnel of some sort— instinctively recognizing it to be a no-man's-land between life and death—a place where time stretched, twisted, and distorted. Because he should have hit the water's surface ages ago. Instead, his downward trajectory had slowed to a snail's pace, allowing him to ponder his life, even as the end of it rushed up to meet him.

And still her face floated above him, peering down. He imagined her outstretched hand, reaching for him as if she could somehow catch him, could somehow pull him back up before he hit the unyielding ocean with the force of a car slamming into a brick wall. But, of course, it was too late for that. With that realization, the excruciating noise returned, and Paul could feel that time and space were about to snap back into their appropriate algorithms.

Paul was falling. But brutal as the impact would be, in his mind he'd already experienced the worst of it.

He closed his eyes and conjured her face once more.

He took his last breath.

And then his world stopped spinning.

CHAPTER 1

EMILIA

Sleep was not as restful as Emilia had hoped. Again and again, the bloated corpses of her ugly past floated up to the surface, proving that no matter how deep you bury a body, it can find its way out of the grave at any time. It went like this all day long, first burning with fever, then shivering with cold until she finally woke to find moonlight streaming through the sliding glass door on the opposite wall of the cabin.

How long had she been asleep?

She swung her legs over the side of the bed and, using the nightstand to brace herself, managed to get to her feet without crumpling to the floor. Suddenly the small space felt oppressively stuffy and stale. Desperate for some fresh air, she took small, careful steps across the carpeted floor until she reached the balcony door. She was grateful when it slid open with little effort and even more grateful when the warm, salty breeze rushed in around her. It brushed her skin and blew through her sweat-dampened hair.

"Oh, God, that's good," she murmured to herself as she stepped all the way out and put both hands on the rail, tipping back her head and inhaling deeply.

Emilia repeated the process until, at last, the fog started to clear from her mind. Bits and pieces of the day began to float back into her consciousness. The last time she could recall being awake was sometime in the late afternoon, when she had gotten up to use the bathroom and splash some water on her face. They'd still been docked in San Juan then.

They weren't now, though. In fact, the ship appeared to be out to sea, moving at a good clip as it sliced across the waves. If it weren't for the winking reflection of the moonlight on the water, there would be nothing but blackness as far as the eye could see.

Turning her back on the water, she pivoted a little too quickly and had to use the handrail to steady herself before continuing back into the cabin. "Paul?" Her voice sounded small and tentative in the silent space. When there was no reply, she tried again a little louder. "Paul? Are you here?"

Nothing.

Okay, she wasn't going to panic. She'd learned the hard way that it was a useless emotion that only served to make a bad situation worse. Dangerous, even. Panicked people made knee-jerk reactions or worse, they made no decisions at all—too overwhelmed by a potent cocktail of terror, anxiety, and indecision to do anything but stand there in the middle of the road and watch the eighteen-wheeler bear down on them at ninety miles an hour. Panic turned even the fiercest creature from predator into prey. She would *not* panic.

She started to flip light switches, taking a good look around for any sign her husband had returned at some point while she was sleeping. But everything was exactly as it had been earlier—the half-drunk glass of water beside the bed, the open suitcase against the wall, his cello perched in the corner. And there was her watch, a custom timepiece made to look like the interior of a piano with real, tiny strings. It was a wedding gift from Paul, and she'd spent a good bit of yesterday marveling at its intricate beauty. Right now, though, it was nothing more than a means to an end—a way to assess just how concerned she should be by her husband's absence.

It was 10:34 p.m.

She sucked in an involuntary breath and closed her eyes for a moment.

"Focus, Emilia, focus," she willed herself.

If she was going to figure out what was going on, she'd have to stay calm and think clearly, despite the fact that she felt like utter crap. Right now she needed help—she needed to talk to someone. So she traded the nightgown for a wrinkled sundress, threw her tangled hair up into a passable bun, and left their cabin for the first time in more than twelve hours. She was grateful to find that the elevator was empty but the information desk was not. An older woman with a smart blunt cut in a silver-gray smiled as she approached.

"Good evening, miss! My name is Greta. How may I help you this evening?"

"Hello," Emilia began quietly, not wanting anyone to overhear their conversation. "I'm hoping you can help me with something . . ."

"Of course!" Greta jumped in, quite eager to be of assistance.

"Right. Well, I think . . . my husband, he seems to be . . . missing. And I'm wondering if it's possible he . . . was left behind . . . in San Juan somehow?"

If Greta was especially concerned or surprised by this question, there was no indication of it on her face. Based on her placating smile, you'd think she dealt with this specific issue at least ten times a day, every day.

"Alright then," she said, turning to a boxy computer setup next to her on the counter. "May I please have your name and cabin?"

"Emilia Winstead, 1623. My husband is Paul. Paul Winstead."

Greta nodded as she keyed the information in. After a few seconds, she looked up at her again, frowning.

"In 1623, I have a Mr. Paul Winstead and a *Miss* Emilia *Oliveras*. Is that you, Emilia Oliveras?"

"Yes . . . I mean no . . ." Emilia paused for a beat before starting again. "Oliveras is my maiden name. We were married two days ago, and there was no time to get an updated passport before we left."

"Ah, okay. That makes sense then. So, Miss Oliveras—"

"Mrs. Winstead," she corrected.

She didn't know why this particular point was bothering her. Maybe because she'd waited so long to be rid of her name; to get a fresh start. And now she finally had, and it was as if it never happened.

Greta's indifferent smile didn't dim a single watt.

"Right. So, may I ask what makes you think he's missing?"

Emilia wanted to be as clear as possible, which was difficult, considering how unclear her thoughts were. She just had to stick to the basic facts.

"My husband disembarked at Old San Juan this morning at ten thirty," she began. "I stayed behind in bed because I wasn't feeling well. At some point during the day, I started to run a fever, and I was in and out of sleep all day. It was only about a half hour ago that I finally felt well enough to get out of bed, and he still wasn't back. There were no signs that he'd *been* back, either. So I . . . I think maybe he never got back on the boat."

The older woman nodded through all this, then leaned forward across the counter.

"Well, the truth is that passengers *do* get left behind from time to time," she said in a softer voice. "And when that happens, we are briefed so we can help with any arrangements that might need to be made in order to get that person on—or their companion off—at the next port." Greta reached over and tapped her computer monitor. "Now, I have the most up-to-date information right here, and I can tell you there has been no such event reported today. So you needn't worry; Mr. Winstead is somewhere on this ship."

The woman seemed to be so confident that Emilia allowed herself to be relieved, but just for a few seconds. Because that's all it took for her instincts to kick in. It didn't make sense. If Paul really had returned from San Juan, then where had he been? What had he been doing all these hours? More importantly, where was he right now? Her concerns must have played out across her face, because Greta patted her forearm, which was resting on the counter.

"Please try not to worry. When couples travel, it's very common for one or the other to stop for a quick drink, or to throw a few dollars on the blackjack table. Also keep in mind that people are quick to make friends on these trips! They start to chat, become engaged in a conversation, maybe have a cocktail and simply lose track of time. I assure you, the odds are much higher that Mr. Winstead is sitting in the sports lounge watching a game than that he's back in San Juan. Now . . ."

The woman stepped back to scan something that was stashed underneath her work station. A moment later, she pulled up a glossy pamphlet, flipping it open before she grabbed a bright yellow highlighter and began marking it up. When she was done, she handed it to Emilia with a smile.

"There now, Miss Oliveras. This is a deck-by-deck diagram of the boat, so you can check some of the popular common areas like the lounges, the theatres, the pools, that sort of thing. Maybe even the late-night buffets? I've marked them all off for you. It's just after eleven, and I'm going to suggest you give it another two hours. If you haven't heard from him by then, you can just come back down here, and we will call for the security officer on duty." The woman stood up straight once more and smiled brightly—clearly proud of herself. "And there we have a plan!" she declared, as if she'd just cured cancer and reversed global warming in one pretty package with a big red bow on top.

If she didn't think it might split her head wide open, Emilia would have laughed. Was this lady actually suggesting she go off on a one-woman pub crawl/scavenger hunt?

Where's Pauldo?

CHAPTER 2

EMILIA

Thirty Years Ago

The Wagon Wheel lounge was the fourth of the cruise ship's twenty-plus bars that Emilia had circled through in the half hour. The others had been smaller and easier to scan. Not this one. The music was loud, and the cigarette smoke was thick. A country-and-western band was set up on a small stage at the far end of the room, playing for a crowd of rowdy two-steppers.

She squinted, trying to distinguish one fake cowboy from the next in search of anyone who bore even a passing resemblance to Paul. Too old, too short, too bald . . . none of them came close. Of course, she knew this was a ridiculous exercise. Paul would never be here or at any other bar at this hour.

"Something to drink, miss?"

Emilia jumped a little when the question interrupted her thoughts, and she wondered how long she'd been hovering there with one hand on the lacquered wooden bar top and the other on the back of a stool.

"Hmm? Oh, no, thank you—" she replied with a faint, polite smile on her face and then started to move away. That was when the sawdust-covered plank floor tilted up, and she swayed unsteadily.

Before she could process what was happening, the man's hand was wrapped firmly around her forearm, and he was guiding her around to the front of the stool, helping her to slide up onto it.

"Here, why don't you just sit for a spell," he offered in a soft southern accent, pushing the seat close enough so she could lean forward and rest her elbows on the cool surface.

"Oh, wow—I'm sorry about that," she murmured, pulling at the single button on the collar of her dress in an attempt to get some air.

"Not to worry, not to worry!" the man assured her. "Here, let me get you a cold drink . . ."

Back on his side of the counter, he used a soda gun to shoot seltzer into a tall glass, then plopped a wedge of lemon and straw in before gently sliding it across to her. Emilia was about to decline when she realized just how hot and tired she was. When was the last time she'd had anything to drink? Or eat, for that matter? No wonder the earth seemed to be moving under her feet—her blood pressure was probably through the floor.

The bartender was dressed in a well-worn cowboy hat, western shirt, and a red bandana was tied around his neck. His lasso-shaped name tag identified him as Josh.

"Thank you, Josh."

She bent a little awkwardly at the waist toward the fizzing, spitting, bubbling beverage until her lips found the end of the straw. It felt so good on her throat, she didn't stop until there were sucking sounds coming from under the ice cubes.

"Here, let's just get you a refill on that . . ." Josh said, and another drink appeared in the time it took her to blink. "Better?" he asked once she'd sucked that one down, too.

She nodded.

"Yes. Really, thank you so much. I think I must be a little dehydrated."

The man nodded his agreement.

"Yes'm. You were looking pretty pale there for a second, but I'm liking the way your cheeks are getting a little color to 'em now you've had a little somethin' to drink."

She straightened up and glanced around the room. It was humming with activity, though most of it seemed to still be over on the dance floor. Periodically a cheer went up from the other end of the bar from Emilia, where another bartender— a woman in cowgirl attire—had attracted a small crowd with her ability to juggle cocktail shakers.

"Hey, you know, I'm feeling much better. And it looks as if your partner down there is raking in some tips—I don't want to keep you from helping other customers, Josh," she assured the man quietly.

He scoffed and waved a dismissive hand at her.

"You're not keeping me at all! We split the tips at the end of the night. That way one of us can rotate out to restock the glassware and maybe refill some of the garnishes like olives and whatnot—which is exactly what I was just fixin' to do."

Emilia's ears perked up.

"Hey, are you . . . are you from Texas?"

The bartender beamed proudly.

"I am at that! Galveston born and raised," he informed her proudly. "What tipped you off? The accent?"

She smiled back and shook her head.

"No . . . I mean, yes—but it was the 'fixin' that caught my ear. My husband's family is from Austin, and we've spent some time visiting there. So I recognize the accent and some of the expressions."

"Well, I tell ya, miss . . ."

"Emilia. Emilia Oli— Sorry, Emilia *Winstead*. My name is Emilia Winstead."

He chuckled and pointed at her as if he'd caught her with a hand in the cookie jar.

"Ahhh . . . so you're a newlywed then!"

"Is it that obvious?"

He shrugged.

"You're still getting used to the name now, aren't ya? And it's a nice one at that—Mrs. Emilia Winstead. Yeah, that's gotta real nice ring to it."

She smiled a genuine, natural smile for the first time in hours. Even now, feeling like crap and concerned about Paul, she couldn't hold back the little jolt of excitement that shot through her whenever she heard her new name.

"We were married in Miami two days ago," she explained. "Then we hopped right on this cruise."

"Well, Mrs. Emilia Winstead, I'm Josh Beaufort, drink-slingin' cowboy. My hearty congratulations to you and your new mister! And where is the lucky son-of-a-gun anyway?"

Emilia stopped short, the smile fading from her face. Was it possible she'd actually forgotten for a few seconds there?

"Ummm . . . well, as it turns out, I'm here looking for him," she told the man in a considerably more subdued tone. "I . . . uh . . . I can't seem to find him . . ." She pulled the map out of her bag and set it down on the bar top. "And, actually, I really should be moving on to the next lounge now . . ."

He nodded toward the glossy booklet with a puzzled expression.

"And what, you're making your way through all the bars looking for him?"

Emilia nodded.

"I am." She cleared her throat, then recounted the same story she'd told Greta not half an hour ago.

He considered her as he listened thoughtfully.

"Emilia, are you sure he *did* get back on the boat?" Josh asked when she'd finished.

"No, honestly, I'm not. Not at all," she said, then sighed before adding: "But Greta insisted—"

He held up his hand to stop her.

"Okay, forget about that for now. I just wanna be sure I'm clear on what you're saying. You're telling me that your husband, man by the name a Paul Winstead, is missing." He pointed down at the floor. "Maybe somewhere right on this here ship?"

Emilia nodded grimly. "Yes, I—I think so."

He let out a heavy, incredulous sigh, then stood up straight and glanced down the bar, catching the eye of a cowgirl/bartender.

"Hey there, Jan? You mind if I take a break?"

When she gave him a thumbs-up, the man came out to the stool and offered Emilia his arm.

"Come on along then, Mrs. Winstead."

She blinked up at him, confused.

"But where are we going?"

"To get you some help. Now."

Emilia shifted uncomfortably in an orange resin chair. She was grateful Josh had been able to escort her down here to one of the lower decks, where the security office was located amongst the crew facilities. She wasn't sure she could have found her way on her own.

"Don't you worry too much, Emilia. They'll track down your husband for you," he told her reassuringly.

She just smiled, unable to take her eyes from the unmarked door along the back wall. The officer on duty had walked through it about fifteen minutes ago, and she'd been watching the big industrial wall clock since then, counting each and every sweep of the seconds hand around its face.

"Emilia, would you maybe like to call someone from your family?"

Her head swiveled in Josh's direction sharply.

"What? No . . . no, that's not necessary. I don't . . . my mother and I haven't spoken in a long time."

"Okay, how about Paul's family then—your in-laws?"

"I can manage. Really, but thanks." Her words came out with just a bit of an edge, and he noticed.

"Are they that bad?" the bartender asked knowingly.

She looked down at her lap.

"Let's just say they're not my biggest fans."

The man scoffed incredulously.

"Darlin', I don't know how anybody on God's green earth could *not* like you. Good Lord, woman, I've known you for less than an hour and I already like you more than I like my *own* family!"

She knew he was looking for a chuckle, but the best she could muster was another weak smile.

"It's a long story, but the upshot is they've got a lot of money, a lot of power. And I come from a poor, rural community in Puerto Rico. I think they had higher hopes for their son."

He frowned.

"Are you saying your husband's family thinks you're . . . what? Some kinda *gold* digger?" he asked, sounding as if this were the most asinine thing he'd ever heard in his entire life.

Emilia nodded sadly.

Before he could comment, they heard the sound of the door opening on squeaky hinges. She was up on her feet and standing at the counter before the young crewman Rolf was completely over the threshold.

"Ah, Miss Oliveras," he said pleasantly, with just a hint of a North European accent.

"*Mrs. Winstead*," Josh reminded him from next to her.

"Oh, yes! I'm so sorry . . . again," the crewman said with a frown. He jotted something down on a pad of paper, then looked up apologetically.

"What were you able to find out?"

"Right. Ah, well, I have confirmed what you were told upstairs, that Mr. Paul Winstead did indeed return to the ship. That was at seven forty-five p.m. So he cut it close, but he *did* make it."

"Okay, great. So where is he now?"

"What do you mean?"

"I mean if he's been on board for the last four hours, then where is he now? And please don't tell me the casino or clubs or midnight buffet."

Rolf looked a bit flustered. Clearly that was exactly what he'd been about to tell her.

"You see, locating his exact movements from the time he returned from San Juan may prove to be a bit difficult . . ."

"Why's that, Rolf?" Josh asked. "Seems to me we've got cameras covering every corner of this ship. One of them musta picked up something."

The officer nodded. "It's true, there are many, many cameras. But we've had a terrible time with them since we left port in Miami yesterday. Several are simply not working, and of the ones that are, the tech people have been turning them on and off as they test circuits and such. But at least we know Mr. Winstead is here somewhere; it's just a matter of time before he turns up."

"Unless he went overboard," Emilia blurted.

That particular fear had been there, bobbing around in the back of her mind like a buoy. Every time she tried to push it down under the surface, it popped up again, unwilling to stay submerged.

Rolf looked horrified at the suggestion, immediately shaking his head emphatically.

"What? Oh, no. No, no," he stressed, his white-blond brows arched high into the real estate of his forehead as he spoke. "No, that's very unlikely, miss. Someone would have seen something. And don't forget there are crew members walking every deck at all hours of the day and night. We have all been trained for such an occurrence . . ." The man paused, his expression morphing to concern in an instant. "Oh, Miss Oliveras—I mean Mrs. Winstead. . . . Please, please do not cry . . ."

Was she crying?

Emilia's hand touched her face, and she felt the damp evidence streaming down her cheeks. From next to her, Josh put a loose hand across the back of her shoulders in a side hug that was respectful enough for someone who didn't know her, but warm enough to bring her comfort. Meanwhile, Rolf stepped back to get a look under the counter, pulling out a box of tissues and pushing them toward her.

"I'm sorry," she whispered, reaching for one. "I'm . . . I don't mean to be so emotional. It's just that I'm so worried about Paul."

Her voice cracked, and more tears spilled.

She wasn't going to panic but, apparently, she *was* going to melt down into a puddle on the floor right here in front of this man.

When Rolf spoke again, his tone was perfectly even, calm, and quiet.

"I assure you, Mr. Winstead did *not* go overboard. Please do not allow yourself to be worried about such a thing."

"Rolf, is it possible to do a page across the ship?" Josh suggested. "I hear 'em from time to time come through the PA system in the bar and our crew quarters."

"Oh, of course!" Emilia jumped in, perking up immediately. If they'd just do something. Anything other than watching the clock and waiting. "What a great idea!"

But the crewman was already shaking his head.

"Not at this hour, I'm afraid. Perhaps in the morning." Rolf affixed a smile to his face once more. "But I am quite sure that will not be necessary. Mr. Winstead will have most certainly been located by that time."

At some point, Emilia had grabbed onto the edge of the counter with both hands. Glancing down now, she could see her knuckles turning white with the exertion.

Enough was enough already.

"Mr. Nilsson—Rolf," she said, locking her eyes on his and speaking in her most direct and sincere tone. "*Please*, Rolf.

Please believe me when I tell you that something is very, very wrong."

She could see him struggling between compassion and regret.

"I am so very sorry, Mrs. Winstead, but it is not in my power to launch a full-out search for a passenger—especially when there is no cause to believe he is in any jeopardy. I tell you what, why do you not go back to your stateroom and rest? For all you know, he could be there at this very moment, worrying about where *you* are!" He reached under the counter, pulled out a sticky note, and jotted some numbers down before handing it to her. "This is my number here. If he has not returned in one hour's time, I will call the security director, Mr. Stenhammer. How does this sound?"

Better than nothing, that was for sure.

"I'd be very grateful if you could do that for me, Rolf," she replied.

Back out in the hallway, Josh led her toward the elevator. He stopped for a moment and looked at her. "Emilia, do you think you could find your way back down here again on your own?"

She thought about it and then nodded.

"Yes, I think so, why?"

"Just so you know—just in case—my cabin is down that way," he told her, pointing to an unmarked hallway across from the elevator. "It's all the way down on the right, number 229. I'm at the Wagon Wheel every night from eight right through 'til five the next morning. Outside a that window, you can usually find me there. You don't hesitate to come find me if you need to, okay?"

She nodded, memorizing everything she could about the location and about the man, hoping she wouldn't have a reason to call on him.

CHAPTER 3

EMILIA

Thirty Years Ago

She felt his warm breath on her face—stinking of cheap beer and cigarettes. She wanted so badly to gag at the stench, but it was important that he believe she was really sleeping. So she kept her eyes closed tight, willing her chest to move up and down in a deep, easy rhythm. He might go away . . . he might not. She was prepared for either. Or so she thought, up until the moment his fingers began to work the tiny pearl buttons at the top of her nightgown . . .

Emilia woke with a start and sat bolt upright, sweaty and panting from another fever-induced dream.

She groaned.

It had been years since she'd dreamed about him . . . about *them*. Still, she wasn't surprised that horrific part of her life chose this moment to resurface. She glanced around the cabin to the alarm clock on Paul's side of the bed to find it had been just under an hour since she left the security office.

She took a deep breath and tried to bring her thoughts to the present, knowing that if she lingered too long in the past, it might somehow grab hold of a foot or a hand and drag her down into its murky depths. That part of her life was over . . . or so she'd thought. Because it was only now she was realizing that escaping the past wasn't as easy as simply starting over in a new place with new people.

She couldn't go back there. Not again. Not ever.

She had to be strong. For her husband.

No sooner had she conjured his face in her mind than there was a knock at the door of their cabin. She rushed to open it, hoping she had somehow manifested Paul. But it wasn't him staring back at her. Instead she was facing a tall man with graying blond hair, perhaps in his fifties.

"Miss Oliveras? My name is Olav Stenhammer, I'm the chief security officer on board. May I come in?"

She nodded and held the door open wide so he could enter. Once he was inside, he took off his hat and held it in his hands in front of him.

"So, I understand your traveling companion is a little late in finding his way back here?"

"He's my husband. And no, I don't believe he's just wandered off somewhere," she told him flatly.

"Well, I just wanted you to know that we have done a thorough check of all the casinos and lounges, as well as the late-night dining rooms. I'm sorry to say there's still no sign of him."

"I told you all that two hours ago."

He ignored the comment. "So now I have a question. I was wondering . . ."

"Yes? What?" she asked anxiously, eager to offer something—anything—that might be helpful.

"Is it possible Mr. Winstead is in someone *else's* cabin? That would certainly explain why we can't find him in any of the common areas."

She stared at him blankly.

"Someone else's cabin? Um . . . no, I don't think so . . . I mean, we don't know anyone on this cruise."

"Ah, well, perhaps he met someone while out on his excursion today in San Juan?"

She couldn't hold back her sigh of frustration.

"I don't understand what you're getting at, Mr. Stenhammer. Why would he be in some random guy's cabin?"

"Well, I wasn't specifically thinking about a man's cabin, Miss Oliveras . . ."

His voice trailed off as his eyebrows arched upward.

It took a moment for the subtext of his question to sink in. But when it did, she practically burst out laughing.

"You . . . you think Paul is in some strange woman's room? In her *bed*? Is *that* what you're implying?"

The tall man shifted uncomfortably, as the incredulity dripped off her words. He turned his hat in his hands for a few seconds.

"I wasn't trying to imply anything. Just throwing out another possibility. You do want to explore *every* possibility, Miss Oliveras, don't you?"

Anger—a relatively rare emotion for her—was beginning to well up from somewhere beneath the yoke of insecurity. Up until this point, she'd wanted to believe these people knew what was best—that they had dealt with just such a situation before and would, eventually, provide a perfectly reasonable explanation for her husband's disappearance and produce him from some secret corner of the ship where missing spouses gathered. But now she was done.

"Missus," she hissed more harshly than she'd intended, backing down a bit on the repeat. "It's *Mrs.* Winstead. Now I'd like to speak with the captain, please." She was firm in the demand, despite the slight quaver in her tone.

Unfazed, the man offered her a regretful smile, as if he were telling her they didn't have the shoes she wanted in her size. "Oh, I'm terribly sorry, but he's off duty at the moment. I'm only meant to interrupt him in the event of a true emergency—"

Emilia abandoned any attempt to sound civil and reasonable.

"This," she shouted shrilly as she pointed to the carpet, "*is* an emergency! A man has gone missing on *your* ship. I think that warrants waking the captain, don't you?"

Stenhammer didn't rise to the bait, a perfectly placid expression securely rooted to his face. That's when he returned his hat to his head.

"You should call down for something to eat. Or perhaps you should have a nightcap?" he suggested, eyes cutting toward the small refrigerator on the other side of the cabin. "I think you'll find the minibar to be very well stocked. It might help calm your nerves."

The condescension in his tone was so clear, and his non-answer so definitive, that she felt her bravado deflate like a balloon.

"Please, leave," she murmured, dropping onto the bed, still messy from where she'd slept all afternoon.

Once he was gone, Emilia went to Paul's cello case, leaning upright in the corner of the cabin. She'd suggested he leave it behind in New York, but he had been adamant about taking it with them on the cruise. He played every single day. Now, she unbuckled the clasps that held it closed and pulled the case open to expose the instrument in its flocked velvet nest.

Her index finger ran along the smooth maple surface until it found the familiar indentation where a falling music stand had gouged it on the way down, marring the cello's otherwise perfect complexion. The instrument wasn't Paul, but it was the only possession he truly loved. And right now, it was the closest to him she could get.

"What am I supposed to do?" she whispered, dropping down onto her knees. "Please, just tell me what to do."

CHAPTER 4

GRACIE

Today

There's this moment at the end of every trial when time just stands still. When, all at once, the cacophony of the courtroom stops, and it's like you're in some kind of tunnel—a no-man's-land between knowing and not knowing; between guilty and not guilty. You hang there in this limbo as a thousand little regrets unspool all around you, waiting to be catalogued even as the outcome is in transit—a soundwave created but not yet perceived by your brain. It is the last moment of not knowing. And then, without warning, it is gone.

". . . Not. Guilty."

I must have replayed the scene in my mind a hundred times since leaving L.A. fourteen hours ago. They are the two words that have kept me sane on this epic—and impromptu—trip back to the tiny speck on the map just over the Oregon border where I grew up. The last thirty miles feel the longest—probably because I could have navigated them blindfolded. The off-ramp leads to the two-lane road that winds back through farms and fields—eerily dark and silent at this hour.

At last I make the left onto Brookbend Lane, easily executing the sharp, unexpected turn onto the unmarked property. The Tesla X winds its way up the long path to the house, its wheels making that satisfying crunching noise on the bluestone underneath them. Then the driveway opens up into the clearing where the two-story Craftsman sits, the drive looping past it and around in a circle with a patch of garden in the middle.

"Oh, shiiiiiiit!" I hiss to myself as the car activates a flood of motion-sensitive lighting from the detached garage.

What the hell was I thinking? Here it's nearly three o'clock in the morning, and I didn't call ahead to say I was coming. I can almost picture my mother rushing through the house, following her progress through the path of lights she creates on her way to the front door. From the back bedroom to the upper hallway, down the stairs, to the lower hallway, passing the living room and kitchen. Half a second later, the exterior floodlights blaze to life, and I can barely put the car into park for the sudden blinding brightness.

"Who's there?" my mother demands in a voice that would make a Doberman cower.

"It's just me, Mom," I call out. "Gracie."

A petite figure in a bathrobe and slippers, my mother steps forward on the front porch, using her hand as a visor against the bright light now blazing around us.

"Gracie?" she echoes tentatively.

"Yes, Mom, it's me," I repeat, stepping directly into a pool of blue/white LEDs so she can get a good look at me.

"Gracie!" she squeals, hurling herself down the stairs and at me with so much force that we nearly both tip over.

"Mom, please," I gasp. "Too. Tight . . ."

Emily Oliver is surprisingly strong for such a small woman. She releases my torso, stepping back to get a better look at me.

"Gracie, honey, what are you doing here? I mean, I'm thrilled to see you, but why didn't you tell me you were coming? You scared the life out of me when you tripped the driveway alarm!"

"It was a last-minute thing. I'm . . ." I begin, and realize I can't possibly do this right now. "God, I'm so tired, Mom,

I've been driving since yesterday afternoon. Can I just tell you about it in the morning after I've gotten some sleep? Please?"

"Right," she agrees with a resolute nod. "I'll get your bed made up while you get your things from the . . ."

Her voice trails off as her eyes land on the Tesla.

"That's . . . quite a car," she says, brows furrowed.

I can almost hear her brain whirring as it calculates what it's seeing, finally spitting out a price tag in the neighborhood of a hundred grand.

I glance at it over my shoulder then back to her with a shrug.

"It's stolen," I tell her, popping the trunk.

"Ah, okay," she replies with a nod. "That makes more sense."

By the time I go inside, use the bathroom, and haul my ginormous roller bag to my room at the top of the staircase, she's just tucking in the top sheet.

"Do you want me to run you a hot bath?" she asks over her shoulder as she leaves the room.

"No, I'll wait until morning. I'm just so tired right now . . ." I call after her with a yawn.

A second later, she's back with an oversized quilt in her arms.

"Here we go," she murmurs, laying it on top of the bed. "There's an extra blanket in the closet if you need it."

"I know. Thanks, Mom."

"And you can find clean towels in the linen closet. And a fresh toothbrush in the drawer in the—"

"Oh, my God," I groan. "I grew up here, remember? I know where everything is!"

Setting foot into this house is like some freaky time/space continuum bullshit happens and I'm transported back fifteen years. She nags, I whine. She mopes, I apologize. Wash, rinse, repeat.

"Alright, alright," she says, lingering in the doorway while I get myself situated under the covers.

I know exactly what she wants.

"Go ahead," I huff, rolling my eyes.

"What?" she asks a little too innocently.

"You can kiss me. I promise I won't bite your head off."

Truth is, I'm pretty sure I need the kiss more than she does.

There's a hint of a smile on her lips now as she comes around to the side of the bed and bends down to brush the hair back off my forehead and presses her lips there. She holds my eyes with hers. I'd forgotten how beautiful they are—how beautiful she is.

"Just tell me this much, Gracie—are you okay?"

I consider the question.

"Not really. But I will be."

CHAPTER 5

GRACIE

Today

I'm not sure how long the phone has been ringing before it finally drags me from utterly asleep to unwillingly awake. I should have just powered the damn thing off last night. But my fiancé is nothing, if not relentless, which is—now that I think about it—how he got me to say yes to his proposal in the first place. But I can't keep it off for long—the work calls will start coming in any time now as they realize I'm not in the office. Today. Or tomorrow. Or . . . for I don't know how long.

I reach over, blindly feeling the top of the nightstand until my hand closes around the phone and I bring it to my ear.

"What do you *want*, Trey?" I demand by way of a greeting.

"I want you to come home," he declares.

"You just want the car."

His pause is a millisecond too long.

"Well yeah, that too. But c'mon, babe, we're good together . . ."

I actually wrinkle my nose. "Did you just call me *babe*? Are we in some seventies softcore porn where you get to bang anyone you want and then come home? Oh, no wait—you banged whoever you wanted *in* our home!"

"Don't be like that, Gracie. I promise I won't see Ju—"

"Don't. You. *Dare.* Say her name to me!" I hiss at him. "Do you really think we can just pick up where we left off? Like it never happened?"

"Well, no . . ." he admits. "I mean, we'll have to change yoga studios, obviously . . ."

I press a palm to my forehead. Has he always been this dim? Yes.

Why the hell have I stayed with him all this time? Definitely something to unpack with a therapist at a later date.

"Just come home, Gracie. Please . . ."

He sounds sweet and sincere. And this, I realize, is exactly where I always make my mistake. I want so much to believe (insert loser's name here) is sincere, that we really can move past the infidelity, or the lying, or whatever it is I've caught him doing.

"Home? Trey, do you really think I'm ever going to spend another night in that place? No way. I can't un-see you and that—"

"Okay, fine, so we'll get a new place—"

"No."

"What do you mean, *no?*"

"I know you're not used to hearing the word, but I suggest you *get* used to it. At least as far as I'm concerned."

"Gracie, stop! Just stop! Don't you think you're overreacting just a little bit? I mean, maybe if you'd been present in our relationship for *any* part of the last few months, then I wouldn't have felt compelled to go looking elsewhere . . ."

I actually sit up, pull the phone from my ear, and stare at it, as if I can't believe what it's just said.

"Are you kidding me with this bullshit?"

A frustrated sigh on his end.

"All I'm saying is that with you, *nothing* is ever good enough. You're like a paper bag with a hole in it—never full. Never satisfied, no matter how successful you are."

"Oh, yeah? And since when are hard work and dedication a character flaw?" I demand.

"They're not. But this—this pathological *need* you have to be the best at whatever you do! At work, in the courtroom—hell, I'm guessing it all started way back with the piano. Maybe if you hadn't been so—"

I'm not sure what he was about to say, because the phone is airborne before he can get it out. The thing hits the wall only inches from where my mother has just poked her head in to check on me.

"Gracie! My God, what's going on in here?" she asks, startled and concerned at the same time. "Are you okay?"

I drop back onto the bed and sling an arm across my eyes. My head is already throbbing, and my feet haven't even touched the floor yet.

"No, Mom, I'm not okay. The engagement's off."

This wasn't how I'd planned on breaking the news to her, and now I cringe, waiting for the backlash, the lecture, the unceasing attempts to get me to reconsider.

"Yes!" Mom gives a whoop so loud that she scares me into an upright position in the bed.

It's followed immediately by a jubilant fist pump in the air.

"Mom, I said the engagement is *off*. We're *not* getting married . . ."

She's grinning from ear to ear.

"Yes, I know! I heard you the first time!" She nods enthusiastically. "That's wonderful, honey!"

Maybe I'm the one who's misunderstanding.

"Mom, I don't . . ." I grind the heel of my palm into my forehead then try again. "Are you telling me you're *happy* about that?"

She clasps her hands together, pulling them close to her heart, the way women in musicals do when they look wistfully off into the distance and sing about their loved one.

"Happy? Oh, sweetie, happy doesn't even start to cover it!

Your father and I were beginning to worry you might actually go through with this one. Oh! Your father! I have to text him right now with the good news!" she tells me, turning back around to leave.

"Hey—wait, hold on a second," I call after her, and she stops, looking back at me over her shoulder. "Are you saying you guys *didn't* want me to marry Trey?"

My mother snorts, scoffs, and laughs simultaneously.

"Oh, sweet Jesus, *no*! He's just . . ." she lowers her voice and gets that *between us girls* tone. "I'm sorry, honey, but he's kind of an asshole."

"An asshole . . ." I echo, brows arched high in surprise.

She nods again, spreading her hands apart like she's describing the size of a fish she's just caught.

"A big asshole."

There's a ringing noise coming from her back pocket. She grabs her phone and looks at the screen.

"Oh, this is your father now!" She holds up her index finger and swipes the screen to speak with him. "Richard, can you hold on just a second? Thanks . . ." She presses the mute button and comes back to me again. "Daddy's coming for dinner—maybe Meg, too. Anyway, I've got the batter ready to go, just come on down whenever you're ready, and I'll make you those pancakes."

She blows a kiss and shuts the door; then I hear her resume her conversation with my father as she goes downstairs.

"Oh, my God, Richard! You are *not* going to believe this! Gracie broke it off with the asshole! Yes, I'm serious!"

CHAPTER 6

GRACIE

Today

Long before my life revolved around crimes and misdemeanors, it revolved around Bach and Beethoven. My mother, a pianist, used to play constantly, and some of my earliest memories are of drifting off to sleep as strains of music floated down the hall and into my dreams. Later on, I'd crawl up into her lap on the piano bench, and she'd help me to press down the keys and walk my fingers up and down the scales. Eventually I grew big enough to get up there by myself, and then there was no stopping me—I was reading music before I could read words. Forget about Girl Scouts or playdates or summer Sundays at the community pool; as the years went by, I chose music over all the things kids my age were doing. It seems ridiculous now to think that she had to nag me to *stop* practicing so I'd go out and play.

Elementary school, middle school, high school—it was all the same. I couldn't have cared less about the school musical, the homecoming game, or the prom. Who had time for BFFs or dating? I had a dream to become one of the best concert pianists in the world. And if you want to be the best, you have to study with the best. And in my mind, the best resided at the very prestigious, notoriously selective Los Angeles Conservatory. The day that early acceptance letter landed in our mailbox was a dream come true. And less than six months later, it was over.

"Gracie?"

My mother's voice pulls me from thoughts I haven't had in over a year—since the last time I was here.

"Hmm?"

"You okay?"

I smile and nod. See, this right here is why I never come home—too many ghosts flitting around. They should figure out they're dead already and just get on with it instead of hanging out, waiting for me to pop 'round every eighteen months or so.

"You know, honey, you're looking a little thin. Have you been eating properly?"

"Em, stop clucking at her like a mother hen. She's a grown woman," Dad chides with a chuckle from the kitchen island, where he's assembling a cheese plate for us.

"I *am* a mother hen, Richard. And she's my chick—no matter how old she is!"

Mom illustrates this point by planting a big kiss on my cheek.

My parents have been divorced more years than they were married but, oddly enough, they get along better and spend more time together than most of the actual still-together couples I know.

"You know how I get during a big case," I explain, swirling the wine in my glass. "I've been living on protein bars, espresso, and takeout Chinese food for the last six months."

She *tsk*s and shakes her head.

"Right—well, we're just going to have to get some good, healthy food into you while you're here, that's all."

"How long *are* you here for?" Dad asks.

I shrug.

"Umm . . . I'm not really sure. A week maybe? If that's okay?"

Mom looks thrilled. "Yes, of course! You can stay as long as you like."

"Here, try this Gruyère," Dad says, handing me a sliver of cheese on a cracker.

I pop it into my mouth, and my eyes close involuntarily as I savor.

"It's good with the wine, right?" he prompts.

I nod and moan at the same time, which makes him chuckle. A few seconds later, he's got me in a side hug, his mouth close to my ear.

"I'm glad you're home, kiddo. We've really missed you," he says, just loud enough for me to hear.

I lean over a few inches and kiss his cheek.

"Me too, Dad."

Technically speaking, Richard is not my father. Not biologically, anyway. That honor goes to some dude Mom met on spring break in college—John Something-or-other from Tampa. She can't remember. By the time she realized she was knocked up, Bio Dad was nothing more than a boozy, blond memory. She and Richard were married when I was four. He adopted me, gave me his name, and became the only father I've ever known.

"So tell us about this case you just won," he coaxes. "I'll bet the partners are thrilled with you!"

I consider this. They certainly weren't too thrilled when I called in this morning and told them I needed to take an unspecified amount of time off for a family emergency.

"Yeah, they were pretty pleased. I can't give you all the details, but something my client did got someone else killed. She didn't intend for it to happen, but it did. The D.A.'s office took a long look at it and declined to prosecute. It was just a tragic, tragic accident. But the victim's family wasn't satisfied, so they went for a civil judgment. They just wanted someone to say that my client was responsible. But you know, in the end it boiled down to intent—did my client mean to harm the victim? And could she have foreseen the circumstances that caused the victim's death? And the answer to both of those was no."

"Oh, my God—how horrible," Mom murmurs, shaking her head. "That must have been a living nightmare for your client, Gracie. I can't imagine how you go on after something like that."

An image of the woman, Lettie, weeping on the stand pops into my mind. That's exactly what this case was for her— one long nightmare. She didn't mean to hit the kid biking home from his friend's house that night. But it was dark and drizzling, and he was dressed in all-black clothes. The rear reflector on his bike had broken off the week before. He was listening to loud music in his earbuds. If any one of those things had not been a factor, then it might never have happened. But it did. And his family wanted someone to pay for the loss of their son. My client may not have meant to take his life, but she would, forever more, be remembered as the person who did exactly that.

"Yeah," I agree softly. "It was, Mom."

The somber mood is dispelled by the electric chime of the driveway alarm signaling my sister's arrival. Less than a minute later, she comes strolling into the kitchen in a short, flowery dress with black tights and a big, clunky pair of lug-soled boots. Her hair is cut into an asymmetrical bob. The frontmost piece—the one that frames her face—has been colored a vibrant cobalt blue. She's the picture of a hip, eclectic artist. It must take a lot of effort to look that effortless.

"The prodigal daughter has returned!" she says when she catches sight of me and comes in for a quick hug-and-release.

"Hey, nice ride, by the way. I never had you pegged as the Tesla type, though."

I shrug. "Yeah, well, like I told Mom last night, it's stolen. So there's that."

Everyone chuckles, not realizing just how close to the truth this is.

"And so . . . what brings you home so unexpectedly?" my sister asks me.

I don't miss the tinge of suspicion in her tone.

"She broke up with the asshole!" Mom says in a singsong voice, while doing a truncated cha-cha right there in front of the stove.

"Really, Mom, do you have to be so happy about it? I'm not exactly celebrating yet, you know?"

"Oh, I'm sorry to hear you broke up with—what was his name? Timmy?" Meg asks.

"No, Trey," I answer.

"So who's Timmy?"

"There is no Timmy."

"Are you sure?"

"Yes, Meg. Do you mean Tibby, maybe? Tiberius?"

She points at me. "Yeah, that guy. So then you *didn't* break up with him?"

"I did, but that was like, I don't know, four years ago?"

"Before Dave," Dad pipes up.

"And after Dmitri," Mom adds.

"Wait, which one was Dave?" Meg asks, then shakes her head. "Know what? I don't care. So what happened with this Trey guy then?"

"He wasn't just any guy," I grumble. "He was my fiancé."

"Hang on—you were *engaged?*" she confirms, surprised. "When did you get engaged?"

I gape at her. "Meg! It was two years ago! I sent you an announcement. How could you *not* know it?" I spin toward my parents. "And what, did you guys like *never* speak about it?

You know, about plans for your daughter's upcoming wedding?" I demand indignantly.

My parents look at each other, then back at me, before shrugging in tandem.

"No, honey, not really," my mother offers weakly. "Honestly, we thought you'd come to your senses eventually and call it off. And now you have! All's well that ends well . . ."

"Oh!" My sister's eyes light up, as if she's just remembered. "Ohhhhh! *Trey!* Of course! The *asshole*! Okay, okay, I got it now."

I throw up my hands. "Unbelievable. I come home for a little comfort, and I get a stroll down Memory Lane with *all* my romantic fuckups. Thanks, guys."

Meg's expression gets serious fast. "I'm sorry, Gracie. We don't really talk, so I guess I didn't realize—you must be really heartbroken. Do you want to talk about it?"

I stare at her for a long moment. My sister is the source of so many emotions in me—and not all of them pretty. But one thing she's never been is insincere. If she's asking, then she really wants to know.

"I came home and found him in the shower with our yoga instructor."

Meg gasps, throwing a hand over her mouth. "He did not!"

"Oh," I assure her, "he did."

"So you lost a fiancé . . . *and* your yoga instructor?"

"Meg, I hardly think that's the point—" Mom says.

I cut off my mother's protest, because that is exactly the point.

"Not just the yoga instructor, but the whole damn studio! How could I go back there and see her? Know she'd been all downward-facing-dog in my shower! I love my shower, Meg!"

My sister is still shaking her head in disbelief as she pulls me into an unexpectedly tight hug. There may be eight years between us, but that's still a much smaller gap than between me and my parents. At least I can count on her having some clue of what I'm talking about.

"I'm sorry, that's just so completely shitty," she murmurs into my hair.

"You know what? Forget about the asshole," Dad says, a little too enthusiastically. "Now that you're here, Gracie, you'll be able to go cheer on Meg tomorrow night!"

"Richard!" my mother whisper-yells.

But he's oblivious.

"What? What did I say?"

I push several inches out of my sister's arms so I can look at her face.

"What is it? What's going on? Did you . . . did you get into Juilliard?"

Her cheeks redden slightly.

"Oh, no . . . I mean, yes. Yes, I was accepted . . ."

"Oh, my God! That's great! So are you going?"

"Um, well . . . maybe. Depends . . ."

"On what?" I ask incredulously. "What could *possibly* make you turn down Juilliard?"

"On whether or not I win the Pacific Coast Piano Competition tomorrow night."

I blink hard and stare at her, wondering if I've misunderstood.

"What? I—I didn't know you'd even entered . . . I mean, that's big . . . that's really . . . huge, actually . . ."

No wonder she's not sure about Juilliard. If she wins, she'll spend the next year on a global tour. And if that's a success, well . . . then she won't need a degree from Juilliard or anywhere else. She'll have leapfrogged right into the life and career of a professional concert pianist.

For a second, all the chatter stops in my head, and it's just her and me in this room.

"Meg!" My exclamation comes out more like a reverent whisper. "Why didn't you tell me?"

I get a one-shoulder shrug and something that sounds like an "I dunno" but without actual words. But she does know. And so do I.

CHAPTER 7

GRACIE

Today

They converted the back sunporch after Meg was born, moving the piano into its new soundproof, climate-controlled home. That way, Mom and I could both practice any time without having to worry about "waking the baby." Because my sister was nothing if not a light sleeper from the day she was born. Later on, when I was at the height of my training, I'd spend four or five hours a day back here in this silent bubble, far from the clang and clatter of an active household.

My fingers wander the keyboard a little hesitantly. It's like they feel self-conscious. Or maybe guilty, like they don't deserve to touch a piano anymore. Not after abandoning it so long ago.

At first I really tried, but when it became clear to all of us that I would not be that one-in-a-million who came back stronger than ever against all odds, I had to abandon my dream by the side of the road. It was just too damn heavy to drag around with me. So, yes, the lying, cheating, mansplaining jackass Trey wasn't wrong when he said I had an obsession with being the best—though I'd hardly call it pathological.

Honestly I think it all would have been fine had it not been for Meg. I'd have gone on with my life, and eventually time would have lessened that pain and disappointment. But it's hard for wounds to heal when someone is constantly rubbing salt in them.

As if I have conjured her right out of my memories, my sister opens the door slowly. Her head comes around it so cautiously that I actually laugh out loud.

"Hah! Mom told you I almost hit her in the head with the phone, huh?"

Meg smiles sheepishly as she comes all the way into the room, closing the door behind her.

"Scooch," she says when she's standing next to the piano bench I'm sitting on.

I scooch.

"You must have drawn the short straw," I say, once she's settled on her half.

"It was rock, paper, scissors."

"You picked paper again, didn't you?" I accuse, poking her ribs with my elbow.

"Shut up," she says, shooting me the side-eye.

"Hey, no one invited you. I was doing perfectly well, sulking back here all on my own, thank you very much."

Rather than reply, she puts her right hand on the keys and starts to play the melody of "Heart and Soul." It was the first duet she learned—simple and fun, till it eventually became annoying as hell. Like right now, as she repeats the same opening over and over again knowing that, eventually, I'll get sick of hearing it. She's not wrong. It's just a matter of time before I "hop on" with her to play harmony. We do this for a while until she adds her other hand, picking up the part I've been playing so that I can shift farther down the keyboard to take on the bassline.

Split between my left and right hands, this bottom part usually has a sort of swinging rhythm to it. But the way my sister slows down the melody causes the whole piece to take on a lighthearted, jaunty feel. It makes me think of the way a horse canters. When she gets bored with the familiar notes, she starts to improvise, adding all sorts of flourishes to dress it up. Not me. I just go on and on, repeating the same finger pattern, the only change when I shift my hands up and down the left side of the keyboard to begin the sequence again but on a different note until she finally brings it all to an end with a bluesy little curlicue.

"That was fun! Wanna do some show tunes?" she asks, with a wide grin that makes me think of her at six, missing one of her front teeth.

She was so freaking adorable that it melted even my cold, cold fourteen-year-old heart. Just a little.

"You could have told me."

I hadn't planned on saying it, but apparently my mouth has a mind of its own.

"Gracie—"

"No, really, Meg. It kind of pisses me off that you all decided *not* to say anything to me. What were you going to tell me if you won? Did you think I wouldn't notice?"

"Can we just not do this right now? Please?"

"No," I insist, not quite ready to let this go. "Do you think you have to hide this kind of stuff from me? That I don't want to see you succeed?"

She considers me for a few seconds, head tilted to one side. Then she shrugs.

"I have no idea what you think when it comes to me and my playing."

"That's not fair—"

"You didn't see your face back there in the kitchen when I told you. You were absolutely gobsmacked! Like it never, in your wildest dreams, even occurred to you that little Meg could pull off something like that."

"Not true!" I object, not a hundred percent certain that it isn't.

She looks away for just a moment, but when she turns back to face me again, I'm looking at a different Meg.

"Gracie," she begins softly, without a hint of her previous irritation, "do you ever think that maybe, just maybe you dodged a bullet?"

The question is so random and vague that it takes my brain a second to dissect it.

"What are you talking about? As far as what?"

"Playing." I think I must have missed something, but then she continues. "It's true, I've been able to do the things you only dreamed of doing. But, you know what? Not every dream is a good one. Sometimes your dreams suck—like those anxiety dreams, or nightmares, or the freaky ones where you're a banana—"

"What the hell are you eating before you go to bed?"

"Will you please be serious? For just a second?"

"We're not talking about dreams, are we," I respond after a long beat.

She huffs, frustrated that I'm not following this bizarro, random tangent.

"You've always just assumed the rest of your life would've been all rainbows and popsicles . . ."

"Rainbows and *popsicles*? Why popsicles?"

"Stop it!" she whines in that singsong way she did as a child. "I'm asking if you've ever considered the possibility that you might have gotten tired of it? All the practicing and the stress, and the sacrifices? You may suck at relationships, but at least you've *had* relationships!"

Ah, okay. Now this is starting to make sense. Meg is twenty-two years old. She's probably seen a lot of other women her age in serious relationships . . . maybe the odd engagement here or there. Of course she'd be wondering if the effort is worth the sacrifice.

"Is that what this is about? Do you feel like you're missing out on something because you put your playing ahead of your social life? Because I can tell you for a fact that you're not—"

Meg shakes her head, starts to say something, then seems to think better of it and settles on a smile.

"You're right. I'm just . . . yeah, I'm just feeling a little emotional right now."

"Of course you are," I agree, happy to slip back into the role of wizened elder once more. "This is a big deal, Meg. But I know you're going to knock their socks off tomorrow night at the finals. And I'll be there to cheer you on. I promise."

She nods, shoulders relaxing slightly. "Good. I'm glad. Hey, so, what you said back there—about the Tesla being stolen? You were just kidding, weren't you?"

I pull a sheepish face. "Well . . . technically . . . I guess if you look at it in the *strictest* interpretation of the law . . ."

Any interpretation of the law, actually.

My sister pretends to be scandalized.

"Gracie Daniels! Did you . . . did you *steal* the asshole's car?"

"I don't think you wanna know the answer to that," I reply. "Especially since I could name you as an accomplice after the fact."

"Ha! And just how would that work? I haven't gone anywhere near that thing!"

I shrug.

"Not yet, maybe. But I thought you might like to take it for a test drive."

She hops off the bench so quick that it almost falls out from under me.

"Well, if I'm gonna do the time, I might as well do the crime," she reasons. "No sense in going down for nothing."

I throw back my head and laugh. It feels good.

CHAPTER 8

GRACIE

Today

I became a lawyer because Dr. Englehardt was a pain in the ass.

He gave me a C on a paper that was worth an A—*maybe* an A minus. Either way, I was sufficiently pissed enough that I cornered him after class and proceeded to deliver a blistering, twenty-minute diatribe on why he was wrong and I was right. In the end, the C stood, but he convinced me to join the university debate team, where I discovered I had a passion for proving people wrong. So much so that I followed it all the way through undergrad and on to UCLA for law school.

And Meg was absolutely right. In all those years, I never once made a point of showing up for a recital, a concert, or a competition. When we were together for the holidays or thrust into an unexpected phone conversation, we adopted a kind of "don't ask, don't tell" mentality. So yeah, I'm a little freaked out that the last time I saw her play in public, she had buck teeth and pigtails. But not now. Now she's a grown woman—confident and poised as she walks out on stage to a packed house. She shakes hands with the conductor and the concert master, makes a quick bow to the audience, and sits on the bench of the Steinway concert grand.

I can still see her sitting on the bench at home, legs dangling so high she couldn't reach the pedals. She doesn't have that problem anymore, that's for sure. Even after all this time, I know this piece inside out, and I have a very good idea of the number of hurdles standing between my sister and the barn-burner of an ending. Nervous for her, I find myself holding my breath right up to the second she nods to the conductor, signaling her readiness to begin. And then the rest is sheer magic.

When the conductor's baton comes down on Tchaikovsky's *Piano Concerto No. 1*, he counts off exactly one-and-a-half beats of super-charged silence before the four horns enter in lockstep to deliver a bold, brassy proclamation—punctuated by the orchestra in a single, jagged slice of a note that serves as an exclamation point.

Hear ye, hear ye!

This will *not* be your garden variety concerto. Not by a long shot.

The orchestra will not just meander around with delightful little countermelodies, filling time until the soloist comes in and starts chewing up the scenery.

We are officially on notice—this is a high-stakes, winner-take-all battle.

When the piano enters, it's usually atop the orchestra. Not here. Not at this moment, anyway. Instead it lays out a series of bold, chunky chords that serve as the framework—the backbone of the concerto. It is a powerful part that requires strength, stamina, and quite frankly, balls. My sister establishes her dominance from her very first entrance, slamming both hands down in a series of stiff, powerful chords that climb up the keyboard octave by octave, three beats at a time. Far above her, the orchestra is spinning a delicate web of gossamer.

In the next moment, though, it's like the piano is propelled out of the woods and into the clearing—alone while the other musicians hover nearby, counting beats of silence. She picks up a complicated rhythm that makes the melody sound slightly out of phase, as if one hand is playing a heartbeat slower than the other. It gets low and rises, rises, rises in intensity until it finally takes control. The piano acts like a harp, gliding the entire length of the keyboard before splitting open and spilling out in a rapid-fire deconstruction of everything we've heard to this point.

While it's not exactly easygoing, she gets to stretch a little bit in the contemplative second movement. But by the time she hits the finale, there is no holding back. This is where you'd better have the stamina, because if you don't, you'll never make it to the end. She is all over the place—leaning forward, adjusting, and readjusting herself to the left, then the right, then back to the middle. Something up there creaks and groans—the piano? The bench? I don't know what it is, but it only adds to the impression that she's pushing this instrument to its outer limits.

When I glance at my mom next to me, it's all right there on her face for anyone to see. Like me. And like my dad. In the moments before he realizes I'm watching him watching her, I see something flash across his face that gets my attention. It's a profound sadness. The kind you reserve for the greatest losses life throws your way. Is it for the marriage that didn't last? Is it for the career he thinks she could have had? Is it . . .

I'm remembering now how my mother used to play late at night when she thought everyone else was asleep. Those were the times when she let it all go—all pretense of being the neighborhood music teacher and the mom egging on her own prodigies. She was so good. Good enough to be on this stage. On any stage. I'd watch her for hours, only slipping away when she started to cry—as she often did. That was a long time ago, but I see that longing now as I listen to Meg and watch my mom.

The memories vanish the second I hear it, my head whipping back around to face the stage.

Wait a second. *Was that . . . ? Did she just . . . ?*

The moment comes and goes so quickly that by the time I refocus on her, she's already closing in on the finish line. Her eyes are closed, her head is back, and her hands take up their position at the bottom of the keyboard, using that bass register as a springboard to catapult all the way up to the top and to the big cinematic finish that has her halfway off the bench as she slams down the final chord along with the orchestra.

No one moves until there is nothing left but the shadow of those last notes. And when that finally fades away, there is a beat of total and complete silence.

That's when everything simply . . . explodes. The audience is on their feet, applauding wildly and yelling *"Brava!"* The orchestra is standing.

My sister smiles and bows and accepts the applause.

She shakes hands with the conductor and gestures to the orchestra musicians. Unlike the two competitors before her, when Meg tries to leave the stage, she's called back twice more for curtain calls.

She already knows she's taken first place.

I already know this is the best thing that could possibly happen to her at this moment.

But I cry anyway, grateful that happy tears look just like sad ones.

"No, I really had *no* idea," I insist, as Mom and I pass the Banana Republic.

It's the day after the concert, and we've dropped my shattered phone at the CELL HELP kiosk. Now, as we wander around the mall waiting for a fourteen-year-old to fix it, I can't help but marvel at Meg's performance.

"Nonsense," Mom replies dismissively. "Of course you did. You've been listening to your sister play piano since she was a little girl."

"Well, yeah, not like *that.*"

She stops right smack in front of the Apple Store, almost causing a ten-person pileup with the shoppers behind us.

"You know what, Gracie?" she begins, putting her hands on her hips and tilting her head to one side. "You act as if this is some miracle from on high. Like she hasn't spent the last two decades with her butt glued to the bench for hours and hours. If you really, truly didn't know what an exceptional pianist Meg is, then it's because you didn't *want* to know."

I put a hand on her arm and guide her back into the flow of foot traffic. "What I meant to say is that I knew she was good. I just didn't know she was *that* kind of good. Like headliner-at-Carnegie-Hall kind of good. Mom, I couldn't take my eyes off of her!"

I guess she's already forgiven me, because when I glance over at her again, she's smiling.

"Yeah, Meg's pretty special," she agrees. "Watching her fingers while she's playing is like watching little humming-birds flutter over the keyboard."

I nod my agreement. It's a good description. And it makes me recall something from last night.

"Um, so . . . did you notice anything strange at the very end of the concerto?"

She shoots me a sidelong glance.

"What do you mean? Strange like how?"

I shrug. "Oh, I don't know. It was like there was this moment when she hesitated. For just this little fraction of a second . . ."

Mom's shaking her head. "You must have imagined it because, believe me, the judges would have picked up on anything that was even slightly off. You heard the other two pianists—competition was tight. The least little hiccup would have knocked Meg right out of the running."

I nod. She's right, I'm sure. But still . . .

"Oh, Gracie, look! Your favorite—Macy's! And it looks like they're having a sale in the shoe department!"

And *poof* go all other thoughts, pushed out by the vision of sky-high heels on the clearance rack that gets my heart racing.

"Oh, wow!" I murmur, reverently taking them into my hands. "Will you look at these beauties!"

She makes a sour face.

"Not very practical. What would you possibly wear with them?"

I consider the question.

"Mmmm . . . a leather miniskirt, probably."

"For court?"

"What? No! Of course not for court! God, Mom, I do find things to do outside of work from time to time, you know . . ."

She looks between them and me doubtfully. "How much are they?"

"Uhhh, let's see . . ." I flip them over to look at the red sticker on the sole. "They're two hundred and ninety-five dollars," I inform her, then wave one in her direction, using it to emphasize my point. "And before you gasp and clutch your chest, that's two hundred dollars off."

"Oh, is that all?" she mutters next to me, looking down at something on her phone. "Well then, I don't know how you can possibly pass up a steal like that," she comments sarcastically.

"Mom, I make a good living. And there aren't many things I spend my money on. And now that the private yoga sessions are out . . ."

I put the shoe back, deciding I'd rather try a pair of over-the-knee boots I've just spotted on a table across the sales floor. She trails me, still looking at her phone.

"Everything okay?" I ask, picking up one of the boots and stroking its rough, deep-green exterior. It happens to be just my size, so I take the liberty of slipping them on, moving to stand in front of a mirror. I turn so I'm looking at my back over my shoulder. Oh, I'm liking these very much.

"Nah, just a couple of missed calls from a number I don't recognize."

"Any messages?"

"Nope."

"Probably just a robocaller then. I get them all the time. You can actually block those—I'll show you later."

"You do know I'm not some doddering old lady, right?" she says as she looks down at my five-inch-heeled feet. "They look slutty," she pronounces.

"What? They do not!" I disagree emphatically.

"Yes, actually they do, Gracie," she insists. "Trust me on this one."

I spin around and look down at her from my newly elevated stance.

"You don't want anyone to see you as a 'doddering old lady,' but you insist on thinking like one. Women actually own their sexuality these days, you know. Getting pregnant on spring break isn't the life-ending event that it was when you had me."

She blinks hard. "Did you just . . . ? Are you saying . . . ? I don't even know what that's supposed to mean!" she finally manages to get out.

This has been on my mind since last night, when I saw the look on her face as she watched Meg.

"Listen, if it happened today," I start, putting a hand on her shoulder to steady myself as I pull off first one boot, then the other. "I seriously doubt you'd have made the same choice again."

Her brows go up, and her mouth forms a perfectly shaped little O.

"Which choice? The choice to *have* you?"

I shrug. "Yeah, you know, the choice to sustain the pregnancy. Okay, maybe it was just the way it was when you were twenty-two. That mentality that 'you made your bed, now you have to lie in it' thing. But what if it happened to Meg?

What if she were to get pregnant right now, when she's just been handed this amazing opportunity? Would you encourage her to give it all up for something so . . . I don't know . . . *ordinary?*"

I watch as my mother's face transitions through progressively angrier shades of red. Rosy, scarlet, crimson. . . . Oh, hell, she's gonna blow.

"If you," she begins, biting off the two venom-dipped words, "believe for a single second that I would have—that I *could* have terminated you, then you really have no idea who I am."

I roll my eyes. "Look, all I'm saying is it's a viable choice these days—"

Mom takes a step closer to me, poking my chest with her index finger.

"I've got news for you, *Graciela Maria*. It was a viable choice back then, too. It would have been the easiest thing in the world to walk into a clinic and have an abortion. But I wanted you more than I ever wanted *anything*—including a career as a concert pianist. I know that's hard for you to wrap your high-paid, high-profile, take-no-prisoners little brain around, but that's just the way it was."

The saleswoman and a few of the other customers are looking in our direction with curiosity. I hold up my palms and drop my volume.

"Hey, okay, why don't you just calm down—"

"How dare you!" she hisses at me.

Oh, hell. I have really mucked this up big time.

"Mom, I'm sorry, I didn't mean to—"

Her phone rings in her hand, but she ignores it, and eventually it stops.

"Yes, you did! You totally meant to belittle my life. You know, the one I gave you and your sister with the happy, stable childhood. Know what your problem is? Nothing is ever good enough. You're always looking for something that's just out of your grasp."

Suddenly Trey's voice is there in my ear:

You're like a paper bag with a hole in it—never full. Never satisfied, no matter how successful you are.

"Mom, please," I try again, doing my best to sound contrite, even though she's kind of blowing this out of proportion. "I swear to you—"

When the phone begins to ring once again, I grab it before she can stroke out right there in front of the Louboutins. I swipe it to accept the call and whisper/yell in my scariest lawyer tone.

"Who is this?" I demand. "What do you want?"

There's a long pause down the line, and I'm thinking about hanging up when a soft, male voice I don't recognize begins to speak.

"*¿Emilia? Emilia, este es Miguel. Lo han encontrado. Encontraron a Paul.*"

Mom snatches the phone back.

"Hold on, hold on," she says, switching off of speakerphone and covering the microphone. Suddenly she looks both pale and flush at the same time. Scared and excited. "Gracie, I need to leave. Now. Get your phone and call for an Uber."

"Wait, what? No, I'll grab the phone quick from the kiosk—"

She's shaking her head adamantly. "No, sweetheart, I can't wait."

"What is it, Mom?" I ask, touching her upper arm.

She offers me a weak smile and then leans in to give me a kiss on the cheek, taking just a moment to stroke my hair.

"I love you so much." The five words come out on a whisper.

And as soon as she's uttered them, she's gone. I stand there in the middle of the shoe department, staring after her, wondering just who the hell this Paul guy is, and why does my mother need to know they've just found him?

CHAPTER 9

MIGUEL

Thirty Years Ago

By the time the tender had docked alongside the cruise ship, Miguel was feeling a little green around the gills. The only thing he liked less than flying in small planes was riding in small boats—or any boats, really. Which was interesting, considering he lived on an island. Luckily, he was able to avoid them for the most part. But then, today was not a lucky day. Today he found himself on a small plane, a small boat, *and* a big boat. Definitely not a lucky day. And it had the potential to get infinitely *less* lucky.

His boss had warned him during their pre-dawn phone call to tread lightly here, especially since there was some question as to jurisdiction. The ship was anchored in international waters, not far from the French island of St. Barts, flying under a Dutch flag. Miguel's presence here was unusual, to say the least. But the missing man was American, and he got the distinct impression that someone much senior to him owed someone much richer than him a big favor. And he was *not* happy to be that favor. Not when there were a half dozen open casefiles on his desk. Not when it involved coming all the way out here to play hide-and-seek with some lost rich kid.

He willed himself to get into a better headspace. Being

pissed at the bureaucracy wouldn't make this go any faster or smoother. Nor would it give him the objectivity he needed right now. Miguel spotted his handler immediately—a tall, lean man with the kind of silvering blond hair that made it hard to pinpoint his exact age, or even his nationality. Norwegian, perhaps? Finnish?

"Detective Alvarez," the man said in a slightly stilted accent, proffering a large hand as Miguel drew closer. "I am Chief Security Officer Olav Stenhammer. Welcome aboard."

Ah, so Swedish, then.

"Thank you," he replied, accepting and matching the firm handshake. "I understand you've got yourselves a missing passenger."

"Indeed," the other man agreed solemnly. "Come, let me take you to our security office. I'm sorry to have to jump right into it, but the captain is quite anxious to be done with this as quickly as possible. We are already a day behind schedule."

"Not at all," Miguel assured him, quite happy to dispense with the pleasantries and get right down to business.

Get on fast. Get off faster. That was his plan.

He had to scramble to keep up with the long-legged man as they made their way from the tendering area, down two flights of stark concrete stairs, and through a heavy door opening onto one of the crew decks. Not unlike the tunnels and hidden cast areas underneath Disney World, this was a surreal juxtaposition of the above-deck fantasyland consisting of posh carpets, gleaming fixtures, and fresh-faced attendants in uniform. This dimly lit hallway, with its utilitarian vinyl composite floor, was more like his daughter's elementary school than a luxury cruise liner.

"So the passenger, Paul Winstead," Stenhammer was saying, "disembarked in the port of San Juan at ten o'clock yesterday morning leaving his companion, a Miss Emilia Oliveras, back in their stateroom. She claims she was too ill to accompany him."

"Miss Oliveras?" Miguel echoed, with a hint of confusion. "I'm sorry, the notes I received said the man was traveling with his wife."

The other man glanced at him sideways when he replied.

"Miss Oliveras *is* Mr. Winstead's wife—or so she claims."

There was no missing the skepticism in his tone.

"And you don't believe her?"

Stenhammer shrugged.

"According to her, they were married two days ago in Miami. But all of her legal identification is in her maiden name. And she has yet to produce a marriage license—said something about it being mailed to them in New York after their honeymoon."

"Well," Miguel began diplomatically, "we get a lot of impromptu weddings in Puerto Rico, so I see this quite a bit. If they were just married, she *would* be traveling under her maiden name, wouldn't she?"

He sensed, rather than saw, a tightening in Stenhammer's already rigid demeanor.

"Detective, married or not, we have reason to suspect Miss Oliveras may not be . . . as she seems."

Miguel opened his mouth to follow up on that statement, but Stenhammer, anticipating this, held up a finger as a trio of crew members passed by, eyeing them with open curiosity.

"Let's continue this conversation when we get to my office, if you don't mind. It's hard to control the rumor mill on a ship of this size," the security chief said in a low voice once the crewmen were out of earshot.

"Of course."

Miguel nodded his understanding. As they walked on in silence, he was surprised to see an entire microcosm existed beneath the waterline. The crew dining room was a more basic version of the giant buffet restaurants the cruisers enjoyed several decks above. There was what looked to be a very well-equipped gym, a decent-sized convenience store, and a bar—

complete with pool table, dartboard, and signs for weekly trivia nights. It had never occurred to him before, but cruise workers needed their downtime, too.

When they entered the security office, Miguel saw a setup not dissimilar to a police precinct, with orange resin chairs lining the wall across from a tall counter. A young woman in uniform with a dark, tight bun sat on a stool, jotting something down in what looked to be a logbook. In one of the corners was a coffee machine with glass carafe, alongside some Styrofoam cups and a shaker full of powdered creamer. The pot looked fresh, and he was tempted to ask for a cup, but thought better of it, instead following Stenhammer to another door adjacent to the counter. The young woman must have pushed some hidden button behind the counter, because there was a buzz and the latch released, allowing them to enter.

He was surprised to find the space on the other side of the door was several times larger than the lobby they'd just passed through, accommodating several banks of video screens monitored by a pair of men seated in the middle of it all. Glancing over their shoulders, Miguel felt like a voyeur as he watched a crowd of people swimming on the top deck, while another feed focused on one of the dining rooms. A third was dedicated to looping through different angles of the casino.

He felt a vague sense of discomfort at the sight of so many people. He'd never understood the appeal of cruising. It was like being trapped out in the middle of the ocean aboard a floating tin can with thousands of people all flocking to buffets like newly minted zombies on the prowl for fresh brain matter. And did they *really* have enough lifeboats for everyone? He shook the thought from his head as they continued through a narrow hallway with a few unmarked doors.

"Offices?" he asked out of curiosity.

"More like the brig."

"Oh! So what does someone need to do to end up in cruise lockup?"

"Mostly we use it to put a scare into rowdy teens or when someone has had too much to drink and gets a little unwieldy."

Unwieldy? Miguel guessed that translated to shit-faced and obnoxious in Swedish.

The security director's office, located at the very back of the suite, was just big enough for a desk and two chairs—one behind it, one in front of it. He took a seat and watched with some amusement as Stenhammer had to turn sideways to get to his own chair.

"Sorry about the tight quarters," he muttered.

"No worries," Miguel replied.

Once he was seated, Stenhammer let out a sigh and jumped right in.

"Detective, are you familiar with the Winstead family?"

"Hmm? Oh, no. . . . Why, should I be?"

"Ever heard of WinCo Oil?"

Lightbulbs erupted in Miguel's head.

"Wait . . . Paul Winstead is one of *those* Winsteads?"

Stenhammer nodded solemnly.

"Second son of Brock and Evelyn Winstead, grandson of John Paul and Clarissa Winstead."

Forget about the term *blue blood*. There was pure black crude running through this kid's veins.

"Holy shit," he muttered.

"Yes, exactly," the other man said dryly. "So, as you can imagine, this situation has become rather high-priority . . . and rather sensitive."

It was all starting to make sense now—the cloak-and-dagger call from his boss at four in the morning, the assignment that wasn't even in their jurisdiction, the feeling that someone far above his paygrade was pulling strings here. It must have shown on his face, because Stenhammer offered up a slightly amused smile.

"I see you're starting to understand how you and I came to be sitting here together. The Winsteads have very powerful friends in very high places."

Miguel nodded thoughtfully. "Have you heard from them? The family, I mean?"

The other man huffed out some cross between a scoff and a snort.

"Oh, yes! And I expect you'll be hearing from them soon, too."

"I see."

"I'm not sure you do. Detective, these people do not like to leave *anything* to chance. In the last several hours, I have spoken with both parents, the lawyer, the accountant, the private detective—"

"Detective?" Miguel echoed incredulously. "They got their own *detective*?"

This time, a chuckle from Stenhammer.

"Oh, yes. And just wait until you hear from the publicist!"

Miguel held up a hand. He'd heard enough. Now he understood why there wouldn't be any jurisdictional challenge. The cruise line would be thrilled for him to take this problem—and the crazy cast of characters who came with it—off their ship so they could pull up anchor and sail off into the sunset. What he couldn't decide was whether or not this worked to his advantage.

"Okay, you know what? Before I speak with anyone else, I need to have a full picture of what happened last night—and when. So why don't you take me through it from the beginning," he suggested, pulling a pen and narrow spiral notebook from his pocket.

Miguel jotted notes as the security director related the previous evening's timeline.

"Okay, so at what point did you decide to do a search?"

"At the point when Miss Oliveras contacted Paul Winstead's father, who then contacted the captain, who then contacted me. Then we did do a full search from stern to bow, port to starboard."

"Including down here on the crew deck? And mechanical rooms?"

"When I say every inch, I mean every inch, detective. We've had crew canvassing passengers all morning—going cabin to cabin. Nothing. The man has simply . . . vanished."

"And you're certain he got back on the ship in San Juan?"

"We are. There are porters on hand to check in each passenger as they reembark the ship."

"And it's not possible someone was slacking off? Or he was mistakenly checked in or anything like that."

"Absolutely not."

Miguel didn't like absolutes. He made a mental note to speak with the crew who had been on duty the night before.

"Right. So then there are only two places he can be—on the ship . . . or off the ship. As in overboard."

Stenhammer nodded, as if he'd expected this conclusion.

"I know it's very common in the movies, but it's actually quite difficult to do. The individual would have to be incredibly determined—as in suicidal, or extremely stupid."

"But it could happen . . ." Miguel pressed.

He noticed Stenhammer's mouth tightening at the corners.

"Well, yes, of course. *Very* rarely a passenger will have too much to drink and attempt some horseplay—climbing the rails, jumping from balcony to balcony and such. But really, the odds are astronomical."

The detective got the sense the man was downplaying the possibility, probably not wanting to cast any aspersions on his employers.

"Like how astronomical?"

The other man looked up as if the answer might be written on the very low ceiling in the very small space.

"Oh, I don't know. . . . Let's see, perhaps one in one-hundred-fifty-thousand people who cruise go overboard each year."

Miguel quirked an eyebrow.

"For someone who doesn't know the statistics, you certainly know the statistics," he commented.

The security chief sighed.

"Believe me, it's an answer I've had to provide several times in the last eighteen hours."

"Did you do a search of the water?"

"No. There was no reason to. At the time."

The addition of the last three words caught Miguel's attention.

"Well, I caught a ride out here with a Coast Guard cruiser, so someone decided there was a reason to search at some point."

Stenhammer met his gaze squarely.

"What I did not know at the time, detective, was how Emilia Oliveras fit into this scenario."

Miguel sat back, crossing his arms in front of his chest.

"And how would that be?"

"She has apparently been . . . involved . . . with Paul for a few years now, and Mr. and Mrs. Winstead have gotten to know her in that time. Let's just say they do not trust her motives in this. At all."

"They think their new daughter-in-law is a gold digger," he surmised.

"They do indeed. She comes from a rather unsavory family background—the mother is serving life in prison for murder, if you can believe it."

Miguel let out a long, low whistle.

Alrighty then. He knew the sins of the mother shouldn't

be visited upon the daughter, but he couldn't deny that, as a father, he'd be cautious if one of his own children were involved with someone who came from such a family. It was time to meet the potential murderess in question and see if his instincts could give him some direction.

"Well, if you don't mind," he began, getting to his feet, "I'd like to speak to Miss Oliveras. Can you take me to her stateroom?"

"No need," the security director informed him. "She's in one of the rooms next door."

Miguel frowned in confusion, pointing over his shoulder toward the hallway they'd walked through to get to the back office.

"She's. . . . You put her in the brig? Where the unruly passengers go? Was she giving you a problem then?"

"What? Oh, no, no. Nothing like that. It was at the Winsteads' request. They believed her to be a flight risk."

"In the middle of the ocean?"

The man held his palms up.

"As I've said, Detective Alvarez, the family can be quite . . . insistent."

Miguel was beginning to get the picture.

CHAPTER 10

EMILIA

Thirty Years Ago

Emilia swung an arm across her face, hinging her elbow over her eyes in an attempt to block out the flickering fluorescent lights above her. Almost as bad as the strobing effect was the maddening hum they created. But she couldn't cover her ears and her eyes at the same time, so she opted for the latter. This was a far cry from the posh honeymoon cabin she'd shared with Paul the night before. Or was it two nights ago? Time was starting to slip away from her, especially now that she was in a room with no access to natural light.

She hadn't fought the request that she move down here to the "security suite," as Mr. Stenhammer had called it. But did they really think she wouldn't know what this place was? The only thing missing in this cell were the bars. The small space had a very cold, sterile feel to it, mainly because of its stainless-steel furnishings, including a card table with four stools—all of which were bolted to the floor, and a sink/toilet combo. Even the cot she was lying on was a stainless-steel platform—sort of like an autopsy table with a vinyl cushion tossed on top of it.

She immediately regretted the comparison.

Autopsies meant bodies. Bodies meant death. And death . . .

She shifted onto her side, hoping to stave off the wave of

nausea that came with the completion of that thought. Maybe she should have asked to see the doctor, but the last thing she wanted was someone poking and prodding her. And the truth was, she just didn't trust them. Any of them. Because now that Paul's family was involved, *they* were most certainly the ones calling the shots. That's how it worked for people who had money and power of that magnitude.

The first time Emilia met Evelyn and Brock Winstead, they were pleasant enough and unfailingly polite. But with each subsequent encounter, things became more strained. It seemed she was good enough to be a freshman fling, but the more serious things became between her and Paul, the less pleasant and polite things were between her and his parents.

They played it smart—neither of them baring their teeth to her in front of Paul. Instead they waited for any opportunity to get in a dig, fuel her insecurity, or be downright offensive. There had clearly been some investigation into her background, because they knew exactly which buttons to push. There were comments about her upbringing—specifically her mother. Evelyn went so far as to leverage her feelings for Paul against her, suggesting she would only hold him back—prevent him from reaching his true potential. Brock, on the other hand, wasn't nearly so mannerly when he actually pulled out his big, leather binder of checks and tore out one of them. It was already filled out and signed. He figured he could buy her off for 50,000 dollars.

He figured wrong.

And through it all, Emilia just smiled placidly, declined respectfully, and refrained from telling Paul the extent to which his parents were willing to go to be rid of her. Because, while she had doubted many things in her life, she never doubted the love they shared from that first year at the conservatory. Well, like it or not, here they were three years later, and she and Paul had eloped. Emilia was now a legal member of their family—a Winstead—and there wasn't a damn thing they could do about it.

Still, this fact had done little to calm her anxiety about contacting them. They needed to know their son was missing. And, more than that, Emilia knew they were the only people who could do anything about that. No matter her feelings toward Paul's parents, she had to do absolutely everything in her power to help him, no matter how uncomfortable it might make her. And it had been uncomfortable. There had been shouting and yelling. The brother—Blaine—got on and called her incompetent and worthless. And that was before she told them about the elopement! But at the end of the day, she knew they were people with deep connections and deeper pockets. Of course she also knew they'd wield those two things against her. And they had. Less than an hour after placing the ship-to-shore call to the Winsteads, she'd been escorted down here to cruise ship lockup.

This had always been a possibility from the moment she picked up the phone, but she'd do it again. Because, in the end, her comfort, her health, and her sanity were all secondary to Paul's safety. She could never have forgiven herself if she *hadn't* called his parents. Not because they had a right to know, but because Brock and Evelyn Winstead had the power to make things happen.

Emilia's stomach churned and, for a moment, she thought she could breathe through it. But when she felt the bile start to climb up from her stomach, past her sternum, and to the base of her throat, there was barely enough time for her to vault off the cot, landing hard on her knees in front of the toilet. She moaned pitifully with each heave—a violent retching that felt as if she were being turned inside out. When she could finally find the strength to haul herself up, she clutched the rim of the tiny sink, swaying as she tried to splash some water in her mouth and onto her face. There was no mirror, which was just as well. She didn't need to know just how awful she looked.

Taking slow, careful footsteps, she managed to sway and stagger her way to the small table and one of its matching stools. A hand to her forehead confirmed her suspicion that the fever was back. She leaned forward slowly until just her head touched the cold, metallic surface. That's when the tears began again in earnest, wicking downward, dripping off the tip of her nose and onto the table.

When she heard the beep and click of the electric lock, she jerked upright abruptly, wiping her sodden face with her hands. There had been so many different people throughout the long overnight hours—variations on the same men asking variations on the same condescending questions. As the night dragged on and she felt progressively worse, there was a point when she could barely process what any of them were saying to her. It was as if somewhere in the space between their lips and her ears, the sentences twisted and flipped, rearranging themselves into a mangled, unintelligible word salad.

The man crossing the threshold right now was different enough that she felt her concentration pull into sharper focus. She was certain she hadn't seen him before—even in those hazy hours—because she would have surely remembered him. For one thing, he wasn't in the starched white uniform. Instead he wore a suit—albeit a slightly rumpled one. Also, he didn't have that European look to him like so many of the other crewmen she'd encountered. He was on the shorter side, though fairly lean, with dark hair that was threaded here and there with glints of silver. Once he'd fully entered the room and the door was closed behind him, the strange man gave her a mild smile. He kept his approach slow and his movements deliberate, as if he were trying to calm some skittish feral creature.

"Mrs. Winstead?" he said softly as he approached. "My name is Miguel Alvarez . . ."

He stopped abruptly, still several feet short of the table, and she watched as he did a visual inventory of her appearance. Who needed a mirror when this man's expression told her everything she needed to know? He reflected back the pitiful, exhausted person she'd become in the last day. Well, let him think that. Let them all think that. Let them all underestimate her. She wasn't done fighting yet, and really, what difference did one more man make in the grand scheme of things?

The detective—what did he say his name was?—closed the distance between them and dropped onto his haunches so they were at eye level.

"Mrs. Winstead," he began quietly, "you really don't look at all well. May I call in a doctor for you?"

"I'm fine," she rasped flatly.

It was a lie. She was *not* fine, and that fact was obvious to them both. But she was grateful when he didn't pursue the matter any further.

"Right," he said as he put one hand on the table, using it to brace himself so he could get back up on his feet. "Okay, well, like I said, my name is Miguel Alvarez, and I'm a detective working out of San Juan. I've come out here to see if I can help with the search for your husband—"

"Have you—have they found him?" she jumped in, suddenly more energetic. "Is Paul okay?"

She hated herself for the desperation that clung to the questions. The last thing she wanted to do was telegraph weakness to this stranger, but she wasn't a good enough liar to pretend she *wasn't* desperate to find him.

The man just shook his head regretfully.

"No, I'm afraid not. Not yet, anyway. But I can tell you they've conducted a full search of the ship, and Paul is not on board. The Coast Guard is out searching right now. You know, on the off chance he somehow . . ." He paused to clear his throat. "In case he . . . fell overboard."

Emilia stared at him, shaking her head.

"I told them," she whispered, more to herself than to him.

"Excuse me?"

She realigned her focus to him.

"I told them hours ago," she repeated, a little louder this time. "I knew he wasn't on this ship, but no one believed me. If someone—anyone—had listened to me and started to search right away, we might have found him. But now . . ."

The sentence died on her lips.

"Emilia . . . may I call you Emilia?" Miguel asked respectfully.

Not trusting herself to speak, she only nodded.

"Thank you—and please feel free to call me Miguel. I understand you're from Puerto Rico as well?"

Another nod.

"Okay, good. That's good. Would you prefer I speak Spanish?"

She shook her head this time, managing to take a shallow breath as she did.

That concerned look was back on his face again, brows drawn inward, lips pursed.

"Emilia, I understand you refused anything to eat or drink earlier. How're you feeling now? Can I have someone bring you some food? Maybe a cup of coffee or tea?"

She was surprised to find the suggestion didn't repulse her—especially considering how violently ill she'd been not twenty minutes earlier.

"Um . . . yes . . . please," she managed to murmur.

"How about eggs and toast?"

This time, her stomach wasn't quite so enthusiastic.

"Maybe just some dry toast," she countered. "And some hot tea with milk? Please."

Miguel gave a single nod of understanding, then strode over to the door, where she watched him turn and yank as if he expected it to just open. Which, of course, it did not. She could have told him that. With some irritation, the man knocked loudly until someone opened it from the other side. Next thing she knew, he was twisted so his upper torso was outside of the room while the rest of him remained firmly planted inside with her. Once he'd conveyed his message, he slipped back in, closing the door before approaching the table again.

"May I sit with you for a few minutes?" he asked, with a tilt of his chin toward an empty stool.

"Suit yourself," she replied apathetically.

Once he'd slipped out of his suit jacket and loosened his tie, Miguel dropped down onto a seat across from hers, leaning forward slightly onto his forearms. From this close up, she could see his eyes. They were dark, rich eyes—kind eyes. She wanted so much to believe that the kindness was genuine, but she knew better than to trust something so superficial. She'd learned a long time ago that there were plenty of people with pretty faces and ugly hearts.

"So how about you tell me how you and Paul came to be here on this cruise?"

Emilia let out a long, slow breath. Well, she supposed she should be grateful that someone finally *wanted* to hear what she had to say. She started with a small, shaky voice.

"We've been together three years, and we were married on the beach in Miami this past Sunday."

"You live there?"

She shook her head.

"No, we live in New York City, but we did it there so we could go right to the port and catch this cruise the same afternoon."

"And who was in attendance?"

She was confused for a moment.

"Where?"

"At your wedding ceremony . . ."

"Oh! No, there was no one. Just the two of us and an officiant—a really nice pastor from a nondenominational Christian church. And we found a couple on the beach who we were able to wrangle into being our witnesses."

Miguel raised a surprised brow.

"So . . . you eloped, then?"

"No . . . not exactly. I mean, we didn't just get up one morning and decide to run off and get married. We did plan it."

"What about your parents?"

She paused, considering how to phrase this.

"My mother and I haven't spoken since I left home years ago. And Paul's parents . . ."

She left the sentence hanging there between them, and when it became clear she wasn't going to elaborate, he pressed gently.

"What about Paul's parents, Emilia?"

She looked down at her hands in her lap.

"Paul was afraid if Brock and Evelyn knew what we had planned, they'd interfere—find some way to derail the wedding before it happened. That's why we didn't tell a soul. Like I said, even our witnesses were strangers."

"Yes, but—"

She looked up sharply.

"Detective, what does this have to do with my husband being missing?" she asked. With the question came a wave of frustration, which brought with it a surge of adrenaline. All of a sudden, she felt a little better—and a lot angrier. "People get married every day. They go on honeymoon cruises every day. They do *not* just disappear every day. One has nothing to do with the other, detective. Paul got off this ship twenty-four hours ago, and I haven't seen him since. What does it matter whether or not the mother of the groom was in attendance at the wedding or not?"

Miguel held up his palms, affecting a calmer tone when he spoke again.

"Okay, look, Emilia, can you please just humor me here? I promise you, I'm just looking for anything—any minute little detail—that might give us a clue as to what happened to your husband."

"They keep calling me Emilia Oliveras. My maiden name," she said, as if he hadn't spoken. "You know, all I ever wanted was to be rid of that name. And now I finally have a new one . . ." She looked at him. "No one will believe me—that we got married."

"Emilia, just listen to me, okay? It's not a conspiracy. Oliveras is the name they have on their manifest, since you literally *just* got married. You have to keep in mind that these guys aren't official law enforcement, so there's only so much they can do." Miguel reached out and put a hand on her forearm. "But *I* am. And I can get those records with a phone call, so please don't worry about that. I promise you we'll get that cleared up. Okay?"

She shrugged noncommittally, once again resisting the urge to believe this man. She'd been lied to before, and look where it had gotten her.

"So, you were married in Miami. But Emilia, even if the Winsteads *had* known, what could they have possibly done from there to stop you two? You're both adults. They have no power to stop you."

She hadn't expected the laugh that came out of her—a jagged-edged, bitter sound that was totally out of character for her.

"Seriously? You're the detective, aren't you? Look where you are! Look where *I* am!" She waved her arms around her to encompass the room. "You can clearly see what kind of influence these people have—the kinds of things they can get done . . . or *keep* from getting done. The Winstead family has very long arms, detective."

Emilia leaned forward, dropping her voice as if she were telling him some deep, dark secret. "Tell me, how *did* you end up here today? I might be wrong, but I'm pretty sure the San Juan Police Department has better things to do than come all the way out to the middle of the Caribbean to talk to some newlywed on a cruise ship—even if she is Puerto Rican."

The detective sat back, crossing his arms across his chest.

"You want to know? I'm happy to tell you, Emilia. My boss called me at four this morning and told me I had to come out here and assist with the investigation into Paul's disappearance. I'm not going to lie to you, I was *not* happy about getting involved in this. Jurisdiction out here is complicated. And, quite frankly, I've already got more on my plate than I can handle. And my boss knows that. But it would seem somehow, somewhere, calls were made, and strings were pulled, and . . . well . . . here I am."

She quirked an eyebrow, the corners of her lips twitching slightly.

"What?" he asked.

"Brock and Evelyn."

He looked confused.

"Paul's parents?"

She nodded.

"Yes, exactly. Brock and Evelyn Winstead. They knew someone who knew someone who knew your boss's boss. Someone who had enough reach—and power—to have you pulled from your other duties for this."

He looked skeptical.

"Okay, I'll admit that's what I think happened, too, but I hardly think it's as nefarious as you're trying to paint it."

She shrugged.

"All I know is that I just kept getting the brush-off every time I asked for help. So finally, I did the one thing I could think to do—I called Paul's parents. Because I knew the *only* way to get anyone to listen to what I was saying . . . was to get the *Winsteads* to say it. And I was right. All of a sudden, everyone was running around, tearing the ship apart looking for Paul . . . and I was put down here in cruise ship jail."

"Okay, you know what? I think maybe you're not feeling well and—"

"No," she said firmly, shaking her head from side to side. "No, no, no. You don't get to do that, *Miguel*." The way she drew out his name made it sound as if she were mocking his earlier attempts to get her to warm up to him. "I don't know exactly who did what to get you here, but I *guarantee* you it's because Brock and Evelyn think it will work to their advantage."

Rather than some understanding, Emilia saw a flash of pity cross the detective's face, and then she knew. Miguel Alvarez may very well have boarded this ship thinking he was an autonomous, impartial third party, but she knew better. He was a pawn just like the rest of them. He just didn't know it.

Not yet, anyway.

CHAPTER 11

MIGUEL

Thirty Years Ago

Something had shifted in this woman from the time he walked in twenty minutes earlier. She'd been pathetically weak and sick. But the longer they spoke, he had the distinct impression her assessment of him had somehow changed. It was as if they had changed places—like *she* was the one evaluating *him*. As if he was the poor, pathetic soul in this room.

He didn't like this change in dynamic.

"I . . . uh . . . I think we've gotten a bit off topic here," he muttered.

"Hey," she began with some irritation, "you wanted to know what happened. I'm telling you what happened. Believe me, don't believe me, I don't really care at this point."

"Alright, go ahead then," he said, even as he dug a small notebook and pen from the pocket of his suit jacket.

"Once we were settled in our stateroom, we didn't come out again until Monday—yesterday—morning."

Miguel, who'd been flipping through the pages looking for a blank one, stopped and looked at her. This statement struck him as curious.

"What, no dinner? No casino? You didn't hit one of those first-night cocktail mixers? This ship is known as the *premier* party ship—"

Emilia stared at him, brows arching high against her fore-head incredulously, as if he were the dimmest person she'd ever met.

"It was our *wedding* night," she told him in a slower, exaggerated manner.

Miguel blinked hard, his face growing warm. "Ah. Yes, of course," he agreed, quickly training his eyes back on his notes. "So—so tell me what you . . . tell me whatever else you're comfortable telling me."

She sighed, shaking her head, and he couldn't tell if it was out of frustration or amusement. She was starting to wind down again, as if she couldn't sustain the level of bravado she'd exhibited there for a brief time.

"We had this gorgeous stateroom with a balcony and or-dered dinner in from room service. Then the next morning—yesterday—we were up early to disembark in Old San Juan. But I . . ." Her voice trailed off for a moment, and she swallowed hard, clearly pushing herself to continue. "But I was really starting to feel pretty awful. I figured a day resting in bed might help me head it off before it got worse. Which, clearly, did not work."

"Emilia, I really wish you would let me call for the ship's doctor," Miguel commented softly.

"Maybe later. Can we just get through this part?"

He nodded, a little surprised she was asking him.

"Yeah, sure. Of course. So you were feeling too sick to go sightseeing in Old San Juan. But then, you're from Puerto Rico, so you've probably seen all that anyway."

"Mm-hmm," Emilia agreed. "And that was part of it, too. I hadn't been back to the island since I left home. I thought maybe I'd be okay with just going to San Juan, because I grew up on the other side of the island. But it was harder than I thought it would be."

"And Paul didn't want to stay in the room with you?"

She seemed a little surprised by the question.

"Oh, no—he was *insisting* on staying. Finally I lied and told him I was dying for *sopa de fideo*. Once he finally agreed to go find some for me, I suggested he take a little while—like just an hour—to do some sightseeing."

"I don't get it. Why so insistent that he go?"

"Because, he's done nothing but talk about going to the Casals Museum for *months*. It's why we picked a cruise that docked in Old San Juan."

"Casals?" Miguel echoed. The name rang a bell in his memory. "As in Pablo Casals—the cellist?"

"You know Casals?"

"My grandmother used to talk about seeing *el maestro* around Ceiba when she was a little girl. He's still a legend on the island."

Emilia seemed to be reassessing him as she nodded slowly.

"Yes, well, Paul is an extraordinary cellist—world class, really—and Casals has always been a hero to him." Now something different crossed her face—something akin to regret. "I didn't want him to miss out on the museum. Not when he'd been looking forward to it for so long. He was just supposed to be gone for a couple of hours."

"But he didn't come back."

The five words he'd meant to be a simple confirmation of facts turned to ash in his mouth—and on her face—as he uttered them.

"Not to our stateroom," she said, unaware she'd dropped her volume to a level barely above a whisper.

Miguel considered her carefully, trying to see the woman behind the sallow skin and the dark circles under her red-rimmed eyes. She was very young, and yet she possessed the hard edge of a woman considerably older, considerably more jaded. One who'd had too much life experience—of the bad variety. No doubt she was a bit of an enigma to Miguel, but there was nothing in his gut telling him she might have been involved in her husband's disappearance.

Was he missing something that Stenhammer had seen?

Or had Stenhammer seen something that wasn't there?

"So, Emilia, you probably should know that the Winsteads have . . ."

When he hesitated, she was all over him.

"What?" she asked, with a fleeting flash of fear. But as fast as that had come and gone, it was replaced by an icy acceptance. "Just tell me, detective. What are they saying about me?"

"You should know that Paul's parents have expressed some . . . concern . . . that you might have been involved in their son's disappearance."

He waited for a gasp of surprise or a cry of indignation.

Instead, Emilia sat there, totally impassive. She had known this was coming. That fact, in and of itself, was a clue . . . he just wasn't sure as to what.

"They think I hurt him," she muttered, more to herself than to him.

"Do you have any idea why they might think that?"

"Yes. They see this as an opportunity to be rid of me once and for all," she told him, with an icy certainty that made the hair on the back of his neck stand up.

Her cool expression hadn't shifted a single millimeter, but now there were tears streaming down her face. Turning back to his suit jacket, he pulled out the small, soft white handkerchief his wife always tucked into his pocket.

"It's clean," he assured her quietly.

She nodded and used the offering to swab the dampness from her face.

"Thank you," she murmured.

When the door opened, they both jumped a little, looking up in time to see the chief of security come in. He didn't say a word, just leaned against the wall next to the door, his hands tucked behind his back as if he were waiting to see what they'd say next.

Miguel looked at the other man expectantly.

"Something I can do for you, Mr. Stenhammer?"

"No. Just observing," he replied coolly.

In the time it took him to glance at the security director and then back at Emilia, her defenses had gone up again. The tears were gone from her eyes as she used them to shoot ice-encrusted daggers at him. Miguel looked back and forth between them.

There was another buzz from the door. It unlatched, and a young man came in, carrying a tray with the tea and toast he'd ordered for Emilia. He stopped briefly to murmur something to Stenhammer, then set the tray gently on the table, offering Emilia a small nod and smile before returning to the door.

"Detective, I'm afraid I must step out for a moment. But I will return shortly," Stenhammer said, already using his key-card to unlock the door from the inside.

Miguel seized the opportunity to speak to the crewman who had delivered the tray and was, himself, just about to exit. He recognized him as one of the trio who had passed him and Stenhammer in the hallway on the way down here. One of the ones the security director was concerned about giving fodder for the rumor mill.

"Uh—excuse me? Could you hold on a second, please?"

The young man turned toward him, brows raised as if to ask *Who, me?*

The detective nodded at the unasked question, holding up a finger. Then he leaned close to Emilia.

"You try to eat the toast, and I'll be right back. Okay?"

She nodded, not bothering to move her gaze from the tray as she did.

Outside in the hallway, he glanced down at the brass name tag pinned to the younger man's uniform.

"Hello, Sven, I'm Miguel Alvarez. I'm a detective from Puerto Rico, and I'm here to investigate the disappearance of the passenger—Paul Winstead. Did you see him on board?"

The other man's deep blue eyes circled the area around him, as if he feared being overheard or being seen with Miguel.

Interesting.

"Ah . . . yes, sir. I was their steward. From the first day they boarded. I delivered room service to the couple. He was very nice, and he gave me a very large tip."

"Did anything about them seem off to you?" When Sven frowned, Miguel realized his command of English might not be as strong as the others he'd encountered on the ship. He tried rephrasing the question. "Were they fighting at all? Did either of them seem angry at the other?"

Sven's face lit up with understanding even as he was shaking his head.

"Oh, no. No, sir. They were . . ." He paused, as if trying to find the correct words. "They were very happy. He was smiling all the time, and she was laughing. They had a nice dinner on the balcony to celebrate their marriage."

"Did you bring them any bottles of wine or champagne? Or did you notice any drinks sitting around the cabin like they'd been using the minibar?"

Sven scratched his head. "You mean did they drink too much? No—not like many other of the passengers, sir. I did not bring them any bottles, and I was the only steward assigned to them since they came aboard. I can ask the maid about the minibar, but I only saw bottles of water in the room. No wineglasses or such things."

Miguel sighed. At least if he could prove one or both of them had been drunk last night, he could consider the possibility of Paul falling overboard accidentally.

"Alright, Sven, thank you. Please let me know if you think of anything else," Miguel said, handing him a business card as he turned to go back inside the door he'd propped open with his foot while they were speaking.

"Em . . . sir?"

The detective turned to face the young man again to find

him looking nervous—which he had definitely not been ten seconds earlier.

"Is there something you'd like to tell me?"

Sven nodded and spoke quickly.

Miguel listened.

CHAPTER 12

MIGUEL

Thirty Years Ago

Cabin 1623, Sven had told him. Miguel was lucky the young man happened to hate Stenhammer and had a soft spot for the young newlyweds he'd been charged with serving. Otherwise he wouldn't have known there was someone already going through their cabin. Through *his* evidence.

By the time the elevator stopped on the sixteenth floor, Miguel was about to lose his temper in a big, ugly way. He'd had plenty of time to stew during the five stops the car had made from the second floor up to this point. During the grueling fifteen-minute trek upward, the doors slid open and shut on children in dripping bathing suits, scantily clad college girls, a trio of seniors on scooters, and a woman whose husband was so drunk, he actually had to get off with them to help her drag him to their cabin.

When he finally reached the correct deck, he didn't need to look at the numbers to find the right cabin. The door was partially open and one of those large, rolling luggage carts was parked outside, already loaded with two suitcases and a few assorted bags. He was about to push the door open but stopped short when he heard a familiar voice coming from inside.

"I don't think we'll have any trouble with the detective. He's rather dim," Stenhammer was assuring someone.

The detective froze outside of the partially open door.

"Well, dim works in our favor right now," said a second voice—this one deep with just the hint of a twang to it. A Texas twang, if Miguel wasn't mistaken.

"I have no doubt I can convince him to arrest her and take her back to San Juan for processing—"

"I wouldn't be too sure about that," Miguel said, stepping over the threshold.

The cabin looked as if a bomb had gone off in it, with drawers open and clothing strewn about—all women's clothing, he noticed. The second man, tall and muscular with light brown hair, appeared to be tossing items into a suitcase sitting on top of the unmade bed.

"Detective Alvarez! I didn't know . . . I thought you were . . ." Stenhammer stammered.

"Maybe not as dim as you thought, huh?" the other man said to the security director with a chuckle. Then he turned in Miguel's direction. "And you must be Detective Alvarez," he said, extending a hand for him to shake.

"And you must be a member of the Winstead family," Miguel replied, leaving the man's hand suspended there until he finally withdrew it with an apathetic shrug.

"I'm Blaine Rockford Winstead Jr. Paul is my little brother, and I'm here to collect his things before they can 'disappear.'"

"This is all evidence. And even if it wasn't, Mrs. Winstead is the rightful owner of the items."

"Missus? *Mrs.* Winstead?" Blaine laughed as if this were the most ridiculous thing he'd ever heard in his life. "Detective, my mother Evelyn is the only Mrs. Winstead. Emilia's nothing more than an itch my brother needed to scratch, if you know what I mean."

He didn't bother to dignify the last comment with a response.

"Well, she seems to think they were married in a legally

binding ceremony a few days ago. And if that's the case, there'll be a record of it filed at the courthouse."

Blaine appeared to be unfazed. "Well, then I suggest you go ahead and give those folks a call. But something tells me there won't be any such document on file at that courthouse . . . or any other."

Miguel wanted to wipe the smug expression right off his face. He turned his attention to the third man in the room to distract himself until he could cool down.

"And you," he said to Stenhammer, "I take it you've been in on this . . . whatever the hell this is . . . since Paul went missing."

The security director seemed to shrink in his starched white uniform. Not so officious now, was he?

"I only did as the captain asked and allowed Mr. Winstead here entry to the cabin so he could retrieve his brother's things . . ."

If there'd been any hope of that lie flying, it came to a crashing halt when Blaine Winstead walked up beside him and draped a casual arm over his shoulders.

"Oh, now don't be so modest! Mr. Stenhammer here has been so helpful, and my family is exceptionally grateful. As we are to you for your help, detective. And I think you'll find my father is very generous with the people who are the most helpful to him."

Miguel couldn't believe what he was hearing. The sheer hubris was astounding. This guy wasn't even *trying* to disguise what his intentions were. Hell, he was broadcasting them!

"Mr. Winstead, I think *you'll* find my job is not to be 'helpful.' My job is to investigate crimes and find out the truth. Like what happened to a young man who disappeared off a cruise ship. Sort of like your brother, right? I can't help but notice you don't seem to be especially concerned about his whereabouts or his welfare."

The transformation was subtle in that it only affected his eyes—they seemed to narrow and harden, even as his perfectly straight, gleamingly white smile didn't fade in the slightest.

"We expect you to do what you were brought out here to do—arrest Emilia Oliveras and accompany her back to San Juan. That's all. Then you can just walk away. Everything else is already in place on that end."

Miguel had to fight hard to keep his own expression impassive. Was this man telling him that someone in law enforcement was prepared to do this family's bidding? It certainly wasn't out of the realm of possibility; police were vulnerable to bribes or, worse, blackmail. He just couldn't imagine anyone he worked with could be capable of that kind of deception or falling prey to that type of coercion.

"I don't walk away from anything, Mr. Winstead. So if that's what you were hoping for, I'm sorry to disappoint you. I was brought out here to follow up on a report of a missing tourist. I've spoken with Emilia and, so far, I have no reason to believe she had anything to do with that. Unless of course there's some evidence I haven't been privy to?"

Stenhammer, who'd been gradually but steadily inching toward the cabin door, stopped short when Miguel fixed his sights on him once more. "Mr. Stenhammer? Did you come up with some video footage of the two of them last night? Hell, have you come up with any video footage of that man even getting back on this boat?"

The other man's face began to redden. Stenhammer opened his mouth to say something—though he'd never know what that was, because Blaine stepped between the two of them. His chest was puffed out now and his legs were spread slightly farther apart. His chin was also tilted back and slightly upward. All, Miguel noted, meant to make himself appear bigger, broader, stronger, and more menacing.

"Listen to me, detective," Blaine warned, moving into

his personal space. "My father's called in a lot of favors and greased more than a few palms to ensure Emilia Oliveras shows up at the police station in San Juan. He's arranged to have a goddamn posse of reporters waiting to catch her 'perp walk' for the five o'clock news. We just have to get her there. And believe me, if you're not up to the job, we'll find someone who is. You boys are a dime a dozen, and I can have another one out here in under an hour—I'll make sure of it. And if you think I'm exaggerating, I suggest you call your superior. He'll tell you the same thing." In an instant, the smiling, affable expression was back in place, and the man's tone was back to friendly. "But I'm sure that won't be necessary, will it? I understand this is a fairly new promotion for you. It'd be a shame to see you get busted back down to beat cop. Or just . . . let go. It'd be a shame if that pretty nurse wife of yours had to support you and your daughter 'cause you couldn't even get a job working mall security."

Miguel didn't flinch. He knew better than to show his hand by getting emotional. He could figure out who was giving out his personal information and kick their ass later on. Right now, he had to figure out which cards to play—and fast. Too fast. He needed more time, so he did one of the things he was best at—he bluffed.

The detective stepped closer so that he and Blaine were almost toe-to-toe. When he spoke again, he lowered both the tone and volume of his voice.

"Tell me, Mr. Winstead. Just how grateful a man is your father?"

Blaine gave his arm a playful shove as he burst out in laughter.

"Oh, detective, I think you'd be amazed at just *how* grateful my family can be!"

He and Stenhammer didn't speak on the way back down to the security office. The security director had lost most of his bravado and now just stood staring down at the floor of the elevator. When they were back downstairs, Miguel held out his hand.

"Give me a keycard. I need to be able to get in and talk to her."

"Oh, no, that is not necessary. I will—"

"Give me the card, Stenhammer. And set me up with a ship-to-shore call so I can figure out the logistics of this with my boss."

He hesitated for a moment but finally just nodded, handing him the requested item and leading him into this office. Five minutes later, Miguel was connected to Captain Delgado. He took the receiver from Stenhammer, staring at him pointedly until he left, closing the door behind him. The detective knew he'd need to keep his voice low regardless.

"Alvarez? What's going on out there?" the captain asked.

He couldn't think of any tactful way to ask the question, so he skipped the tact altogether.

"What the fuck, Captain? You sent me out here to help them set up this woman? These people aren't even looking for Paul Winstead . . . which makes me think they already know where he is . . ."

"Miguel . . ."

"And he knows about my family! He knows Hilda is a nurse and that I have a daughter and—"

"Miguel! Just stop!"

"But I—"

"I mean it, Detective Alvarez. Not. Another. Word!"

Delgado could have a wicked temper, but Miguel had never been on the receiving end of it before. It was more than a little unnerving. Several seconds passed in tense silence before the captain spoke again, this time in a considerably calmer voice.

"You seem to have forgotten that before I was a captain, I was a detective—and I was a damn good one at that. Good enough that *I* never made the rookie mistake of assuming I was the smartest person in the room."

What the hell was that supposed to mean? He wasn't willing to risk opening his mouth again to ask the question.

"Here's how it is, Detective Alvarez," the man continued once more, "my phone rings in the middle of the night, and I'm told to send someone out there to evaluate a missing tourist. Except it's not our jurisdiction. The FBI's supposed to get that call, but for some reason, my boss's *boss's* boss is ordering—not requesting—but *ordering* I send a detective out there. Thing is, I have a problem with people who believe they can buy anything and everything they want. I have an even *bigger* problem with the cops who are giving these people a reason to believe such a thing is even possible."

"Oh, thank God! Captain, I'm so glad—" he burst out, but was shut down by a vicious hiss from Delgado.

"Shh! Listen to what I'm telling you. It's important."

There was a long pause on the other end, and for just a moment, he thought he'd lost the call. But then his boss spoke again.

"Do you remember, maybe five years ago? That woman who stabbed her husband thirty-seven times?"

An image popped into his head. She was tall and thin with a streak of white in her hair. She'd been a spiritualist of some sort—tarot cards, spells, fortunes, and the like. Miguel's mother would have called her a *bruja*—a witch.

"Yeah, yeah . . . she claimed the 'spirits' made her do it, because he'd been abusing her daughter—his stepdaughter. Turns out the kid had told her what was going on, and she didn't believe her, so the girl ran away from home."

"Exactly. The defense tried to find her so she could come back and testify. It might have been the difference between manslaughter and murder."

"Right. I remember now. Why? Did you work that case, Captain?"

"I was the lead detective. Believe me when I tell you—crazy lady or not—the guy had it coming to him. We found a whole *stash* of photos he took of maybe a dozen girls, including the stepdaughter."

"Oh, God, what was her name again? Esmerelda?"

"Imelda," Delgado corrected him. "Imelda Oliveras."

For a moment Miguel thought he'd misheard.

"Oliveras," he repeated.

"Oliveras. The daughter—"

He finished the sentence for his boss.

"Was Emilia Oliveras."

"Now you understand."

But did he? Just because she'd been a victim of sexual abuse didn't mean she wasn't capable of killing her husband. In fact, given what her mother did, some people might say she'd be more inclined than most. Delgado must have been following his unspoken train of thought.

"I can't think of a detective I trust more than you, Miguel. You're smart, you're fair, and your gut is almost always spot-on. I knew if I sent you out there and let you do your thing, you'd come back with the answer I needed."

"You wanted to know if she could have done it."

"Exactly. I know what I think. The question is, what do you think?"

He knew the answer the second he heard the question.

"It's a setup," he growled. "The brother told me as much. The security director is taking payment, and I was told that if I didn't bring her in, someone else would come out here and do it. To top it off, the girl is violently ill, and she was begging the crew to help her find Paul long before the Winsteads got involved. No. No way she's got anything to do with his disappearance. And, for the record, I believe they were married."

"Right. Well, I can tell you two things that I know to be fact. What you do with that information is up to you."

"Okay . . ."

"The first thing is that if Emilia Oliveras stays on that boat, she'll be arrested and brought back here to San Juan. The second thing is that if Emilia Oliveras is brought back here to San Juan, she doesn't stand a snowball's chance in hell."

CHAPTER 13

MIGUEL

Thirty Years Ago

Miguel found Stenhammer in the hallway, peering into Emilia's cell through the glass pane in the door. He joined the man and took a look for himself. The woman was curled up on her side across the ridiculous vinyl cushion they called a bed. He could see her shivering from here.

"You know, you could at least get her a blanket," he commented. "Or did the Winsteads forbid it?"

"Don't judge me," the other man replied in a low voice. "You have no idea what these people are capable of."

Miguel scoffed. "Please, a little dramatic, no? I hardly think that puffed-up, entitled cowboy upstairs is going to have you killed."

"No, of course not. But you heard him—they have connections, they have power . . ."

"They have nothing unless you give it to them, Stenhammer. So why don't you just man up and tell me the truth. Paul never got back on this ship, did he?"

The security director turned to face him. "You seem to think I have a choice here. If I don't placate them I could lose everything—my job, my home. Again, I don't think you appreciate the lengths they'll go to to get what they want."

Miguel cut him off with an incredulous scoff.

"Don't I? You were in that cabin, you heard him. He knows my wife's name and what she does for a living. He knows I have a daughter. And how *is* that by the way?"

Stenhammer shrugged. "They run a check on everyone they deal with. Or perhaps someone you work with gave him the information? Does it really matter?"

It did to him, but he'd have to get that sorted later. There were more pressing issues for the moment. He glanced at Emilia again. She hadn't stirred from her position.

"I'm taking her to the ship's doctor," Miguel announced.

"That won't be possible," the other man said. "She's not to leave this room until you're ready to take her to San Juan for processing."

"I wasn't asking, Mr. Stenhammer. Where is the doctor's office located?"

"I'm afraid I can't allow it."

Miguel sighed with his impatience, as if the security chief were a wayward child.

"Why don't you go and take care of your VIP guest—help him load up that fancy helicopter he flew in on, and I'll see her to the doctor's office myself. If Junior asks what the holdup is, just tell him you wanted to get that fever under control so she looks a little less pathetic when she gets in front of the cameras in San Juan. They want people to believe she's capable of making her husband disappear, don't they?"

He seemed to consider this and then nodded.

"Yes, this makes sense. Fine. It's on third level, aft starboard. You can't miss it. But I want a report in one hour's time, detective."

"Frankly, Mr. Stenhammer, I couldn't give a flying fig what you want."

"Emilia, vamos. Tenemos que sacarte de aquí. Ahora."
Emilia, come on. We have to get you out of here. *Now.*

When the woman finally opened her dark eyes, they were glassy and unfocused.

Miguel dropped down to his haunches and put his mouth close to her ear. He was certain Stenhammer would have someone keeping an eye on them.

"You were right," he whispered as loudly as he dared. "I have to get you off this ship right now, but you have to help me. You have to get up . . ."

If she took any satisfaction in being told she'd been right all along, she didn't show it. She only nodded, swinging her legs over the edge of the cot. But she began to sway unsteadily as soon as she was on her feet. Damn. How was he going to get her out of here if she couldn't even walk? She was a small enough woman, but he wasn't sure he could carry her all the way up and out to the tender. And even if he could, they would most certainly draw attention to themselves.

Sensing the dilemma, she grabbed onto Miguel's hand and placed it on her upper arm, wrapping his fingers around it tightly. He was confused until he realized what she'd done. It looked as if he was transporting her somewhere—like a police officer would handle a suspect. Excellent idea. He led her back the way he had just come, taking a beat before stepping out into the waiting area once more.

When the detective turned the knob and pushed the door open, he was met by complete chaos. No fewer than ten people were crammed into the little waiting room, all of them yelling at the same time. The melee seemed to center around two very drunk women who were, even at that moment, clawing against security officers as they tried to get to each other.

Miguel said a silent prayer of thanksgiving for the perfectly timed distraction and quickly navigated Emilia through the throng and out to the hallway. He found them a shadowy doorway where they could stand unseen for at least a few minutes while he figured out what their next move would be.

He'd had to get her out of there so quick, there hadn't been time to sort out the details before.

"Now," he said, more to himself than to her. "If we take the elevator back up to the main lobby, we might be able to—"

"There," Emilia whispered, pointing to a small, unmarked hallway directly across from them.

He looked at her quizzically.

"What? What's down there?"

"Two-two-nine."

Miguel didn't know what that meant, but he didn't have a lot of time or options at the moment, so he helped her down the corridor past what must be crew cabins. When they reached the one she indicated, he knocked. There was no response, so he knocked harder. After a few seconds, a muffled voice came from inside.

"Hold yer damn horses! Someone *better* be on fire if you're waking my ass up at—"

The door flew open on a bleary-eyed, bed-headed man wearing nothing but his boxers and a very pissed-off expression. He blinked hard at them and shook his head slightly, as if he thought he might still be dreaming. Then he squinted and focused in on Emilia.

"Mrs. Winstead?"

"Hi, Josh," she managed to whisper. "Mind if we come in?"

"What? Oh! Yes, of course! Please . . ."

He stepped back, holding the door open for them. Once they'd cleared the threshold, the man stuck his head out into the corridor, looking both ways, presumably to see if anyone had seen the two of them go to his door. Miguel liked him already.

"Detective, this is Josh; he's a bartender and he was with me last night when I was trying to find Paul. He's the one who got me to the security office."

And that had worked out wonderfully, hadn't it?

"You have a roommate?" Miguel asked, nodding toward the bunk beds taking up most of the tiny space.

"Ahhh . . . no. I mean yes. I do share the cabin, but we work opposing schedules. He won't be back here till four or five. And who are you again?" he asked, giving Miguel a once-over.

"Josh, this is Miguel; he's a detective from San Juan. He's going to help me," Emilia said.

"Help you how?"

The detective filled him in on the events that had transpired after the man left Emilia at her cabin the night before. As he listened, Josh's face morphed from concern to incredulity to rage.

"Hang on there just a sec. Emilia, are you saying that after I saw you last night, they put you in the *brig*?" She nodded. "So this all's been going on, and your Paul is *still* missing?"

"Yes, he is," Miguel jumped in impatiently. "Look, I'm sorry, but we don't have a lot of time here. Paul's brother is already upstairs, and we have a very small window before someone starts looking for Emilia. I need to get her off this ship without anyone noticing. Is that something you think you can assist us with?"

The bartender seemed to consider this as he scratched his unruly hair.

"Depends; you got transportation outta here?"

"I do—for now. There's a tender waiting to take me out to rendezvous with a Coast Guard cruiser. But I've got to find a way to get her out there before anyone figures out she's not where she's supposed to be."

Josh straightened up suddenly, seeming to grasp the emergent nature of the situation.

"Yeah. Yeah, I reckon I might could do that. Tender's up on deck four. We can use the back stairwell. The tricky thing'll be getting her aboard without the tender captain *knowing* she's aboard. There ain't much room to hide a person, on one a those things."

"Okay," the detective began thoughtfully, "what *wouldn't* look suspicious accompanying me back to Puerto Rico?"

"Don't know . . . somethin' needs transporting to one of the ports for some specific reason? Maybe somethin' that can't be repaired here on the ship?"

Miguel looked up abruptly, something occurring to him. "Emilia, any chance you'd fit in Paul's empty cello case? I just saw it up in your cabin, and it looked pretty big. I could lie and say I'm bringing it back to San Juan for safekeeping or evidence or whatever."

He could see how hard it was for her to focus on this simple question. After a long beat, she shook her head slowly.

"No. The neck is too narrow."

He let out a frustrated sigh.

"Hey, just hang on there," Josh said, wagging an excited finger at them. "What about one a those big cellos—what d'ya call it? A bass! What about a bass case? Them suckers are pretty big."

"I . . . yes, I guess that could work," she agreed. "But where are you going to find one of *those*?"

Josh was already pushing past them in the tiny cabin, throwing on some jeans and a T-shirt.

"Oh, honey, this place is lousy with musicians! We must have a dozen different bands on board to cover all the different lounges. Hell, they got an entire orchestra playing for those big fancy shows they got going every night! Now I gotta buddy, Caleb—he plays that bass in the jazz club that's next deck up from the Wagon Wheel. And just so happens he owes me a big favor."

"Emilia, you okay with that?" Miguel asked, hopefully. "It's a tight space to be in for more than an hour. If you've got claustrophobia or anything like that . . ."

"I don't care if I have to ride out of here in a coffin," she replied acridly. "Please just get me the hell off of this ship."

By the time Josh and his friend had prepped the case—pulling out some of the padding and drilling tiny airholes—Emilia seemed more than happy to get in, barely able to stand on her own at this point. It also helped that Caleb the bass player had given her "a little something" to help her relax. She was out cold when they sealed up the case and gently rolled her up and out to the tender.

Miguel felt better the moment they pulled away from the floating dock, but he knew better than to count his chickens. Every minute or so, he glanced behind them, half expecting to see Stenhammer and Blaine Winstead chasing them down in a powerboat a la James Bond. But there was nothing. No one. And before long, the ship was just a speck on the ocean.

CHAPTER 14

MIGUEL

Thirty Years Ago

Several hours later Miguel tapped his fingers on the kitchen table nervously. He would stretch periodically, tipping his chair to the far left so he could get a glimpse down the long tiled hallway to the guest room, where his wife had taken Emilia over an hour ago. He didn't know what he expected to see there, but it was something to do while he waited, going over the day's events in his mind. He'd already had three *cafés con leche* and was seriously contemplating a fourth when the phone rang.

He knew it was Captain Delgado before he even picked up the receiver, and he was ready.

"Detective Alvarez."

"Captain?"

"So, I just spent an hour dealing with a very pissed-off Swede called Hammerhead."

"Hammerhead?" Miguel echoed. It took him a second to understand. "Oh, do you mean *Stenhammer*? Olav Stenhammer, the security chief on the ship?"

"That would be the one."

"And what did he want?"

"Detective, Emilia Oliveras is gone."

Miguel was good at this. He could play dumb all night

long. As, apparently, could his boss. This call was clearly for someone else's benefit. Someone who was likely listening on another extension.

"I'm sorry, gone?" the detective confirmed with appropriate incredulity. "My God! She was sick, but I didn't realize she was *that* sick . . ."

"She's not dead, Alverez, she's just missing from the ship. And, as Officer Clawhammer pointed out, you were the last one seen with her."

"Me?"

This time he didn't have to feign his surprise; he didn't think Stenhammer had the *cojones* to file a complaint against him. Not when he was up to his eyeballs in this thing himself.

"Yes, you."

Miguel let out a long sigh.

"Okay, sounds to me like he's trying to shift a little blame."

"Yes, well, that may be, but according to this guy, you were seen escorting her from the security offices, and then she just . . . vanished. Next thing they know, you're headed back here without so much as a wave goodbye."

He scoffed.

"The man stepped out of the interview for what was supposed to be a few minutes, then never came back. I dropped the woman at the sickbay so the doctor could have a look. And when I went back down to the security office so they could page him, there was a full-on circus going on down there. A rowdy bunch of tourists trying to claw each other's eyes out. They wouldn't have noticed Cindy Crawford walking out of there naked with a patch on her eye and a parrot on her shoulder. By then I was done, so I got myself down to the tender and left."

He could hear Delgado trying to cover a snort of laughter with a faux cough. He didn't do a very good job of it, and Miguel smiled, almost wishing he was there to see for whose benefit this performance was. Probably the boss's boss. Maybe even someone from the Winstead camp.

"So you're saying the woman was *not* with you in the tender?" Delgado asked pointedly.

"Um, well, not that I could see."

The other man sighed. "Alright, well, I appreciate your efforts out there, Alvarez. Be sure to file a report for me tomorrow."

"Right, will do. Goodnight, Captain."

He hung up and turned around to find Hilda watching him with interest. His wife hadn't asked any questions when he showed up with a sick young woman whose picture was, by then, starting to pop up on the later newscasts. It seemed like the best option, given his wife was a traveling nurse who kept medical supplies.

"Well, how is she?" he asked, rushing to her.

"How do you think she is?" she replied with some irritation. "The poor girl's husband is missing, and now her in-laws are telling the world she killed him! As if that's not bad enough, she's sick. Sick enough to be in the hospital, Miguel, not in our guest room."

He lowered his voice, not wanting their daughter to overhear this conversation.

"You have to just trust me on this, *mi amor*. Right now, this is the safest place for her."

The irritation on his wife's face was replaced by concern.

"*Safer*? Does that mean she's actually in danger?"

"She was so long as she was on that ship," he began slowly. "That's why I couldn't leave her there."

Hilda put a soft hand on her husband's arm.

"Of course I believe you. What I don't understand is how this started out as a favor for your captain and ended up with us harboring a fugitive?"

"She's not a fugitive," he said firmly. "She hasn't been

charged with anything. Hell, they still don't even know what happened to Paul Winstead."

"Well, for someone who isn't a fugitive from the law, you're certainly taking great pains to hide her from it. I heard you, you know. When you were speaking with Captain Delgado on the phone just now. Miguel, you lied to him. You told him you didn't know anything about her disappearance from custody. And yet"—she waved a hand toward the hallway where the bedrooms were—"here she is under our roof."

He leaned forward and kissed her on the cheek. "Honey, you don't have all the information—"

"No, no. Don't you 'honey' me. I know I don't have all the facts, but I know one thing—you shouldn't have brought this trouble into our home—where our five-year-old is playing with her dolls in the other room."

The detective didn't know how to make her understand— to make her *see* what he was feeling. But he knew he had to try. Because without his wife's cooperation, everything would fall apart—and fast. He put both of his hands on her shoulders and met her green eyes squarely.

"*Mira*—look, Hilda, it's *our* girl—our Alicia—who I'm thinking about right now."

"Miguel—"

"No, no. Please just hear me out. Think about it, Hilda. What if it was *her*? What if, God forbid, Alicia found herself alone, sick, and unable to trust the people who were supposed to be looking out for her?" Miguel had to stop so he could swallow the hard lump forming in his throat. He was surprised to find himself getting so emotional. "I know I'd be down on my hands and knees praying to Jesus Christ Himself to send our girl someone to watch over her—to protect her. To get her someplace safe."

She looked at him for what felt like a very long time until, finally, he saw the shift in her expression.

"But Miguel, do you *really* believe you can't trust your own squad with this?" she asked quietly.

He considered telling her about his earlier conversation with Delgado but decided the less she knew, the better. "All I know is that, right now, *I'm* the only one I trust."

She sighed.

"Okay, so what's your plan then? Someone will figure it out eventually, Miguel—if they haven't already. And when they do, your career is over."

The detective had no illusions. It was just a matter of time before someone came sniffing around here. And he couldn't have that.

"I know you're right. And I give you my word I'll find a safe place for her to go once she's well enough. But tell me, how sick is she?"

Hilda crossed the kitchen to put some more water in the kettle.

"Ah, well, she's been out of it for the most part, so I've had to do a little detective work of my own. But I'm fairly certain she has norovirus," she told him over her shoulder. "It can be rampant on those ships. That's the most pressing issue, anyway. I already gave her some Tylenol for the fever, and I'm going to go grab an IV kit and saline bags from my travel kit. Once she gets some hydration, she'll feel much better."

"Thank God it's not something serious."

"Ah, well . . . not the norovirus anyway. But I suspect there's an underlying condition that would account for the vertigo, the violent nausea, and the sudden, severe dehydration—something called hyperemesis gravidarum. It's not super common, but I've come across it enough times to recognize it."

"And how serious is this—this hyper thing?"

Hilda smiled. "Hyper-em-eh-sis grav-ee-darum," she repeated phonetically.

He rolled his eyes and shook his head, smiling. "Okay, okay, fine Dr. Dictionary. How long will it take *that* to resolve?"

She shrugged.

"I don't know. My guess is five or six months maybe—I'll have a better idea when she's more alert. She didn't happen to mention how far along she is, did she?"

Miguel stared at his wife blankly, somehow unable to grasp what it was she was telling him.

"How far along . . . ?"

"*¡Ay, Dios mío!*" she exclaimed with some exasperation. "And you call yourself a detective? Miguel, that young woman is pregnant!"

CHAPTER 15

GRACIE

Today

"Gracie, she must have said *something*!" my sister is insisting. "How could you just let her leave the mall like that?"

"What was I supposed to do, Meg? Hurl myself in front of the car? She wouldn't wait for me to pick up my phone from the repair kiosk, so she told me to catch an Uber and left me standing there. That's when I called you and you called Dad."

"I didn't call Dad. I thought you called him."

We both turn to look at our father, who's rubbing his temples.

"Dad?" Meg presses. "How did you know to meet us here?"

"Because she called me on her way to the airport and asked me to come."

"Wait, wait, wait—the airport? She's actually left town?" I ask, incredulous.

"But where did she go?" Meg wants to know. "Couldn't she just wait for us? I don't understand any of this—"

"Please stop," Dad says quietly.

"Who is Miguel? And since when does Mom speak Spanish? And—"

"Okay—just stop! *Both* of you!"

I can count on one hand the number of times our father has

raised his voice at us. It's so jarring that we both stop and stare at him. He runs a hand through his hair nervously and starts to pace the kitchen. When I glance at Meg, she just shrugs.

"Dad?" I say softly.

"Gracie, I'm not *your father!"*

The words feel so much like a slap that I actually put a hand to my cheek. A second later, he's in front of me, pulling me into his arms. He's shaking. Oh, my God, is he . . . ? He's crying!

"I don't . . ." I begin, but he cuts me off.

"I mean, of course I'm your father," he murmurs into my hair. "I couldn't love you more if we shared DNA. But we don't. Your father—your biological father is a man named Paul Winstead . . ."

I push away from him so I can see his face. "The guy from Tampa? The spring break guy's name is Paul?"

He looks so miserable as he shakes his head. "Jesus Christ, Emily," he mutters, rolling his eyes upward, invoking my mother from her seat on the airplane. Then he takes a deep breath and pauses, as if willing himself to calm down before continuing. "No, honey, there was no one-night stand on spring break. Your mom—her real name isn't Emily, it's Emilia. And she was married once. Before me. To your father—to Paul . . ."

I have heard a lot of crazy shit in the courtroom over the years. So much so that I can't recall the last time I was really and truly surprised by something someone said. Until now. Until this.

"They attended the Manhattan Conservatory together," he continues. "He was a cellist and, of course, she was a pianist. Paul's family had a lot of money—oil money. And let's just say they weren't especially fond of your mom. They thought she was a gold digger—"

"Mom! *Our* mom?" Meg exclaims from the other side of

the kitchen island. "A *gold* digger? What's wrong with those people!"

"I know, sweetie, I know. Paul never believed that, and they eloped against his family's wishes. But he . . . well, he disappeared while they were on their honeymoon cruise in the Caribbean."

He goes on to explain the wrath of the evil Winstead family—like something out of an old western movie—and their determination to hold my mother accountable for murder. When he's finished, I drop onto a stool, trying to soak in this twisted, convoluted and, quite frankly, far-fetched story.

"She really had another husband?" Meg confirms, as if she might have gotten that rather pertinent point wrong.

"She did," he agrees.

"Before you," she adds.

He nods. "Yes, before me."

"And—you knew all this? All these years?"

I don't realize just how hurt I am by this realization until I hear it in my own question.

"I did," he agrees quietly, looking down to study his hands. "She told me when we started seeing one another, but it had to be a secret—from everyone. There were some very real safety concerns that were a consideration here. Especially when you girls were young. Eventually the story died down . . . but we could never assume the threat had gone away. Those people were hell-bent on making Mom pay, and if they'd tracked her down and discovered they had a grandchild . . ."

He lets the thought die, but I decide to resuscitate it.

"If they'd discovered they had a grandchild what? They would have wanted to know me? So I could have had grandparents. Maybe aunts, and uncles, and cousins . . . I wouldn't have been living here out in the middle of Nowhere, Oregon feeling like my entire life has been a joke that everyone was in on except for me?"

My heart is starting to pick up speed in my chest, and I can feel my pulse in my neck and temples.

"You don't understand," Richard insists. "They would have *taken* you from her. They would have painted her as an unfit mother—a killer, even—and they would have made certain she never saw you again."

"Pffft," I scoff. "Please. Do you know how hard it is for grandparents to get custody over parents? What it takes to declare someone an unfit parent? No way anyone could make that argument against her."

"I'm telling you it didn't matter, Gracie!" he stresses, his voice growing louder. "You've got to consider that this was thirty years ago! They had more money than God, and they had absolutely no problem using it to grease whatever palms were necessary—the police, judges, the press—even the crew of the cruise ship was involved. They would have stopped at nothing to see your mom charged with murder and have you taken away from her. So she ran before anyone even knew she was pregnant. She fled the Caribbean, changed her name, and came to live out here. Later on, I fell in love with her . . . and with you."

"But you didn't stay together," Meg observes quietly. "Was it . . . am I the reason? You were happy before *I* was born . . ."

"What? Oh, no, honey! No, no, no . . ." Dad says, stretching across the island so he can brush her hand with his fingertips. He sighs deeply, then continues. "I loved your mom. And she loved me. But Paul was the great love of her life. He still is. No matter how hard I tried, I couldn't compete with a ghost. So we split, even though we still loved each other very much. We still *do* love each other very much."

"And her real name is Emilia Oliveras," I confirm. "But she changed it to Emily Oliver."

"Yes. Then we were married, and she became Emily Daniels."

"But I still don't understand why she had to leave," Meg comments.

It's an excellent point. What was it, exactly, that precipitated this shit show?

"Right," Richard starts slowly, as if he'd been hoping we might forget to ask this question. "That call she got—when you were in the mall, Gracie? That was someone she knew back then. Something happened and he has reason to believe Paul might be alive down there in Puerto Rico. Now she's gone to see for herself."

Very often when I'm listening to a witness give testimony on the stand, something specific jumps out at me. Usually something that seems innocuous enough to gloss over. That's what's happening here. As intrigued as I am by the "dead husband sighting," that isn't the part of his explanation that catches my attention.

"And that's her only connection to Puerto Rico?"

He pauses, clearly not expecting the question.

"She was born there," he tells us with some reluctance. "Spanish was actually her first language."

I stare at him and then smile, shaking my head. This is starting to become comical—how little we know about our own mother.

"Of course she was born in Puerto Rico. Because God forbid she even tell us the truth about that," I snark, and continue before I can be chided for the comment. "Okay, fine. And if it *is* him? What's supposed to happen then?"

He stares at me for a long moment.

"Your guess is as good as mine, Gracie."

This answer does not sit well with me.

"But *is* it?" I challenge. "See, because from where I'm sitting, you haven't had to guess about much. You've been privy to all of this for decades. And the only reason you're telling me . . ." I pause long enough to gesture between myself and Meg. "The only reason you're telling *us* anything now is because you don't have a choice. I get the feeling you'd have been just as happy keeping this little secret buried indefinitely."

My father considers me impassively before he speaks again, and I have to admit I'm a little taken aback by how much his tone—and his attitude—have cooled when he finally does.

"Gracie, this was your mother's story to tell. These were *her* secrets to keep. You're right, I would love to be anywhere but here right now having this conversation with you. And yet, here we are. Because I respect your mother, and I respect the choices she's made."

Well that makes one of us.

I know he's gone when I hear the driveway alarm from downstairs. A few seconds later, Meg's footsteps are headed up the stairs toward my room. I've already got half of my stuff crammed into the roller bag when she comes in unannounced.

"What are you doing?"

"Packing."

"Listen, I get it, you're hurt, you're confused, you're angry. And every single one of those feelings is appropriate under the circumstances."

"Well, thank you very much, Dr. Phil. I don't know what I'd do without you to 'validate my emotions.'"

When my sister speaks again, her voice is icy, and it bothers me more than I'd care to admit. "Right. Do what you always do. Just push everyone away so you can suffer in silence. Really loud, really *obnoxious* silence, by the way."

"What is that supposed to mean?" I stop packing long enough to glare at her.

"It means you're acting like a martyr."

I scoff. "Am I now? Well, Meg, if you think I'm exaggerating how upsetting all of this is, then you're not as smart as I thought you were."

She flips me the middle finger and stomps out, slamming

the door behind her. A minute later, I can just make out the sound of her screaming into a pillow. When I enter her bedroom, I find her face down on the bed.

"Meg?"

"What do you want?" she grumbles.

"You okay?"

"It doesn't matter," she replies petulantly.

"Yes it does. I'm sorry. Here you've been trying so hard to help, and I'm just being a bitch . . ."

"Yes," she agrees. "You are."

There's a long, awkward pause before I finally just spit out my request.

"I need you to take me to the airport."

She raises her head and looks at me over her shoulder.

"Pfft. Yeah, like that's going to happen."

"Please?"

"Sorry, I'm not smart enough to drive a car. Or navigate to the airport. Or breathe. Hell, I'm not smart enough to *live!*"

Her face goes back to the pillow, and I come all the way inside, taking a seat on the bottom left corner of the mattress.

"I'm sorry. I didn't mean that to sound the way it came out . . ."

Now she flips all the way over so I can see her when she shoots daggers at me with her eyes.

"Yes. Yes, you did. So don't even try and walk it back. We both know that you may say things that you regret, but you *never* say anything you don't mean, Gracie."

She's right. I don't. I sigh and try for a reasonable tone.

"Meg, there's something really wrong with this whole thing. It just doesn't smell right. You know?"

My sister looks suspicious, like I might be trying to lure her into a trap.

"What do you mean?"

"I mean, why now after thirty years? Where's this guy been all this time? His family's got all that money but wasn't able to find Mom? I don't know, this is all just a little too . . . random. And convenient."

She considers me for a few seconds.

"It is," she agrees. "You think it's a scam?"

I shrug. "Wouldn't be the first time I've come across something this elaborate. And Mom isn't . . . well . . . the most savvy person. I don't think it'd take much for someone to use her insane past to drain her bank accounts or steal her identity . . . maybe worse."

Alarm flashes across her face.

"Oh, my God! You're right . . . she really is kind of gullible."

I nod my agreement. "I love her, but yes. Definitely. So I'm going to go down there to make sure she doesn't do anything stupid like blow her life's savings on some guy in a Speedo pretending to be her long-lost dead husband."

Meg squishes her face in distaste, probably envisioning the scene I've just painted for her.

"You're going now?"

"I am if you'll take me. The Tesla's out of juice, and it's damn near impossible to get an Uber out here."

"And you really think she might be in trouble?"

"Not a doubt in my mind."

She nods and gets to her feet. "Okay, just let me throw a few things in a bag—"

"Whoa—stop right there," I say, holding up my palms. "You're not coming with me."

"Yes, I am."

"No, you're not," I push back harder.

Meg stares at me for a long moment. "Gracie, I'm not eight years old anymore. I know it's easier for you to think of me that way. You probably resent me less if you still think of me as some stupid little kid. But I'm not. I'm a grown-ass woman. And if our mother needs help, then I'll be damned if I'm going to stand by and do nothing."

Pigtails and buckteeth.

She's right, that's exactly what I see when I look at her. Even now after everything she's accomplished.

"Okay, fine. But if you get in the way or if it feels dangerous at any point, I'm sticking you on the first flight back home."

"Deal. Thank you, Gracie," she adds with a grin so sweet and genuine, it actually thaws my heart a degree or two.

"Hey, you can cover the tickets on your credit card, right?"

And back into the freezer it goes.

CHAPTER 16

GRACIE

Today

It's quiet in the cabin now at four o'clock in the morning. The lights are dim, save for a few non-sleepers such as me who are reading or working on laptops, or scribbling in notepads. Occasionally one of the flight attendants will stick a head out from the galley to check that everything is as it should be.

But everything is not as it should be. Not in my world, anyway.

I rub my temples and sigh, flipping up the lid on my computer. Again. The lid I just slapped closed not five minutes ago. Because maybe more information about the disappearance of Paul Winstead will have just magically migrated to the web in that time. Unfortunately, digitizing archives hasn't been a priority for every news outlet, but I have been able to track down a handful of items referring to the case, including a few articles from Puerto Rico where the investigation was launched and Texas where Paul Winstead was from. There was also a brief mention in a *Wall Street Journal* profile of Brock Winstead with a grainy family picture including two good-looking boys in their teens. Considering all the press this must have gotten, I was disappointed to find just three television clips on YouTube—all featuring the brother,

Blaine, prominently. He's the kind of sneering little prick I hate—totally confident in his ability to do or say anything with impunity. Because that's what billions of dollars could buy you thirty years ago. And, to some extent, today.

The family makes a number of statements in which they refer to the kind of "questionable company" their poor, naïve boy had gotten himself involved with when he entered the seedy underbelly of the classical music world. A tiny bark of laughter slips out before I can stop myself. That is one of the most ridiculous group of words I've ever seen strung together into a sentence. The "seedy underbelly" of the classical music world? Seriously? What the hell did these people think he was doing? Snorting coke off his cello? Trafficking violinists to work in sweatshop orchestras in third-world countries? Were they afraid he was in on a ring of counterfeit Stradivariuses? Or would that be Stradivarii? Absurd to the point of being hilarious.

Oh, but the Winstead clan wasn't laughing.

Through their lawyer and publicists, Blaine Rockford "Brock" Winstead, Sr. and his wife Evelyn bemoan how hard it's been to keep their children safe from predators disguised as friends and young women hoping to seduce them into marriage or, worse, ensnare them with an unplanned pregnancy—all to get a foothold to the family fortune. How ironic that my mother kept *her* unplanned pregnancy a secret from these people for fear that *they* would prey on her!

I can *not* believe this kind of nonsense flew, even back then. It's such a clear distortion of the facts and a blatant manipulation of the media. Even if they had been able to get Emilia—I have to keep reminding myself she and my mother are the same person—indicted and in front of a jury, it would have taken a lot of bribing and coercing to get twelve people to overlook the fact that there wasn't a single shred of evidence.

One thing is for sure, I'd have had a field day with this case if I'd been the defense attorney. And had I not been in utero at the time.

"Hey, you okay?"

Meg's groggy voice pulls me from the depths of my rabbit hole. I close the laptop again, shifting in my sister's direction.

"It's like there are a thousand tiny pieces to this puzzle and they're all white. I can't figure out where to start or how to sort them. You know what I mean?"

She nods and yawns at the same time.

"Uh-huh. You can't see the big picture. But I think that's just because you're actually *missing* some of those pieces. I think once you've got everything you need, it won't take long for you to snap it all into place."

"The question is how am I supposed to find those missing pieces?"

"You don't have to find them alone. That's why I'm here," she tells me through another yawn. "Besides, you dig, and you dig, and you dig until you find the truth. It's what makes you such a great attorney. You won't stop until you're satisfied that you know *exactly* what went down."

I stare at her for a long moment.

"What? Am I really off base?" she asks when I don't immediately respond.

"No. I'm just surprised by how spot-on you are."

She nods, as if this makes perfect sense.

"What surprises me is how calm you're being about all of this. I mean, considering you found out like five minutes ago that your father was more than a sperm donor during a hookup."

I shrug.

"It's my process. I have to be like that for court cases. I have to focus on the facts and worry about the emotions later."

"I'm not so sure that's healthy."

"It's probably not. But I owe it to my clients to give them the best representation I can. Me getting caught up in the drama . . . and the *trauma* of their lives, their stories clouds my judgment. I'll cry with them later. First I've got to help them get out of trouble."

"And do you think Mom is in trouble?"

"I don't know. I hope not. But I've been giving that some thought, and I think if we still haven't heard from her by the time we land we should go straight to the police station. There must be some old case files there. Something that might point us in the right direction. Whether or not they'll let me see them is another question. It might still be considered an open investigation."

My sister's brows shoot up in surprise.

"Wow, really? After all this time?"

"Oh, yeah. Absolutely. It might be inactive, but they haven't solved it, so it's probably classified as one of their cold cases."

"Huh. Interesting. You really are good at this law stuff."

I smile. She smiles back.

"Thanks. And you're really good at the music stuff."

Her smile falters just enough to be noticeable.

"I'm not wrong, am I?" I prod softly. "You hesitated on the Tchaikovsky. You were actually considering throwing the competition, weren't you?"

Now that I've presented my witness with my theory, I watch her for the telltale reactions of the guilty.

Meg looks away for a few seconds at something over my shoulder.

"When I was performing, I found myself thinking about how easy it would be to mess it up. To tank my whole career with a single note."

"I hardly think you'd have done that with a silver medal instead of a gold. Not that it matters, because you played it perfectly and you won the whole damn thing."

"I did. But in that moment—like right there on stage? I don't know, it could've gone either way. Even *I* didn't know what I was going to do . . . until it was done and everyone was on their feet applauding."

I can see she's both perplexed and pained by this.

"Meg, do you not want to be a concert pianist?"

"I've worked for this my entire life."

"That's not what I asked," I say, shaking my head.

It's there, right under the surface. We're so close to what we've been dancing around for so long.

"I . . . I don't know. For the longest time, it was *all* I wanted. And then, well, you know . . ." She lets the thought fade as she turns away to look at the pitch black through the window next to her.

"It's okay, you know," I tell her quietly. "It's okay that you kept going when I couldn't."

This is the first time I've ever said these words aloud, outside of my therapist's office. They've always been there, and she's always needed to hear them. But the bitter, selfish, envious part of me—the petulant teenager in me—wasn't willing to give her this absolution.

When Meg turns back to face me, her eyes are bright with tears she's fighting to hold back. And then the first one slips past her defenses—a tiny hairline crack in her hard-shell exterior that, in an instant, splits off into a thousand smaller fissures, spiderwebbing its way around her until the entire façade of the confident young woman falls away. Left behind is nothing more than a pile of rubble around the feet of a stricken eight-year-old girl.

In the four seconds it took for her to accidentally slam the car door on my hand, my sister *literally* ripped my dream from my grasp. I know Meg well enough to know that the guilt has, at times, consumed her. Just as the rage has, at times, consumed me. Those are perfectly normal, totally expected emotions in a case like ours. But what the hell kind of fucked-up soup of feelings am I—are *we*—supposed to have when she then goes on to live that same dream? *My* dream? I reach out and put a hand on the little girl's arm and smile reassuringly, telling her without telling her that we're going to be okay.

CHAPTER 17

EMILIA

Thirty Years Ago

Emilia lay awake, staring up at the ceiling in the Alvarezes' bright, cozy guest room. She'd spent most of the last three days sleeping as bags of saline dripped into her veins. She'd even had the strength to shower on her own today, without the help of Miguel's wife. Thankfully the worst of the nausea seemed to have passed, as well, and she'd been able to keep down broth, crackers, toast, and apple sauce. And now as she smelled whatever it was that Hilda had on the stove for dinner, she could feel the slightest stirrings of hunger starting to return.

She wondered how much of that was due to her healing and how much was some hardwired response to the news she was pregnant? Now that she knew, had she somehow tripped a switch activating her latent maternal instincts? Her hand moved to her stomach—still perfectly flat. No one would guess the secret. Not yet, anyway. But she wouldn't be able to hide her condition forever.

Emilia wanted desperately to be overjoyed by the thought of carrying Paul's child, but she didn't have the luxury of celebrating the news just yet. This baby's father was still missing, and no one seemed to be any closer to discovering what happened to him. Well, perhaps Miguel would have some news for her when he returned from work today. The press around this case had exploded almost overnight as Paul's family launched a full-out media blitz, painting her as a shrewd, money-grubbing seductress intent on clawing her way into the family.

They were calling her a "person of interest" in Paul's disappearance, splashing her name and face on the front page of every newspaper and the top of every newscast. And while she had yet to be officially charged with anything, a substantial reward was being offered to anyone with information leading to her whereabouts. Finally Hilda had taken the television out of the guest room and refused to bring her anymore papers, insisting she needed to be resting—for the baby's sake. And that's what this all came down to now.

In the span of less than a week, her entire life had changed in a profound and permanent way. This was, by far, the most significant turn of events—which was saying a lot considering the magnitude of everything she'd been through in this small slice of time. The moon was no longer the source of her gravitational pull, the sun was no longer the body which she orbited. Emilia's entire world had shifted on its axis, and now everything—every single breath she drew into her lungs— was for the child she carried.

The instant she knew about its existence, something extraordinary had happened within her—physically. It was as if steel had leached into her bones, coursing through her veins as pure, white-hot molten strength—laying flaming waste to any fear she'd been clinging to. Emilia's body was fortified, her instincts sharpened, her nerves cold and calm. Everything was different now. And anyone who valued their life had best stay the hell out of her way or prepare to be destroyed.

The creak of the guest room door opening made her look up. There was a tiny face peering in at her.

"Can I come in?" the little girl asked.

When she nodded and patted the bed next to her, five-year-old Alicia Alvarez threw the door the rest of the way open and flung herself toward the bottom of the bed. She slipped under the bottom edge of the covers and crawled up the length of the mattress, like some subterranean creature making its way toward her. Emilia couldn't help but laugh when the girl popped up next to her, perfectly tucked in.

"Well, hello there, beautiful girl!" she said, flipping on her side so they were face-to-face on their respective pillows.

The child had started visiting that morning, when Hilda had proclaimed Emilia to no longer be contagious. And she'd proved to be the perfect medicine at the perfect time.

"Hello!" Alicia replied with great enthusiasm. A moment later, she produced a baby doll from under the covers.

"Who's that?"

"Graciela!" the little girl declared. "She's my baby."

"Oh, I see. And what a beautiful name you picked!"

"I know," Alicia said with the *Well, duh!* tone of a teenager.

It made Emilia smile.

"What are you doing?"

"I helped Mommy make dinner."

"You did! What are you cooking?"

"Arroz con pollo," she began, pausing to think about the rest of the menu. "And . . . tostones, and . . . salad, and . . . bread . . . Hmm. Yeah, that's it."

"Well, that sounds like a lot! What a helpful young lady you are. Your mommy and daddy must be very proud of you."

"They are," she informed Emilia with a very serious nod for emphasis.

"Yes, they are!"

They both turned to see Miguel standing in the doorway watching them. Emilia wondered how long he'd been there.

Alicia flew out from under the covers, hurling herself off the bed and into her father's arms.

"Ooof!" he huffed when he caught her. "*Mija*, you're going to be too big for this soon!"

"Neverrrrrr!" the child declared gleefully. "Never, never, never! Papi, you have to catch me always. Even when I'm old like you and Mama!"

"Old? Well, thanks for that," Miguel replied, smothering her face with kisses. "You're lucky you're so cute, kiddo. Now go see your mama, she needs your help setting the table. Says she can't do it without your special folded napkins."

The moment he put Alicia back down on her feet, she scampered out of the room without so much as a glance back at either of them.

"Mamaaaaa . . . I'm cooommmmming!"

Emilia held up the baby doll, left behind in all the excitement.

"Hey! You forgot Graciela!" she called after the girl, but it was too late.

Miguel laughed and shook his head.

"Graciela, huh? Yesterday it was Marisol. The day before that it was Eugenia."

She chuckled, and he pulled up a chair to sit next to her side of the bed.

"How are you feeling today?" he asked.

"Pretty tired still, but so much better than yesterday. Miguel, you guys have been so amazing," she told him for the tenth time.

He waved away the compliment for the tenth time.

"You can thank Hilda for the healing touch."

"And Alicia for the cheering-up, and you for the . . ." She paused, her voice softer when she spoke again. "And you for *everything*. For saving me, Miguel. That's what you did, you know . . ."

He shook his head.

"I'm trying, Emilia, but we're not out of the woods yet. We have to talk about what comes next . . ."

"I know," she agreed. "I've been giving this a lot of thought, and I keep coming to the same conclusion."

"Alright. And what's that?"

"I need to leave. For good."

The man dropped down into the small chair next to the dresser.

"And by 'for good,' you mean . . . ?"

"I have to start over someplace far away from here. Someplace Paul's family won't be able to find me."

Emilia found herself holding her breath as Miguel considered her, stroking a bit of stubble on his chin.

"That's pretty drastic."

She nodded. "I know. But I can't see any other way. Unless you have a better suggestion?"

"Well, I'm not saying that's not the right decision, but you should consider all of your options. You could stay here and fight. But let me be clear here based on what I've seen so far, you'll likely be charged, and I'm skeptical you'll get a fair trial. But if you want to go that route, you will not be alone, Emilia. Hilda and I will be there every step of the way, fighting with you. It is, however, entirely possible you will give birth in jail while you're awaiting trial. The choices will then be to place the child in foster care or with family. Now, I've met Paul's brother Blaine, and he's a real piece of work. If the parents are even half as bad—"

"They're worse," she cut in. "Well, Brock is, anyway. He's ruthless."

"And the mother?" he asked.

Emilia shook her head. "I don't know. She goes along with whatever he wants. I get the sense that she's just checked out most of the time—and he likes it like that, so he makes sure she has easy access to pills or booze or whatever."

"Right, okay. Well, we could help you get out of state in hopes you'll have a better chance of fair treatment somewhere else . . ." His voice trailed off as she shook her head.

"Miguel, they got to the captain of a Norwegian cruise ship in the middle of the Caribbean in the middle of the night. It doesn't matter where I go, they'll find someone to help them get what they want. And, no offence, but you and Hilda—amazing as you are—are no match for that kind of money."

"It sounds to me like you've made up your mind then," he observed.

"Well, talking through all this with you definitely helps me to see the way things are—not how I wish they were. Paul was a disappointment to his father because he didn't want anything to do with WinCo. And Blaine? Well, he's just out for Blaine. No, there's absolutely no doubt in my mind that if Brock Winstead were to discover he's got a grandchild, there wouldn't be anything—or anyone—that would stand in the way of him taking custody. Another heir. Another chance to 'get it right.'"

Miguel nodded resolutely. "There it is. I'll start putting together a plan—"

She held up her hands to stop him.

"No, you've already done too much, risked too much. I can take it from here; it's not the first time I've had to start over. I can do this alone."

He stood and offered her a smile that came up just a hair shy of pitying.

"That maybe so Emilia, but remember, you're *not* alone anymore."

When she followed his gaze to her belly, she knew he was right.

CHAPTER 18

MIGUEL

Thirty Years Ago

The note was stuck to his phone when he got into work. He draped his jacket over the back of his desk chair and made his way to the windowless office in the back corner. Captain Delgado was waiting for him.

"Miguel, good. Come in, and please close the door behind you."

He did as he was told, perching on the seat across the desk from his boss.

"What's going on? Everything . . . okay?"

"Well . . . there's been a development in the Winstead case . . ."

Without warning, Miguel's gut felt like it was in freefall off a fifty-story building.

"Did they find him? His body?" he asked slowly.

"No, not yet," Delgado replied. "You look pale, Miguel, are you okay?"

The detective nodded, feeling relief flood his system.

"Uh, yeah—I'm fine, thanks. Then what is it, Captain?"

His boss leaned across the desk and lowered his voice.

"It is my understanding that a grand jury here in San Juan will charge Emilia Oliveras in connection with Paul Winstead's disappearance by the end of the day. Once that announcement comes out, there will be a big press conference. One that I will be holding personally along with Brock and Evelyn Winstead. If Emilia hasn't turned up by then, we've been instructed to prepare for a full-on manhunt. After that, the press on this will explode, and there won't be a corner of the island where she can hide. Do you understand what I'm telling you, detective?"

Holy shit. So much for relief.

"Yes, I believe I do," he replied slowly and quietly.

The captain was telling him they were screwed. Warning him that if he didn't turn over Emilia to police custody before she was officially charged, he could be accused of harboring a criminal. Jesus, this was bad. Really, really bad . . .

The other man tapped on his desk lightly, snapping him out of his thoughts.

"Focus, detective," he warned, waiting for Miguel to meet his gaze before continuing. "The San Juan airport and docks are already under increased surveillance, and by *nine o'clock* tomorrow morning, so will every other airport and dock."

Wait, wait, wait . . . no, he was telling Miguel what he needed to know in order to get Emilia off the island!

"Nod if you understand me," his boss ordered. When the detective opened his mouth to speak, Delgado cut him off abruptly. "I need you to tread very carefully here, Miguel— for both of us. There are certain things I am compelled to report, and once I cross over that threshold from *suspecting* something to *knowing* it, there's no going back."

"I understand."

Delgado sighed heavily. "Right, so our official orders are to track down Emilia Oliveras before she can find a way to leave the island. Because if she did, somehow, manage to get away in that very narrow bit of time, it would bring our investigation to a standstill—especially since she hasn't been charged with anything."

"And if she didn't manage that? If she maybe came forward and decided to defend herself?" Miguel ventured, curious to get his superior's take.

He let out a long stream of air as he thought about it.

"This thing is about to blow up, and believe me when I tell you, it will take a miracle to knock these jackals off the trail—even if she did manage to get off the island. And I mean a bona fide, sent directly-from-Jesus-Christ-Himself kind of miracle. If we bring her in—or even if she comes in on her own—I think it's over. She'll have been tried and convicted in the press before she ever sees the inside of a courtroom. So if Emilia Oliveras is the kind of woman who prays, I hope she's down on her knees right now. Because, quite frankly, that's her best shot."

When Delgado stood and offered his hand, Miguel rose and shook it.

"I uh . . . I appreciate this, Captain."

"Don't thank me yet, Miguel."

His boss's tone stopped Miguel mid-shake.

"There's something else you need to know . . ."

CHAPTER 19

EMILIA

Thirty Years Ago

Emilia stirred reluctantly when she felt someone shake her shoulder gently. She'd fallen back into a deep sleep after breakfast and was surprised when she woke to find Hilda leaning over her and Miguel standing at the foot of the bed, looking grim.

Oh, no.

"They found him," she guessed. "They found Paul's . . ." She couldn't even utter the rest of the sentence.

"No, Emilia, it's not that," Miguel told her. "It's . . . we need to get you out of Puerto Rico. First thing tomorrow morning, in fact. And there's a lot to do before then."

She sat up abruptly, her heart leaping into her chest. They both seemed to be calm, but there was no mistaking the urgency behind his words.

"Wait . . . what? I thought we'd have a few more days to get this sorted out. What happened?" She knew the answer as soon as the question had left her lips. "Oh. They're here, aren't they? And they're coming for me."

Miguel and Hilda exchanged glances.

"If they're not already, they will be before the end of the day."

Under the blanket, she pulled her knees up to her chest,

wrapped her arms around them, and then rested her forehead on top. Last night she'd been so confident leaving was the right answer, but now, in the cold light of day, she was less certain.

"Um, yeah, okay. Except I haven't really thought this all through yet. The details, I mean. . . . Like where can I go that they won't track me down?"

Hilda took a seat next to her on the bed and laid out the framework of a plan the two of them had devised.

"My oldest and dearest friend, Erica, has a farm in Oregon. She has plenty of room, and she's been so lonely since her husband passed two years ago. I didn't tell her everything, but she knows enough, and believe me when I tell you she is thrilled by the idea of having company—and especially having a baby to fuss over again. It's a win-win."

Emilia could help out during the busy summer and pumpkin picking seasons, keeping the baby with her all the time. She could start again.

"The thing is," he was saying, "it will be a little like witness protection. You'll have to change your name—I'll go get you some new identification this afternoon. But you must be careful, Emilia. No one can know who you are or where you come from. Ever. And . . . you'd need to stay off the radar entirely."

He was telling her that her dream of being a renowned concert pianist was over. Well, sad as it was, that was the least of her problems at that moment.

"Okay. Yeah. I can do that," she agreed, using her hands to wipe away the tears that had slipped down her face. Crying, like time, was a luxury she didn't have at the moment. "What do I need to do first?"

A look passed between Miguel and Hilda. There was more. How could there be more? How could this get any worse than it already had?

"What is it?"

Miguel reached around to grab something off the dresser. A newspaper. He handed it to her and read the print painted across the first page.

Family resemblance? Woman wanted for questioning in Winstead disappearance is the daughter of a convicted killer.

Emilia dropped the paper as she scrabbled out of the sheets, a hand pressed to her mouth, and ran for the bathroom.

"You're sure you have everything you need?" Hilda asked for the third time, twisting around in the front seat so she could see Emilia behind her.

"Turn around, *mi amor,*" Miguel murmured. "We don't want it to look as if there's someone in the back seat."

"*Oye,* Miguel, do you really think anyone is out here at this hour of the morning? In a parking lot in Fajardo?"

He shrugged.

"I don't know, Hilda. But I'd hate to end up in jail because I guessed wrong on that one. Besides, if she needs anything else now, it's a little late. She *has* to be on this ferry."

His wife nodded and faced forward.

"Yes, I think I have everything," Emilia said quietly from the back, where she was hunched down on the seat below the window line.

And that was fine. She didn't want to catch her reflection in the glass. She didn't want to see the strange woman looking back at her—the one with the shoulder-length, golden brown hair created by a surprisingly adept Hilda. Once it was all blown out, they had topped off the look with a pair of clear, wire-framed glasses.

Miguel had snapped a couple of pictures of her and disappeared, returning with a driver's license and birth certificate. She didn't ask where he could find such things at such an early hour and in such a short period of time. As a police officer, he'd likely come across some very talented criminals.

Perhaps ones who owed him a favor—or hoped to cash in on one from him in the future. However he'd done it, Emilia Oliveras was gone. She would spend the rest of her life as Emily Oliver. It was just close enough so it would still catch her attention when someone called her by the name. She'd do her best to keep to herself and avoid conversations, but if pressed, she would tell people she'd been working in Puerto Rico as a nanny before relocating to live with her "Aunt Erica," really Hilda's friend.

"Right, so you remember the travel plan?" Miguel asked.

She closed her eyes and ran it down in her mind—there were several moving parts to keep straight, and the nausea had been particularly brutal this morning.

"I take the ferry to St. Thomas. Then a cab to the airport where I fly to Miami. There's a bus station there at the airport, where I'll catch a bus to Seattle. Erica will pick me up there, and then she'll drive us back to her home in Oregon."

"Exactly," Miguel said.

Hilda pulled a thick envelope out of her bag and, without turning away from the windshield, she threaded her hand between the two front seats and passed it back to Emilia.

"Emilia, this is enough money to help you get a start. Erica is so thrilled to have you and the baby, but I'm sure there will come a time when you want to be out on your own. This will help you do that. You should have enough here for a little car and to put down the deposit on an apartment when the time comes."

Miguel had warned her against trying to access any of her bank accounts or credit cards. Any cheap P.I. could track her that way, and the Winsteads wouldn't be using just any cheap P.I.

Tears pricked Emilia's eyes. Again. She was so tired of crying.

"I don't know how to thank you . . ." she murmured.

"You don't need to," Miguel said firmly. "Just go and make

a life for yourself, Emilia. We'll communicate through Erica, just to be safe. I don't know if anyone in my precinct—or above—will be keeping an eye on me. But I swear to you, I will do *everything* I can to find out what's happened to Paul."

"Keep taking those antibiotics," Hilda added. "And the Tylenol every six hours. We don't want the fever to come back. Get as much sleep as you can—I put a little travel pillow and blanket Miguel stole when we flew to Europe a couple of years ago . . ."

"I did not steal anything! It's not as if they put those things out again for other passengers to use . . ."

"Regardless," his wife said pointedly to her husband before turning back to Emilia, "sleep on the plane and the bus. There are plenty of snacks in the bag that goes under your seat, and I tucked some separate cash into an envelope there for when the bus stops for meals."

"Okay . . ." she whispered through the tears.

They'd been quiet for a long minute when the ferry came into sight out on the water. Emilia took a slow, shaky breath.

"Oh! I almost forgot . . ." Miguel said, reaching into his pocket for something. "Emilia, let me see your hand."

She did as requested, stretching her arm over the console between the two front seats, palm upward. He pressed something heavy into it, and when she pulled it back to examine it, she found her watch. The one Paul had given her. A hand went to her mouth as she stared down at it.

"How did you . . . ? Where . . . ? I don't . . ."

He looked back at her in the rearview mirror.

"Your cabin steward. Sven? You two left quite an impression on him. When he was told to let Paul's brother into your cabin, he saw the watch on the nightstand. Then when he realized the guy was pawing through all your things, he slipped it into his pocket. He asked me to get it to you, but with all the excitement, I'd forgotten about it until I found it in my coat pocket last night."

She put the delicate timepiece on her wrist and looked down on it, remembering the way Paul had affixed it to her wrist himself. It was all she had left of him now.

Then she remembered and put that same hand to her belly.

No, it wasn't *all* she had.

CHAPTER 20

MIGUEL

Thirty Years Ago

They spent the majority of the hour-long ride from the ferry in Fajardo back home in silence. Periodically Miguel saw his wife swipe at a tear, then turn away, pretending to look out the window. Periodically Miguel himself swiped at a tear and pretended to adjust the air vent on his left. He wasn't even certain what it was, exactly, that they were crying about. Emilia was going to get out from under the Winstead family once and for all. She would have her baby far away from all of the ugliness that was unfolding in the media here and beyond. Even if she'd gone back to her life in Manhattan, this story would have plagued her, as would her in-laws. And God only knew what they'd do once they found out about the baby.

But there was still the fact that the woman had lost her husband—*literally* lost him. And until the day his remains were found washed up on some tropical beach or caught in some fisherman's net, for the rest of her life a part of her would always wonder if he might, somehow, still be alive out there somewhere. And what if he did surface? As long as there was no body, there was a chance Emilia would not be charged with her husband's murder.

"Miguel?" Hilda's voice was soft next to him, as if she could tell he was deep in thought.

"*¿Sí, mi amor?*"

"The marriage certificate."

He glanced at her. "What about it?"

"Do you think it's possible those people would back off if it was found?"

Blaine Winstead's words echoed in his mind.

"*Something tells me there won't be any such document on file at that courthouse . . . or any other.*"

"Not likely," he told his wife. "Things like that tend to disappear at moments like this, never to be seen again."

"Okay, fine. But let's just *say* you find it—"

"Me? Now you've got *me* finding it?" he teased.

"Say *you* find it," she repeated in a sterner tone meant to be a warning to him, "and log it into evidence or whatever. What could they say then?"

He raised his palms slightly, gesturing as much as he could without taking them off the steering wheel.

"Honestly, Hilda, I say better it stays missing. Otherwise they could claim she married him for his money and bumped him off on the honeymoon."

"*¡Jesu Cristo!*" Hilda exclaimed, horrified. "So it's hopeless, then?"

Miguel put the car in park, turned it off, and shifted in his seat to face her.

"Short of Paul Winstead himself walking through the precinct doors, there's nothing. The Winsteads are always going to have the upper hand so long as they hold sway with the media. And this is such a salacious story! Of course the news outlets are tripping all over themselves. Everyone wants to be the first to break the news of new evidence, or a new theory, or whatever nonsense the family wants to put out there."

"Okay, so, how do you shut them down then? How can

you keep them from printing whatever they want—even if it's not true?"

Miguel chuckled.

"Repeal the First Amendment, maybe?"

"Ha-ha-ha," Hilda replied, unamused.

"Seriously, there's nothing. They can spin it all as 'theories' or cite anonymous sources or whatever bullshit tactics they want. At this point," Miguel said, shaking his head sadly, "it's like Captain Delgado said to me—it'll take a miracle to get those vultures in the press to stop chasing her. No, I'm afraid this is going to go on for a good long time—either until they get bored with the story or something juicier comes along."

"Pfft. Well, my love, I know you're not a big believer in miracles. And, honestly, I can't imagine anything juicier than what they've got now," she lamented. "Come inside and have a coffee with me before you leave for work. You have some time yet."

He glanced down at his watch. He did, actually, which was why he was so surprised to find the phone in the kitchen ringing once they'd barely crossed the threshold. It wasn't even six-thirty yet. Hilda answered it, listened, then put a hand over the receiver.

"Miguel, it's Captain Delgado—he wants to speak with you. He says it's urgent."

"Urgent?" Miguel echoed. That wasn't a word his boss used very often. When he placed the phone to his ear, he heard a lot of noise in the background. Far too early for there to be that much activity at the station. "Captain? Everything okay?"

"No, Miguel. I'm afraid not. I know it's early, but I need you to come in immediately."

The sickening feeling started somewhere around his stomach, rapidly scaling upward through his body until he could actually taste the bile. In the time it took for Delgado to give him the details, a dozen different scenarios played out in Miguel's mind.

They'd found Paul's body. They had intercepted Emilia and arrested her. They had some kind of proof he'd helped Emilia get off the island. They had some kind of proof that Emilia really *had* killed Paul . . .

"Miguel, we have a missing child in La Perla—a seven-month-old named Marianna Ruíz . . ." Miguel put a hand out onto the counter to steady himself. "Her father woke up in the alley out back of *El Gallo Rojo*, beat to hell and the kid missing. The stroller has been found in a dumpster nearby. I want you to take the lead on this one. You up to it? Because every second that ticks by . . ."

He didn't need to finish that sentence, because it was something every cop knows from Day One. When a child goes missing, the first twenty-four hours are the most critical. The more time that goes by, the colder the trail gets, the less likely it is they'll be recovered. Recovered alive, anyway.

"Yes, Captain, of course. I can be at the station in—"

"No," Delgado cut him off. "Go straight to La Perla, Miguel. We've called in every beat cop to canvas the neighborhood. All the radio and TV stations are breaking into programming to get her name and picture out there. I'm sending out extra patrol to keep the rest of the press at bay so you can work. This could very well be national news by tonight."

When he hung up, Hilda had his *café con leche* ready to go in a travel mug and a muffin wrapped up in a paper towel. He saw the concern—and the question—in her expression.

"A baby has been kidnapped," he explained. "As of right now, Emilia Oliveras is out of the headlines, and there isn't a damn thing the Winsteads can do about it. So I guess we got our miracle."

But at what cost?

CHAPTER 21

GRACIE

Today

"Are you sure we shouldn't just get a room and dump our stuff?" my sister asks between panting breaths as we drag our bags up the very steep cobblestone streets of Old San Juan in search of the main police precinct.

Somewhere over the Atlantic, I messaged Mom and let her know we were coming but she has yet to reply. And so I have yet to secure us a room at any of the myriad high-rise hotels lining the beach here.

"We have no idea where Mom is," I tell her. Again. "I don't want to check in then turn around and check out two hours later."

"But what if we can't get a room later? Where will we sleep tonight?"

"Huh?" I ask distractedly, pausing to yank my rolling duffle out from the storm drain where its wheels have become wedged. I nearly fall backward when it finally breaks free. This is freaking exhausting. "Listen," huff once we're moving again, "I seriously doubt we'll have trouble finding a room here in San Juan if we need one, so let's just wait a little longer, okay? Just until we hear back from Mom and we've spoken to the police."

But *will* the police speak to us? That's the question of the hour.

"I suppose," she mutters. "At least the scenery is beautiful."

She's certainly not wrong about that! To our left is the craggy shoreline of the Atlantic, where the water is somehow translucent and brilliantly colored at the same time—an ombré of aquas and blues culminating in bubbling white foam heads that hit, dissolve, pull back, and start all over again.

To our right are row after row of two and three-story townhouses, each painted a different color of the rainbow from brilliant orange to lemon yellow, mint green, and rich terra-cotta. The window shutters, entranceways, and balcony doors are all that dark brown/black wood associated with the Spanish Colonial period where these houses originated. Bright white trim lightens the weight of the wood while accentuating the pop of each color on the block. They are by far the most vibrant, joyous homes I've ever seen, and I can't help but smile when I look at them.

"Okay, so, is it terrible that, in the middle of all this, I'm just itching to explore this whole island?" Meg asks guiltily.

"Hah! You plucked that thought right out of my head," I inform her. "And no, of course not. This place is absolutely stunning! Look at all the eye candy everywhere—the beach, the water, the neighborhood . . ."

"The shops, the restaurants, the music," she adds with a wistful look toward a central square where a guitarist is playing in the shade.

"We'll find some time," I assure her. "When this is all . . . sorted."

She glances my way again. "Gracie, how did this all happen? How did we not know about this part of her life? Is Mom just that good of a liar?"

I shrug.

"I guess she'd have to be wouldn't she? I keep wracking

my brain, trying to remember something—anything—that would have been a clue to her past. Something I should've caught. But I can't think of a single thing."

My sister shakes her head. "I've been doing the exact same thing and I'm coming up empty too. So, yeah, I guess she *is* that good of a liar. But this," she waves her free hand, gesturing to our vibrant tropical surroundings, "being here now, following her on this insane hunt for a man who went missing like five minutes after they got married? This is some serious Dateline NBC shit right here."

"I don't buy it," I announce to both of our surprise.

"What? That they were married? That he went overboard?"

"That he's back. I'm telling you, I don't like this at all. No way somebody goes missing for thirty years and then suddenly just 'pops up' out of nowhere. Not in this day and age. There's something wrong with this, and we're going to get to the bottom of it."

She doesn't look convinced. "But isn't that what she came here for? Don't you think *she'd* be the one to know if there was something fishy going on?"

I scoff. "Please, you know Mom."

"I thought I did . . ."

"What I'm saying is—yeah, I believe something happened back then. What little information I could find online proves that. But what happened exactly? I don't know."

"Well, Dad told us—"

"Dad only knows what she told *him*," I interject.

Before she can protest further, we're standing in the parking lot of our destination.

There's a uniformed officer about my age manning the counter when we walk into the police precinct. He glances our way, looks down at something on his screen, then his eyes boomerang back again.

"Did you see that?" Meg murmurs from next to me.

"No," I lie. "What?"

"That guy totally did a double-take when he saw you!"

That's what it looked like to me, too, but I was hoping I was wrong. Apparently not. He's a good-looking guy with a shock of dark, wavy hair that's just a little bit disheveled, as if he runs his hand through it periodically. As we approach, his smile is a little tentative.

"*Buenas tardes, señoritas*," he says, giving my sister a cursory glance and polite nod before fixing his attentions on me.

"Good afternoon. Do you speak English?" I ask him brusquely, so as not to encourage any flirting.

No such luck. His smile broadens, undeterred by my cool manner.

"Yes, yes, of course. I am Officer Carteres. What may I do for you today?"

"I'd like to speak with someone about a cold case, please."

It's a statement, not a question.

His smile fades just a little.

"May I ask why?"

I shift slightly, and he quirks an eyebrow.

"Be nice to him!" Meg whisper/hisses. "He's cute!"

He doesn't notice, thankfully, and I swat at her with a hand behind my back. This is so *not* the time to be playing cupid!

"I believe we have information that could be useful," I continue.

"And may I ask which case that is?"

"Does it really matter?"

"Oh, for God's sake," my sister mutters, stepping forward around me. I watch her put on her sweetest smile. "Hello, officer. My name is Meg Daniels, and this is my sister, Gracie Daniels. We were just wondering if there might be someone from your cold case squad who we could chat with for a few moments? It really is rather important."

"Ah, well," he starts slowly, running his hand through his

hair, just as I suspected, "we don't have a cold case squad . . . exactly. But I tell you what, if you'd please sign in here and have a seat, I'll see if I can find someone who is free to speak with you."

"Yes, that will be fine," I reply, jotting our names down on the clipboard.

We sit in some resin chairs, and I watch as the guy spins the form around to read our names. A second later he picks up the handset of his phone, dials a few numbers, and says something. He frowns at whatever the person on the other end of the line is saying, tries to interrupt, then stops to listen, glancing over his shoulder to find us watching him. At last he hangs up.

"Someone will be with you shortly," the officer tells us, as a man with a bloody nose steps up to the counter.

We sit there in silence for a good fifteen minutes before an unmarked door opens and a tall, slim man in his forties stands at the threshold looking out. He glances at us, scowls, then makes his way over to Officer Carteres.

"*¿En serio?*" he begins, muttering just loud enough that we can hear him. I guess he figures we're too dim to catch the drift of his little tirade because it's in Spanish. "*¿Me arrastras hasta aquí para tratar con un par de turistas que quieren jugar al detective? ¿No crees que tengo mejores cosas que hacer?*"

"*Pero detective, parecen creer que tienen . . .*" the younger man protests, but he gets shut down almost immediately.

"*Tengo diez casos reales sobre mi escritorio esperando ser resueltos.*"

The man glances at us again, then turns to go back the way he came.

Meg is clearly perplexed, because she doesn't speak a word of Spanish.

I am clearly pissed, because I do.

"*¡Oye!*" I call out loudly, getting to my feet. The man

stops and turns toward us again. Carteres looks concerned suddenly. "First of all, we are *not* a couple of *'turistas'* here to play detective and, quite frankly, I don't care if there are ten *thousand* cases on your desk! That's not our problem, it's yours." I can just make out my sister gaping up at me in my peripheral vision. "We came here because we have information about one particular case. The Emilia Oliveras/Paul Winstead case. But hey," I put up my palm and shrug at the same time, "if that's not of interest to you, I'm sure another precinct might be interested in listening to what we have to say . . . or perhaps the *San Juan Daily News* might like to speak with us?"

The man looks as if he can't decide whether to be annoyed or impressed. In the end, he goes with both, holding open the door he was about to walk through and tilting his head toward the hall on the other.

"Alright then," he says with an exasperated sight. "Let's hear what you have to say." We follow him back to a small, windowless office stacked high with cardboard file boxes.

"So who'd you piss off to get stuck working out of the file storage room?" I ask, scanning the names and numbers that have been written on each box in Sharpie marker.

He frowns. "What are you talking about? We have an entire basement for file storage. Those are just some of the cases I'm working on at the moment."

Wow. I guess this guy wasn't kidding when he said he had a lot of work on his plate right now. Regardless, there's little room left for much more than a desk and two folding chairs, which my sister and I perch on while he closes the door behind and takes a seat behind the desk, hands folded on the blotter as he considers us.

"Now, what is it you want to speak to me about in regard to the Winstead/Oliveras case after all this time?" he asks, skipping any pleasantries.

"Do you run the cold case squad?" I ask.

He stares at me for a long moment before replying.

"I *am* the cold case squad, Miss Daniels. Now, please, as you can see, I'm very busy. What is it you think you have in regard to that investigation?"

I feel my jaw tighten. Fine. He wants the condensed version? I'll give it to him.

"Yesterday our mother received a phone call from a man claiming to have found Paul Winstead. It really rattled her—but she refused to talk about it. Next thing we know, she's hopped a plane from Oregon to Puerto Rico. Meanwhile, she's not picking up her phone or answering text messages. Quite frankly, we're concerned for her safety."

"Her safety?" he echoes.

I nod. "We're concerned that she might be the target of some kind of scam. It's been thirty years for God's sake—why now? It's just too incredible. She might have come here under duress—maybe someone is threatening or extorting her. We just don't know, so we were hoping you could maybe give us some guidance here. Is this something that happens?"

"Is what something that happens? Do we have a ring of blackmailers contacting random people and telling them they've located someone who's been missing for decades in an attempt to lure them here for some nefarious reason? No, I can't say that I'm aware of such a scheme."

Well, when he puts it like that, it does sound a little far-fetched. Before I can form a response, he continues.

"Clearly I'm missing a piece of the puzzle here. What connection does your mother have with this case?"

Meg and I exchange glances. Yeah, maybe we should have mentioned that right at the beginning.

"Our mother *is* Emilia Oliveras," I say softly.

The detective blinks hard, his expression unreadable as he leans forward, resting his forearms on the desk blotter.

"Okay," he begins slowly. "Now you've got my attention."

A half hour later, we're comparing Emily Oliver's driver's

license with an old file photo of Emilia Oliveras. The resemblance is too strong to be a coincidence. This is when I realize that I've never seen pictures of my mother when she was a young woman. She was so soft and delicate. But even more striking than her youth and her beauty is the vulnerability that radiates off the image. The Emilia Oliveras of thirty years ago is nothing like the Emily Oliver of today. I'm pulled from these thoughts by the detective, who's considering the two with a much sharper eye.

"Well, at first glance they certainly look like the same woman," Raña is saying. "Still, it's not something that would hold up in court."

"It might," I pipe up. "If you got an expert in facial recognition technology to come in and present an overlay so the jury could see how the bone structures are identical." I nod toward his great wall of cardboard boxes. "Now if there happened to be any DNA tucked away in one of those files of yours—maybe from something that belonged to Emilia that's still in evidence—then we could run an analysis to prove it definitively."

He stares at me blankly. "Well, that's very . . . specific."

"She's an attorney," Meg informs him, not looking up from the printouts of the two photos on the desk in front of us.

"Ahhh. I see," he replies, nodding as if this makes perfect sense.

"Sorry," I say with a sheepish shrug. "I probably should have disclosed that earlier. I just didn't want to risk alienating you."

"Why would you being an attorney alienate me?" he asks, perplexed.

"I'm a defense attorney."

When that statement hangs out there for a while, his brows go up expectantly.

"And?"

"And . . . not everyone likes a defense attorney. Some people think that all we do is defend dangerous criminals and get them back out on the street."

He considers this.

"Okay, well, I'm not one of those guys. I've seen plenty of innocent people charged over the years—none of them my cases, thankfully—and it was the work of good defense attorneys that exonerated them. Plus the fact that you're familiar with the legal system is helpful, actually. You get the whole 'burden of proof' thing. Now, as to DNA, one thing we could do is run a comparison of your DNA with Imelda's. That would be a close enough relationship to confirm the connection."

"Who's Imelda?" Meg asks before I can.

The detective looks from her to me and then back again, growing more incredulous by the second.

"Imelda Oliveras. Emilia's mother. Your grandmother."

CHAPTER 22

EMILIA

Today

After living in the Pacific Northwest for so long, Puerto Rico appeared as a never-ending buffet of eye candy to Emilia. She devoured the lush greenery as it flew past the windshield of her rental car—the palm trees; the plants with huge, waxy leaves; the bright orange and pink blooms. Periodically a roadside stand popped up with spray-painted signs offering *frutas*, piña coladas, and the giant pork rinds called *chicharron*. So much had changed . . . and yet there was an undeniable familiarity, as if she'd never left. Now that she was there, she realized just how much she'd missed it.

The sense of belonging was so potent that it bordered on euphoric. This was still home, even if she'd had to abandon it all those years ago. Unfortunately, it was impossible to return to the place without returning to all of the ugly memories she thought she'd buried once and for all. It wasn't that her life in their little community had been all bad. In fact it had been nice for much of her childhood. Better than nice, actually. Those were the years when it was just her and her mother. But then the devil himself came to live right under their roof, laying to waste any happy memories she'd had and obliterating any chance of them in the future.

Before *him*, Emilia had wholeheartedly believed her mother

could summon *los espiritos* and harness their powers. But looking back, it occurred to her that if Imelda really *had* been connected to the spirit world, one of them would have tipped her off about what kind of a man she'd married. And what he was doing to her daughter. Or maybe they had, and she just didn't listen. After all, she didn't listen when Emilia told her.

In some ways, she wondered if she was, herself a spirit. Thirty years ago, Emilia Oliveras died so abruptly that there'd been no time to process the loss. And even if there had been time, there was no body, no coffin, no funeral for closure. She had no choice but to keep moving forward, to find a way to get past her past.

With the help of Miguel, Hilda, and Hilda's friend, Erica, she'd moved 4,000 miles away—to the opposite end of the country—and prayed to God that would be far enough. Not that the prayers brought her much confidence. The last time she'd left matters up to the Almighty, He'd left her hanging, and that wasn't a risk she'd been willing to take again. Not with a child to worry about. Even after the Winsteads finally ceased their relentless campaign to destroy her life, Emilia couldn't let herself be lulled into a false sense of security. Not when their money gave them access to the best investigators, the most confidential information, and the keenest surveillance.

What she had not anticipated was that at some point, she would need to grieve that girl who died. Because grief wasn't something you could just stick in a box and toss in the back of the closet, dusty and forgotten. It had all the time in the world to lurk there in the shadows, hiding in the silences. Grief was where hope died. Grief was where ghosts were born.

And there were plenty of ghosts out and about now as she navigated her rental sedan through the San Juan traffic, south toward Yauco—where the Alvarezes had moved after his retirement from the police. She'd spent most of the eleven-hour journey trying to write her thoughts on paper for her daughters. In the end, all she had to show for it were several crumpled balls of half-written paragraphs, because there were simply no words for what she was experiencing and there was nothing she could say that would make them understand her past life . . . her past *lives*. Well, at least she'd have plenty of time to sort it out before she saw them again. She had decided to turn her phone off altogether so as not to hear the incessant buzzing of their calls or see the constant barrage of text messages demanding answers. They were grown women now and Richard, God bless him, would tell them what they needed to know for now. Hopefully enough to keep them from fretting too much. Either way there was nothing to be done about it right now. She'd worry about the future later. Right here, right now in the present, she had a date with the past.

Emilia turned off the AC, reached up, and pushed the button that opened the sunroof. Then it all spilled in—the warm sun, the salty breath of the sea, and the ghost of the girl she once was.

She was a little startled when, instead of the handsome young detective with the rising star, she found herself face-to-face with the much grayer, timeworn retired version of Miguel Alvarez. Of course, he was probably thinking the same thing now as he peered at her under the kitchen lights. She wasn't a frail young girl anymore. Her body had settled and thickened with childbirth and gravity. And she had plenty of her own grays and fine lines. Not that it mattered who they'd been then or who they were now. Their lives were going to be inextricably linked until the day neither of them walked the earth.

Hilda set down cups and put a sugar bowl in the center of the table. "Miguel, why don't you take out some of those *galletas* I picked up from the bakery yesterday?"

He did as she asked, finding a white waxed paper bag on the counter.

"How're you holding up?" Miguel asked after a few moments, as he leaned down close to set a plate of cookies next to the sugar bowl.

She shrugged.

"Oh, about as well as you might expect under the circumstances—not that *anyone* ever expects to be in these circumstances."

He nodded and took the seat across from her, joined a moment later by Hilda to her husband's left.

"Right. Okay, well, might as well save the catching up and the pleasantries for later and get right down to the matter at hand." He paused long enough to pull a phone from his pocket. A few swipes later, he set up an image on the screen, turning it so she could see. "I received this attachment in an email yesterday morning. I tried to reply almost immediately, but the message just bounced back. Whoever it was sent this out and then deleted the account immediately. I'm sure there's a way to trace it, but I don't have ready access to that kind of information since I retired. I could probably call in a favor and get some help but, for now, the fewer people involved in this the better. As I told you on the phone yesterday, I didn't even want to forward the photo to you, for fear someone might intercept it somehow. Maybe a bit paranoid but . . ."

"I know," Emilia assured him. Then she took a long, slow breath, reaching out with a single, shaking hand. "May I?"

"Please," he replied, passing it to her.

She wasn't sure what she'd been expecting, but it wasn't this totally innocuous photo of two women in burgundy scrubs with their arms around each other's shoulders, smiling for the camera. One of them was wearing a tiara with the words Birthday Girl spelled out in faux-rhinestones. What was she meant to see?

"Miguel, I don't—" she started to say, but stopped short

when her focus shifted from the foreground to the background. There she spotted the partially blocked image of a man in profile. He was sitting on a chair, looking out a big window, a cello resting against his shoulder. She looked up to find Hilda and Miguel watching her intently.

His brows were raised into the unspoken question.

Is it Paul?

She nodded.

"Um . . . yeah," she murmured and sniffed, reaching for a napkin to wipe her face, now damp with streaming tears. "I've been seeing that man's profile, the set of his jaw, his eyes—all of it—since the very first moment I laid eyes on my daughter Gracie. And every day after that for years."

The detective sighed. "I'm relieved. I was afraid I'd brought you all this way—that I'd brought this all up for nothing— that it was a hoax. But I had a feeling . . ."

Emilia extended her arm across the table and put a hand on his forearm. "Miguel, your instincts are what saved me in the first place. When you called, I knew without a doubt that you'd found him."

"Well, we haven't exactly found him yet. But at least now we know to be looking for him. And I'm sure there's a clue in here somewhere. I thought maybe between the three of us, we could figure it out. And if necessary, I have a close contact in the San Juan PD who could help."

"Do you think that's a good idea?" Emilia asked as a pang of concern hit her.

It was a knee-jerk reaction, she knew, from all those years of staying under the radar. There was no statute of limitations on murder. But if Paul really was alive, then there *was* no murder. And there never had been.

CHAPTER 23

CÉSAR

Thirty Years Ago

It was supposed to be a quick job—easy money. And God knew he needed some of that right now. Thanks to his ex-wife, forty percent of his already paltry paycheck was skimmed right off the top for alimony. Alimony that he wouldn't have to pay if she'd just hurry up and marry the *pendejo* she was shacking up with. But why bother when he could sit around collecting unemployment while César worked overtime to pay for a house he didn't live in anymore. So when these side jobs came up, he usually jumped at them. Especially when they were this lucrative.

This one had come through the friend of a friend, and he doubted he'd be able to trace it back to its origin if he tried. But what he did know was that he got paid half upfront, and even if the party reneged on the back end, this was more money than he'd ever been paid for a job before. And who knew if this one might lead to more work? Still, he'd just hit his forties and, while still physically imposing and stronger than most, he was getting a little old for this shit.

It would be a scorching ninety-eight degrees today, but for the moment, he was sitting on a bench in the shade overlooking the pier, a warm, salty breeze rustling the newspaper in his hands. Not that he minded, the thing was just for show anyway—an easy, inexpensive way to look inconspicuous as he waited for what turned out to be more than two hours. Luckily he was patient. He would spend the whole damn day there if he had to, until the passengers reembarked and the massive cruise ship pulled backward out of the dock toward its next port-of-call.

Legalities aside, César considered himself to be a decent man—a man of his word. He never resorted to violence unless absolutely necessary, and he had never once killed anyone. He didn't think he could live with another man's blood on his hands. So he cherry-picked his jobs, only taking the ones that suited his rather loose moral code. He'd built a reputation as a discrete, honest man who never left a job unfinished. Which was why he would sit there all day if he had to, waiting for the *turista* to emerge from the massive cruise ship. Regardless of whether or not the man turned up, it was important that he be able to say he'd seen *every single* person who came and went from that boat while it sat in the dock today.

That's not to say he didn't wonder if this was an exercise in futility. Perhaps something had happened on board that necessitated a change in plans? The vast majority of the cruisers had disembarked between eight and nine that morning in a huge group, but he had what his mother had called *vista de lince*—the vision of a lynx, and he had not caught sight of the *turista* whose picture he had paperclipped inside the newspaper for quick reference.

He'd been contemplating walking to the coffee cart about a hundred feet away when he spotted the lone figure coming down the gangplank at ten-thirty. A quick check with the picture confirmed the features, the sandy blond hair, the six-foot-two frame. This was definitely him. The only thing unexpected was the fact that he was alone. There was no woman with him, which had been the expectation, not to mention his biggest concern. He didn't "do" women. And now, thankfully, it looked as if he wouldn't have to.

César watched the young man look up and down between the map in his hand and the street sign on the corner in front of him. Apparently deciding he was on the correct path, he turned left onto Calle Marina, then veered right onto Calle de la Tanca. He waited until there was a good distance between them, then stood up from the bench, folded the newspaper, slipped it under his arm, and began to follow.

Tracking the *turista* wasn't hard. He headed straight for the Museo Pablo Casals, exactly where he'd been told the man would likely go. He knew the place well, having brought his own son Javier there a number of times. The acquaintance who'd called César with this opportunity had known that his Javi played the cello—the same instrument as the *turista*. It was this uncanny coincidence that had catapulted him to the top of the list for this lucrative gig.

Once the man went inside the tiny building that housed the museum, he walked around back to the car he'd left in the alley. The old junker was untraceable and he planned to dump it as soon as he'd completed the assignment. Now he jiggled the keys in the trunk lock, cursing under his breath when it didn't open immediately. When it finally clicked at last, releasing the latch so the trunk could swing up, he reached in and pulled out the instrument he'd borrowed from his son. Then he gave the lid a good hard slam and took a seat on a bench in direct sight of the museum.

At last, a full hour after walking in, the young, blond man stepped out into the square, shielding his eyes from the blinding sun. César held his breath, glancing over the top of his newspaper every few seconds to see if the man had noticed him. For a second, it looked as if he might just turn and walk the other way without even glancing in the direction of the bench. But then the man's eyes passed over him, cut left, and returned. He started to walk toward the bench. César shook the paper slightly, making a big show of turning the page before pretending to read, waiting until the man was so close that his shadow fell across the paper. He looked up to find the *turista* smiling down at him.

"*Hola. ¿Como estás hoy?*" he asked in anglicized but understandable Spanish.

César always liked it when the tourists made some attempt to speak Spanish.

"*Muy bien, gracias a Dios. Y tú?*"

A moment of panic crossed the man's face.

"Ummm . . ."

"I speak English, too," César assured him in a heavy accent of his own.

"Oh, that's great! Thank you, I appreciate it. My Spanish isn't very good . . . yet. My fiancée—actually, my wife now—she's been teaching me. But I've got a long way to go," he said with an apologetic smile. "I, uhhh . . . I couldn't help but notice your cello there," the man said, with a nod toward the instrument.

"Ah, yes," César replied with a knowing nod. "It's the . . . how do you say? The *violoncello* of my son."

The *turista*'s eyes lit up.

"Your son plays the cello?"

César nodded enthusiastically.

"I play too," the man declared proudly, and César feigned surprise.

"Oh, *sí*? *¡Que bueno!* How good this is!"

"Why do you have the cello out here?" he asked, again looking toward the case on the cobblestone square.

"Ah, well, I bring it to have one of the strings replaced. I do not know how to do this for him, and the man who do it in the music store is no here right now. They sell me the string, but I have to wait for him to come back from lunch so he can fix for us."

"Really? I mean, I could do that for you . . . if you want . . ."

César considered himself to be an exceptional judge of character, and every instinct was telling him this was a good and generous man. This didn't sit well with him. He was used to dealing with sketchier characters who were suspicious by nature. He was used to having to work harder than this to manipulate them, because they weren't the kind of men to offer help without an incentive. This was almost too easy.

"Oh, yes? Oh, this would be wonderful! I, um . . . I put the string in the car. You can do there?"

"Yeah, sure," the man agreed. "We can set it up right on top of the trunk. It shouldn't take more than a few minutes. Your son will have to tune it when he gets it back to school, though. Hey, what's his name?"

The question took him by surprise.

"*¿Como?* Emm . . . sorry?"

"His name—*el nombre de tú hijo*," the man managed to say slowly.

"Ah, yes. Javier. *Se llama Javier.* We sometimes call him Javi."

"Javier," the *turista* repeated slowly, as if rolling the single word around in his mouth. "That's a good name. A strong name."

César could only nod. It was exactly what had attracted him to the name in the first place, and it was the only one he and his wife could agree on.

"Yes, he is a good boy," he replied, trying not to show his discomfort as he got to his feet.

He tucked the paper under his arm and was reaching for the instrument when the man held up a hand.

"Please, let me. This is going to sound strange, but I feel more . . . balanced . . . when I'm carrying one of these," the *turista* explained with a smile.

He returned the smile, then directed him toward the alley where his car was parked.

There was a split second—a hair's breadth of time when he considered not doing it. But then he remembered he was a man of his word. And he never left a job unfinished.

"*Ven*," he said, with a nod in the direction of the alley. "Come. I show you."

Once the *turista* was bent down over the open trunk, fingers working to open the clasps, it was just a matter of a quick jab with the needle full of sedative. An instant before he collapsed, their eyes met. There was something in the rapid progression from confusion to understanding to betrayal that unnerved César from the moment he saw it all swirling there in his eyes. It bothered him still even now that they were parked on the cargo ferry, safely hidden amongst the vast pallets and containers and a few other cars as the great vessel prepared to head out into international waters. This particular ship traveled amongst all the Caribbean islands delivering cargo to various ports. There would be a few stops before finally reaching their place of disembarkation, St. Croix.

He took a few deep breaths and closed his eyes, hoping to shake the malaise festering in his gut. He hadn't intended on falling asleep, but he must have done exactly that, because when he woke, the sun was already low in the west, making its way toward the horizon.

It wasn't until he stretched there in the front seat that he caught a glimpse of something in the rearview mirror. César twisted around in the driver's seat so he could confirm what he thought he'd seen. A moment later, he was out of the car and rushing around to investigate the open trunk. That stupid latch! Why hadn't he done more to secure it? There weren't any crewmen walking the deck that he was aware of, but anyone could have seen the man unconscious there and—

He stopped in his tracks, staring down at the empty trunk in disbelief.

There had been enough sedative in the syringe to keep the *turista* knocked out for hours.

"*¡Maldita sea!*" he hissed into the darkness. *Goddammit!*

He took a deep breath, willing himself to calm down and take stock of the situation. He had to find the man before he was spotted by someone on the upper decks. The Coast Guard would be called in, and then César would be well and truly fucked. He looked behind him to the rear of the boat, then he looked forward. Then he began to walk, allowing his gaze to sweep from side to side across the ship's interior as he made his way closer and closer to outside of the ship—toward the sound of the waves.

The man probably wouldn't have attracted his attention had he not moved between two containers, temporarily disrupting the light between them and catching César's eye. Reaching into his jacket pocket, he felt for the extra syringe and gave silent thanks that even if he had screwed up, he'd at least had the good sense to bring a back-up. He turned sideways and continued creeping with his back sliding along the ribs of the huge container. When, at last, he ran out of real estate to hide behind, he took a deep breath and swung himself hard around the corner.

What he'd not anticipated was the possibility that the man would be *right* there.

The momentum César had generated sent him careening headlong into the *turista*, knocking him down onto the deck. The younger man began to scrabble backward like a crab until he was just under the chain at the end of the deck. The one put in place to secure cargo from going over the side and into the ocean below. He grabbed it quickly and hauled himself up. All the while, César came closer, one hand up as if to convey he was not a threat to the man.

But they both knew otherwise.

He had to call out in order to be heard over the sound of the ship's bow cutting across the waves.

"Come back this way. There is no need for you to be afraid. No one is going to hurt you. I am just dropping you somewhere."

"Who sent you?" the man called back, his voice strained with his panic. "What do you want?"

For every inch César closed between them, the other man edged back and away. But he couldn't see what César could—that he was about to hit the terminus of the chain, where it had been anchored to a concrete pole. And that there was a good two feet between that pole and the sidewall of the boat. It wasn't much, but it was enough. If the *turista* backed up to that space, there would be nothing between him and the water below.

"You need to stop now. You have nowhere to go, and you will fall if you keep going. Just stop now . . . please, I don't want you to be hurt."

"Really? You drug me and throw me in the trunk of a car, and I'm supposed to believe that?"

"I don't know anything about your situation," César confessed. "I know only what I need to know to deliver you. But they promise me no one will hurt you."

The laugh that came from the other man gave César chills. It was sarcastic and frantic and furious all at once. He'd never heard anything like it in his life and he hoped to never hear it again.

"No? And you believed these people you work for? The ones who're paying you to kidnap me? Are you taking me someplace where no one will be able to find my body after they get what they want?"

César stopped but the *turista* continued to move, his steps unbalanced and uncoordinated from the sedative. He had to find a way to get him to calm down enough to be aware of his surroundings.

"No one is going to kill you in St. Croix . . ."

Something shifted in the *turista*'s expression.

"St. Croix?" he echoed, his tone indicating recognition. Recognition of what, César didn't know.

"Yes! Yes, St. Croix," he repeated, thinking this had somehow brought some clarity to the younger man and that he might relax just a bit.

He thought wrong.

"No. No way," he yelled. "I'm not going to St. Croix. I'm not going anywhere. Not with you. Not with anyone—"

He'd actually started moving faster, in clumsy, jerky movements, one hand gripping the chain behind him. There were barely three feet left between him and the potentially deadly gap.

"Please! Please, just stop. There is a space there," César said, pointing behind him. "If you go any more, you will fall through the space."

"Like I'm going to trust you!" the man shouted, moving a few more inches.

César felt his breath catch in his throat.

"Stop!" he yelled.

But it was too late, the *turista* had run out of chain. Unfortunately his body didn't know that until the support he'd been leaning into was gone, and there was nothing between him and the edge of the deck.

In a last-ditch effort, César threw himself forward, his fingers searching for some bit of flesh or clothing to grab onto. Something—anything to disrupt the pull of gravity. But his grasp came up empty, and an instant later, Paul Winstead disappeared before his very eyes.

César lay there, staring for a long time afterward, unable to tear his eyes away from the last spot he'd seen the man. Finally he managed to get himself up, slowly walking to the edge, hand firmly on the chain. There were tears rolling down his cheeks as he peered out over the edge of time and space.

CHAPTER 24

GRACIE

Today

"She's a murderer?" Meg asks for the third time. "An actual *killer?*"

I, on the other hand, am less surprised by this turn of events. Because I know that the fact that you've killed someone does not, in and of itself, make you a bad person. You just don't always know what drove someone to that point. Something tells me this is one of those situations.

Detective Raña nods as he flips through the pages of a folder pulled from yet another file box, this one brought up from the basement archives.

"Afraid so. The victim was her husband, Sergio Braga. She testified that she came across his stash of his pornographic photos and she went into a blind rage."

"Pfft. Well, that's hardly a reason to kill someone," I comment.

He looks up at me. "This wasn't stuff out of a magazine. These were photos that *he* took—of actual girls. Teenagers. Imelda recognized some of them. Including Emilia."

Meg and I stop breathing at exactly the same moment, suspended there in that place after you hear something but before you understand it.

"Oh, my God!" she gasps after a long few seconds.

Raña realizes what he's done—again—almost immediately, removing his reading glasses and shifting in his chair so that he's facing us fully.

"I'm so sorry. That was very insensitive of me . . ."

Meg shakes her head. "Um, no, it's okay. It's just a—a surprise, is all."

Something about this doesn't sit right with me, above and beyond the obvious. "So how did she end up in prison for life?" I inquire. "I know that was a long time ago, but with something like that—where there's, you know, *evidence*, the jury and the judge are apt to be more lenient."

"Ah. Yes. Well," he says slowly. "Perhaps they would have been more sympathetic had she not lain in wait for him one night when he came home drunk. Then she ambushed him with a knife. Stabbed him twenty-eight times."

"Right. Wow," I murmur, trying to keep myself from imagining what that crime scene must have looked like. "So she pled guilty?"

He glances down at the papers in front of him. "Let's see . . . looks like a plea of 'not guilty by reason of transitory mental defect' was entered."

"What does that mean?" my sister asks from next to me.

"Not guilty by reason of temporary insanity," I explain.

Before we can debate the merits of the woman's case any further, Raña's cellphone rings from on top of his desk. He quickly grabs it and excuses himself, only to return a minute later holding the phone in his hand.

"I know where your mother is."

"Hey, slow down!" Meg says from the passenger's seat of our newly acquired rental car.

"I don't want to give Mom a chance to dodge us again," I explain, making a quick lane change as if to prove my point.

"Are you sure you're not thinking *he* might be there? That you don't want to give *him* a chance to dodge you?"

I shoot her a sideways glance before answering her question with a few of my own.

"Do you think it's possible the guy went missing on purpose? That maybe he didn't want to be a father, or his family finally got to him . . . or maybe he regretted marrying her?"

Meg lets a long stream of breath pass her lips, as if she's releasing air from an overinflated tire. "I suppose anything's possible, right? But damn, that would suck for Mom. Because then she would have spent the last thirty years in love with a man who left her to take the blame for a crime that never even happened."

"You're more sympathetic than I am," I comment. "I'm still pretty furious about all of this—about the lies."

She's scowling in my direction.

"Seriously? After everything we just found out back there—everything she endured—you're *still* angry with her?"

"Yes, Meg, I am. Unlike you, I can't just let things go and pretend that they never happened, that everything is perfect and wonderful and fine."

It's a profoundly bad choice of words, and I regret them immediately because they pry open a door that was nailed shut years ago. And my sister walks right through it.

"And there it is," she says in a voice that's uncharacteristically cold and detached. "It's always just right there under the surface, isn't it?"

"I don't know what you're talking about," I lie.

"You're never going to forgive me, are you? For ruining your life. Am I right, Gracie?"

I'm smart enough to know I should stop right where I am. Maybe I can't stuff the genie back in the bottle, but I sure as hell don't have to take it out for dinner and a movie either. Which is exactly what I do.

"No, Meg, I don't blame you for ruining my life. I blame you for stealing it," I inform her flatly.

And *there* it is. The words I've never spoken aloud.

Meg lets out some kind of scoff/laugh combo.

"I didn't steal a damn thing. I worked my ass off for *years* to get where I am, and if you'd bothered to check in every once in a while, you'd know just how hard it was for me."

"I know exactly how hard it was because *I did it first!*" I spit back at her, even as I'm making an aggressive pass around a small pickup truck that's moving slower than I want to go.

When she's quiet for a few beats, I think she's going to be the one to let it go. I'm wrong.

"That's the thing," my sister begins slowly, cautiously. "You didn't, did you?"

I shoot her a sideways glance. "What? What did you just say?"

"Oh, you worked your ass off, too. And you got into the LA Conservatory—which is no small feat. But you never got to go. You never had to do a jury or a recital. You never had to get into a graduate program or compete at a semi-professional level, did you. In fact, you know what, Gracie? It's like you're frozen in time at seventeen years old—where you had infinite potential and no obstacles, no competitors. In your mind, you were unstoppable."

"Except I wasn't, was I?" I hiss back at her, clutching the steering wheel so tightly that my knuckles are turning white. "You did a pretty good job of stopping me. I was good enough to go all the way, and I sure as hell wouldn't be whining about what I had to give up to do it."

"Yeah, I wouldn't be so sure about that," she tells me. "You were good, but you have absolutely no concept of what it takes to be good *enough*—so good that you stand out over every other exceptional pianist—because there are a *lot* of them."

I don't remember making a conscious decision to pull the car off the road. I just kind of end up there, idling in the shoulder of the rural highway, turned completely to the side so I can look into my sister's eyes. So she can see my face.

"You're wrong. I *always* knew how hard it was going to be—but obviously you didn't. And here you are, poor little prodigy, all grown up, and now you have to go out into the big, bad world."

"And here *you* are, Gracie. A *brilliant* lawyer. You love it, and it's clearly what you were meant to do. Not music. Not piano." She shakes her head adamantly. "No, I think of the two of us, you definitely got the better end of the deal."

For some reason, this just pushes all of my buttons at the same time, and before I can stop myself, I let loose some of the razor-sharp edge that makes me so good in the court-room.

"You looking for permission to quit, Meg? Feeling bad because you insisted on taking what was mine and now you want to throw it away? Don't! Because I don't give a shit anymore. An opportunity taken, an opportunity stolen, an opportunity squandered . . . they're all the same to me at this point. Just different degrees of opportunism."

I face forward once more, start the car, and pull back out onto the road. Then I turn on the radio so I don't have to hear her crying next to me.

CHAPTER 25

BLAINE

Thirty Years Ago

Why should Paul get to be happy?

That question was the crux of every ugly word and deed that had passed between Blaine and his brother in the last five years. When they were kids, they'd been each other's best friend, swimming in the Caribbean, snowboarding in Vale, and exploring exotic places all over the world. But something changed when Brock began to involve them in the business. Their father had no intention of raising a couple of spoiled trust fund playboys. He wanted to mold his heirs in his own image to ensure his vision for WinCo would be executed even after he left the company or this earthly plane—whichever came first.

Except Paul wasn't interested in the oil business. All he wanted to do was play his cello and play house with Emilia. Neither of those choices was acceptable to Brock, which meant neither was acceptable to Blaine. Because Brock was the final authority on all things Winstead—including his children. Besides which, Blaine would be damned if he was going to be the only miserable one. If he had to shoulder the burden of being Blaine Rockwell Winstead's son, so did his brother. They were in this shit together for the rest of their lives. So when he got wind that Paul had filed for a marriage license, he knew he needed to do something, and fast.

That was how he'd come up with the plan. Blaine had been certain that if he could just get Paul away from the gold-digging slut long enough, he could make him see reason. Make him see that his first loyalty was to *them*—to his family and, by extension, to the business. That nothing else mattered. He decided to keep it a secret so that he could surprise Brock—show him that his eldest son had the initiative and problem-solving skills needed to take over the company someday. Hopefully it would also buy him a month or two in the old man's good graces. Except something had gone terribly wrong, and suddenly Paul was missing *for real*—as were the people Blaine had hired to take him.

He knew there was a problem when his brother wasn't delivered to the rendezvous in St. Croix by the evening. Several fretful hours later, Brock, in a rare moment of parental concern, had phoned from Texas to tell him about Emilia's frantic ship-to-shore call in the middle of the night. It had been a spur-of-moment thing, him throwing out the possibility that Paul's bride had been involved, but Brock ran with it. And Blaine made damn sure to be on that ship first thing in the morning to push that narrative, even if it meant bribes, blackmail, or threats. But when Emilia managed to get off the ship—with the help of that detective, he was sure—she took with her Blaine's last best hope of finding Paul before his father or the press or anyone else found out *he* had been the one to set this clusterfuck in motion in the first place.

Tens of thousands of dollars and several private investigators later, there hadn't been a single lead. It had been six weeks at this point, and he was just desperate enough to go see Emilia's insane, murdering mother Imelda in the women's penitentiary outside of San Juan. If she could lead him to her daughter, then maybe *she* could lead him to his brother.

He had nothing to lose.

Thanks, once again, to his surname, the warden had made the arrangements—though driving past the barb-wired walls and the towers with the armed guards had given him a brief barrage of second thoughts. And being a VIP hadn't excluded him from the particularly unnerving experience of being searched for contraband and having several of his personal items temporarily confiscated. Now, as he passed by the entryway to one of the cellblocks, he was a little alarmed to find himself the subject of catcalls and lewd gestures from a handful of female inmates. The guard escorting him didn't even seem to notice.

He felt a little better when they finally reached the tiny meeting room meant for inmate/attorney consultations. There was just enough room for a metal table flanked by backless benches, all bolted to the floor so, presumably, no one got bludgeoned to death with a piece of furniture. Not that Imelda was the bludgeoning type. In fact, he knew her to be the stabbing type, though she didn't look it, he noted, taking a seat directly across from her.

She was dressed in bright yellow prison-issue scrubs, and he guessed her to be somewhere close to his mother's age. She bore a striking resemblance to her daughter with angular cheekbones and the same deep, dark brown eyes. Blaine couldn't help but notice the interpreter sitting next to her—a considerably younger woman with long dark hair tied back in a ponytail. Behind thick, black-framed glasses were eyes in a striking shade of green. He wondered fleetingly what someone like that had done to land in a place like this.

"I am Claudia," she said in heavily accented English. "I will translate between you and Imelda."

"Are you a murderer, too?" he inquired bluntly.

If the woman was offended by the question, she didn't show it.

"No, I don't kill nobody. I get mixed up with a man who bring a lot of drugs here from other countries."

"Ah, so a drug mule then," he paraphrased disdainfully. "And a junkie too, I'll bet."

The interpreter didn't bat a single long, dark eyelash.

"Yes, exactly. I testify against him and come here for five years. But I don't take the drugs anymore."

He nodded brusquely and got to the matter at hand. "I'm looking for Emilia," he said coolly. "Does she know where her daughter is?"

Claudia held up an index finger, then conveyed his question to Imelda, who responded in rapid-fire Spanish.

"Imelda say that she has not heard from Emilia in many years," the interpreter said, causing him to scoff.

"Really," he said skeptically. "Well, that's convenient."

"Convenient?" she echoed, not understanding his sarcasm.

"I don't believe her," he tried again slowly.

Without comment to him, she conveyed this sentiment to Imelda, and listened to the older woman's response then turned back to him.

"She says Emilia will never forgive her."

Well, now this could be interesting. Blaine leaned forward.

"Forgive her for what?"

"For not believing Emilia when she tell Imelda that her husband was . . . hurting . . . her." Claudia paused, keeping her eyes glued to his as her brows went up. "You understand what this means, yes?"

He shrugged disinterestedly.

"You're saying Emilia's stepfather was a pervert and now her mother is in jail for carving him up like a Thanksgiving Day turkey. Tell me something I don't know."

Neither woman looked pleased with him as his comments were translated. When Imelda's response came, it was punctuated by a few hand gestures that didn't need explaining.

"She say to tell you that Sergio would not listen to what she say to him either, and look what happen to him."

Blaine laughed so hard that he actually snorted. When he finally caught his breath, he raised his palms up toward the ceiling while addressing the older woman directly. "Lady, you really *are* delusional! What do you think you can do to me from in here? Or from anywhere, for that matter? Do you have any idea who the hell it is you're talking to right now?"

This time, Claudia didn't wait for Imelda's words, because she had a few of her own.

"Is *very* dangerous to speak this way to Imelda," she hissed at him. "She is an *espiritista*. This mean she talk to the ghosts—the spirits—and they do things she ask for. You do not want her to be angry with you, because then *los espiritos* will be angry with you. And *they* find you no matter where you go!"

Was this chick seriously threatening to sic a ghost on him?

Blaine folded his arms across his chest and quirked a challenging eyebrow.

"Huh . . . and were the spirits angry that she knew her husband was screwing around with her teenage daughter and she didn't do a damn thing about it?" he shot back in an equally menacing tone.

"*¡Sí!*" Imelda replied, nodding adamantly and pointing at him.

"Yes," Claudia said, as if he couldn't figure out the two-letter word. "I know from her that *los espiritos* they would not come to her for a long time. Not until Sergio was dead and she was here in the jail. But now they come back to give her information you need."

"Right, right. So is this the part where she offers me information in exchange for money? Or does she think I can convince the governor to pardon her? Because that's not gonna happen."

Imelda seemed to understand him without the benefit of translation. She leaned across the table, dark eyes flashing and spittle-soaked words flying from her mouth in Spanish.

Whatever the hell the old bat was saying it clearly made the translator very uneasy which, in turn, made Blaine uneasy.

"Imelda say you need to stop being so ... so ..." She seemed to be digging deep for the word. Failing to find it in English, she threw it at him in Spanish. "*¡Arrogante!*"

"Yeah, no need to translate that one," Blaine muttered, getting to his feet. "I can't believe I thought I could actually get something useful here. What a colossal waste of time."

He was about to head back to the door when Claudia reached out and grabbed his wrist hard.

"*¡Oye!* She knows! Imelda knows *you* are why Paul is missing!"

Blaine froze but managed to keep his expression totally impassive.

"I don't know what the hell she's talking about."

Imelda just smirked and said something, flipping a hand in his direction dismissively.

"What? What did she just say?" he demanded from Claudia.

"She say you *do* know, and you are acting like a little *pendejo* now when your brother need you. If you walk out from here, you will never see him again."

Blaine swallowed hard, trying to maintain his façade of calm indifference as he looked back and forth between the two incredibly pissed-off women. Suddenly he was wishing he hadn't asked for the guard to wait in the hallway rather than come inside with them. Now he figured he had about two seconds to make a decision. He could walk out that door and go back to looking for a needle in a haystack. Or he could do something he *never* did. Ever. He could take a chance on something he couldn't see—something he couldn't understand. A moment later, the decision was made for him when Imelda herself spoke to him in slow, deliberate English.

"You. Have. Nothing. To. Lose."

It was the thought he'd had not ten minutes ago—verbatim—and it made the hair on the back of his neck stand up on end. Without further comment, he nodded once and waited for Claudia to continue.

"Right. So Imelda, she ask *los espiritos* what she can do to get the forgiveness. And they tell her to give a message to you."

"To me?" he asked incredulously. "The spirits have a message for *me*?"

Now Imelda began speaking again in earnest. He caught a word here and there, but most of her monologue was lost on him until Claudia was ready to translate it.

"Imelda says the spirits they show her *la nena*."

"*La . . . nena*? What is that? What does it mean?"

"It means the little girl," she explained.

"What little girl? Paul is with . . . a little girl?"

The younger woman shook her head.

"No, no . . . *los espiritos* sometimes send symbols that you must interpret for yourself. She say you will know when *los espiritos* want you to know."

Before he could respond, he heard the door behind him open, and a female corrections officer stepped inside the cramped room.

"Time's up, ladies," she said, beckoning Imelda and Claudia, who stood immediately.

Blaine looked to Claudia while pointing to Imelda.

"Hold on, that can't be it—some cagey spirits and a little girl. Can't she give me anything else?"

He hated the way his tone had shifted from skeptical to desperate. He was never desperate. Or, at least, he'd never been desperate before now.

Imelda made her way around the table to join the officer. She paused just long enough to say something to Claudia over her shoulder before stepping out into the hallway with their escort.

"Yes, she has one more thing to tell you," the interpreter began.

"Finally," he murmured under his breath with an impatient sigh. "What is it?"

"She say this will make you a better person."

He couldn't hold back the acerbic laugh.

"A better person? Great. Well, thanks for that. I feel so much better knowing I have the thumbs-up from a convicted killer. Now I can finally be happy."

Claudia smiled right in the face of his sneer, her eyes locking on his.

"No, not yet. But someday," she said. "Someday soon."

The farther Blaine got from the prison, the more he was able to convince himself the entire encounter had been nothing more than a sham. Imelda had just been trying to screw with his head. And that Claudia . . . well, who knew what the hell she was after? All he knew for sure was that he wanted to get back home to St. Croix to a good stiff drink, and a hot meal. Unfortunately he had to endure a forty-five-minute flight with Chatty Chad, the pilot next to him.

At first, he gave one- or two-word replies, hoping the guy would get the hint. No such luck. He was perfectly content to prattle on about all the little landmarks on their flight path.

"Do you like the beaches?" he asked Blaine, not bothering to wait for a reply. "This island below us, Vieques, has some of the most beautiful beaches in the world! Have you been?"

Blaine looked out the window with disinterest.

"Nope."

"Oh, and they have wild horses and a nature preserve, too. It's *very* beautiful. They call it *La Isla de Nena*."

Blaine's head snapped around to face the man.

"What did you just say? The name of the island, I mean?"

"Vieques," the pilot replied with a smile.

"No, no—the other name. La . . ."

"Oh! *La Isla de Nena*! Yes, yes. The island of the little girl. It's called this because Vieques is like *la hermanita* . . . the little sister of Puerto Rico."

Was it possible? Could *his* little brother be somewhere down there with the little sister?

CHAPTER 26

MIGUEL

Today

Miguel was sitting out on the front porch in a wrought-iron rocking chair when David Raña pulled into his driveway. He stood to greet his old friend—the one who had taken his place when he retired from the San Juan P.D. Miguel offered a hand and a broad smile when they met at the door.

"*Buenos tardes.* I appreciate you finding the time to come out here now that you're a celebrity!"

Miguel had been both amused and proud when the profile piece about his friend had come out in the paper.

Raña groaned and rolled his eyes. "It was supposed to be an article about cold cases—not about me. You would not believe the shit I'm getting for it at work. Every day I take down photocopies that someone has taped up all over the building and somehow more magically appear the next day. They're merciless."

Miguel chuckled. Those were the kinds of things he missed about the job—the pranks, the laughs, the camaraderie. "Well, come my friend, have a seat. I really do appreciate you coming. There's something I need to talk to you about."

Raña dropped down into the second rocker, leaning forward so that his forearms rested on his thighs. He nodded toward the rental car he'd just parked next to in the driveway.

"Does it have something to do with your company?" he asked

"Well, actually, as a matter of fact, it does . . ."

"And that would be Emilia Oliveras?"

Miguel stopped rocking. "I'm sorry, but . . . what would make you ask *that*?"

Raña sat up again and glanced at him. "Her daughters. They showed up at my office this morning telling quite a story about a strange phone call their mother, *Emily*, received yesterday before jumping onto an airplane to come here. To see someone named Miguel."

Miguel was at a loss. He'd spent the last two hours trying to figure out how to explain everything to his old friend, but it would seem he needn't have worried about it. Before he could calculate a response David continued. "You never mentioned to me that you were the original detective assigned to the Emilia Oliveras case when Paul Winstead disappeared. When *she* disappeared."

"There was no Emilia Oliveras case," he replied coolly. "She was never charged with anything."

Raña shrugged.

"I think we both know things might have been very different if Marianna Ruíz hadn't gone missing right about then. Everyone was so caught up in *that* story that it took the air out of the Winstead investigation."

Miguel felt a small wave of irritation, and it came through in his tone.

"I think we both know that you were too young and too involved with your own . . . *situation* to have an appreciable memory or understanding of that time. Now tell me, why are you here, David?"

Raña let out a long column of air as he folded his arms across his chest. "I'm here because, as far as I can work out, someone who knew where Emilia Oliveras has been living called to tell her they'd found her long-lost husband of thirty years ago. She came here, not realizing her daughters were trailing her. They, in turn, came to see me, afraid she was walking into some sort of hoax or scam. Only it's not a hoax or a scam, is it? *That's* why you called and asked me to meet you out here."

Miguel considered the other detective for a long moment before shifting his gaze out toward his banana tree, noting the fruit was almost ready to be cut.

"No," he replied without shifting his gaze. "It's not a hoax—at least I don't think it is. Two days ago, someone sent me a picture that has a man in the background. He's playing the cello, and he looks a lot like Paul Winstead from the side—but I never met the man in person, so I called Emily—Emilia—and she came right away." He paused, refocusing on the man in the rocker next to him. "So where are the daughters now?"

"On their way here."

Miguel sat up straight and pointed to the tiled floor beneath them.

"Here? Like to this house? When?"

The other man glanced down at his watch.

"I should think any time now. I gave them your address and dropped them at the rental car agency. Then I hightailed it out here so you and I could have a little time to talk this through before they arrived."

"You could have called ahead," Miguel noted with some irritation.

Raña shrugged. "Again, I know you. I was fairly certain if I did that, Emilia—Emily—would be gone by the time I arrived. What I want to know is why *you* didn't call *me*? I could have helped you get to the bottom of this."

Miguel sighed and turned to look at his friend. "I would

have. In fact, I'd planned to speak with you later today, because I do need help figuring out who took this picture—and where. But then Emilia arrived this morning, and I didn't see any point in involving you until I knew for sure that it was him."

"Okay, well, I'm here now, and I'll do whatever I can to help you. But there's something else . . ."

"Really?" Miguel half-chuckled. "More than a man coming back from the dead after thirty years, and his wife who's been on the run all that time finally coming out of hiding? What else could there *possibly* be?"

"Imelda Oliveras."

The name stopped Miguel mid-rock once more. "What about her?"

"I guess Emilia told her daughters that her own parents were dead. So they had no idea who I was talking about when I mentioned Imelda to them."

Miguel let out a long, low whistle. "Well, that's going to make for an uncomfortable reunion."

"Considering how upset they were about all these secrets, I think you're right. But listen, I called over to the prison to get a status check on Imelda—she's been released."

"She's been—released?" Miguel echoed with surprise. "I thought she had a life sentence with no chance of parole? *¡Dios mío!* She's not coming here, too, is she?"

Raña held up his hands. "No, no. Nothing like that. Imelda was released directly to hospice on compassionate grounds. She doesn't have long to live."

Miguel sighed and shook his head without comment. After a moment, he got to his feet. "Well, come inside so I can show you the picture. Maybe you'll be able to spot something in it that I missed. And I guess I'll have to let Emilia know her girls are on the way . . . and find a way to tell her about her mother . . ."

The screen leading into the house opened abruptly, and Emilia stepped outside.

"Tell me *what* about my mother?"

"I still cannot *believe* Gracie and Meg followed me here!" Emilia was saying from her spot at the kitchen table. "How did they seem to you?"

It was much as it had been earlier this morning, except now Raña sat across from her.

"They seemed very . . . tenacious. And the older one, well, no offense, Emilia, but she's really something."

When Emilia started to laugh, Miguel found himself smiling. It wasn't a sound he could recall ever having heard before, and he quite liked it. He quite liked this woman that the slight, unimposing younger version of Emilia Oliveras had grown up to become. He was curious to see if her girls were anything like her. He hoped so.

Hilda came bustling in from the hallway.

"Alright, here's the laptop," she said, setting her MacBook on the table and pointing to the screen. "David, that's the picture right there."

Curious, Miguel came to look over his shoulder. "You really think there's something there that will help?"

Raña looked up at him. "If we're lucky, your man—or woman—left a trail of digital breadcrumbs for you to find." A moment later, he was using keyboard shortcuts to bring up a menu Miguel hadn't even known existed.

"Right, so there's something called EXIF—exchangeable image file format. Essentially it's information that's attached to the image. Time, date, location, that kind of thing. So let's just do a little scrolling through the metadata . . . ahhh . . . and there it is . . . Rincón," Raña told them.

"Rincón?" Hilda echoed. "That's only a half hour from here!"

"But where in Rincón?" Emilia wanted to know. "It's not exactly a tiny village. Is there any way you can pinpoint it?"

"Not with what I have here," the younger detective explained. "But maybe if we can zoom in on this picture a little more, we'll spot something that might help us narrow it down."

Using the trackpad, he began to pull the image at its corners, enlarging it as he went. Then he started to examine it inch by inch.

"Wait!" Emilia said, loud enough to startle them all.

"Do you see something you recognize?" Raña asked her, craning his neck to look at her standing behind him now.

"There . . . right there." She pointed to the cello. "Can you make that part any bigger?"

He complied, then adjusted the screen slightly so she could get a better look at it.

"Oh—oh, my God!" Emilia gasped, a hand flying to her mouth.

"What? What is it, Emilia?" Miguel asked, putting a concerned hand on her shoulder. "What are you seeing?"

"That indentation," she whispered, pointing at the screen with her free hand. "That's *Paul's* cello! No doubt in my mind!"

Raña and Miguel exchanged looks.

"So it must be him then," Hilda surmised. "This must be the proof, no?"

Raña shrugged and ran a hand through his hair.

"Well, it's not exactly DNA evidence, but it's a start—"

"No, no, you don't understand!" Emilia cut in with sharp impatience, grabbing Miguel's arm and pointing again. "It's *Paul's* cello!"

That's when it hit him.

"*¡Jesucristo!*" he murmured under his breath as Raña and Hilda looked on in confusion.

Miguel and Emilia were the only ones who recognized the significance of this because Miguel and Emilia were the only ones who'd been there that day on the boat. *Whoever* the man in the picture was, there was only one way he could have come to be in possession of that cello—and that was from the Winstead family themselves. Which meant they knew exactly where Paul was—and likely had all along.

CHAPTER 27

BLAINE

Thirty Years Ago

He couldn't take his eyes off the sculpture on the doctor's desk—a plaster-cast brain sitting in the palms of two cupped plaster hands. It had been a good place to park his gaze when he couldn't stand to look at the doctor's pitying expression or listen to his parents' pitiful questions. Again and again, his eyes wandered back to it.

Dr. Jack Epstein was the fifth neurologist they'd consulted—each one having been offered so much cash that they didn't even scoff at taking a quick jaunt to the Caribbean to examine Paul in person, or the ridiculous nondisclosure agreement Brock had required. Proof, once again, that if you put enough zeros on the end of a check, you can get pretty much anyone to do pretty much anything.

A superstar out of Johns Hopkins, Epstein was repeating, verbatim, the same opinion that had come from the doctors at Columbia Presbyterian, UCLA, Mass General, Cleveland Clinic, and Mayo over the last week. That's how long it had been since Paul was airlifted to a private hospital in the Bahamas. Up until this point, his parents had stubbornly refused to accept the brutal truth—that Paul would never be Paul again. But now they were all out of second opinions, and it was time to play the hand they'd been dealt. That his brother had been dealt.

"Doctor, are you saying there's nothing more you can do?" Evelyn asked in a tight voice. "No special trials or experimental anything? You can't do some surgery to relieve pressure . . . somewhere?"

Blaine saw the regret on the doctor's face before he heard it in his tone. It was how they'd all looked, how they'd all sounded. There was nothing shocking here—and not just because he'd heard this song and dance several times before.

He'd known where this was headed on the day he chartered a flight to Vieques, picked up a car, and set out in search of his brother. All thoughts of Imelda being a fraud were suspended, at least temporarily. There was only one hospital there on the island. And while he was not a religious man by any stretch of the imagination, Blaine found himself attempting something resembling a prayer as he parked the car. It was a plea to something greater than himself that the wacky psychic woman was right—that he would find what he was looking for on this tiny speck of land in the ocean.

Inside, the small waiting room was full, and it took several agonizing minutes before he could even approach the counter. When he was finally standing in front of a woman not much older than himself, he pulled out the picture of Paul in his wallet.

"I'm looking for my brother," he said quietly. "*Mi hermano.*"

She looked down at it, then up at him, and for one heart-stopping moment he was sure she was going to shake her head no. But she didn't. She crooked a finger at him and he followed her into the back and to a small room at the end of a short hallway. There was a curtain that prevented anyone from seeing the bed—and the patient in it—from the hallway. Blaine closed his eyes as she pulled it open slowly—afraid Paul wouldn't be there. And afraid he would be.

But there he'd been, looking small and crumpled—head wrapped in gauze, both legs and one arm in casts. He'd been unconscious and intubated, a machine breathing for him. But he'd been alive. Though now, apparently, the definition of alive was being called into question by his father.

"So there's no hope of him being anything more than a vegetable?" Brock asked the doctor bluntly.

Epstein took his time responding. When he did, his eyes were squarely on Brock's.

"As I've said, Mr. Winstead, the brain is a tricky business, and I want to be very careful to manage your expectations here. It's very unlikely Paul will be able to live a wholly independent life, as he did before. But that's not to say he won't be able to have a good life—a full and productive life. So much will be dependent on Paul's attitude as he begins the painful, slow process of recovery. And so much of that will depend on the family's attitude throughout this, as well. He'll take his cues from the people closest to him, and he's going to need a lot of positive emotional support and love."

"I just have to know," Brock began, "would this have been a different outcome if someone had actually bothered to get my son to a real hospital?"

Blaine couldn't help rolling his eyes. As usual, it was all about who was to blame and how to make them pay. If only he knew the truth about how this had all *really* been set in motion.

Dr. Epstein sat back in his chair, clasping his hands and resting them on his stomach.

"Mr. Winstead, all I can tell you is what I'm sure every other doctor you've consulted has said—your son appears to have fallen from a height that could have very easily killed him but somehow did not. His skull was fractured, and there was extensive swelling to his brain. Several bones were broken. The hospital in Vieques might not have been as big or as well-equipped as you're used to, but I assure you Paul had excellent care while he was there. I can't say with any certainty that he would have fared any better had he been brought here to my ER. All things considered, there is much to be grateful for."

His father scoffed.

"And what, exactly, should we be grateful for? That our son doesn't have the mental capacity of a kindergartner? That he's going to need someone to wipe his ass the rest of his life? That he'll never be able to claim his place in our family business? Because I have to tell you, *doctor*, I'm not seeing too many reasons to thank God, or you, or some rinky-dink doctor in some rinky-dink hospital out in the middle of nowhere. As far as I'm concerned, it would have been better for everyone concerned if Paul *had* died."

Blaine sucked in a breath.

Evelyn let out a pained sob.

And Dr. Jack Epstein lost his ever-loving shit.

The man straightened up in his chair so abruptly that the three of them jumped. Then he leaned so far across the desk that Blaine was sure he was about to come right across to grab his father by the necktie.

"You paid for my opinion, *sir*, so I'm going to give it to you," Epstein practically snarled. "I believe Paul will have a better outcome than most people in his situation that is due, in no small part, to the care he received after his accident— whatever the circumstances might have been. Now I think maybe you should try exhibiting a modicum of gratitude for his situation instead of looking for people to blame it on."

"Holy shit," Blaine muttered under his breath, his pulse picking up considerably at the unexpected thrill of seeing Brock get his ass handed to him.

Sporting a shade of crimson from under his collar right up to his hairline, Brock raised a finger and proceeded to point it in the other man's direction, poking the air sharply.

"I'll remind you there's a non-disclosure agreement in

place, Dr. Epstein. If I see anything even close to that quote anywhere in the press, I will own your practice, your first-born child, and your ass."

Much to Blaine's surprise, the doctor shrugged.

"I'm not worried, Mr. Winstead. I don't have to tell any-one anything, because people like you always show their true colors eventually. It's just a matter of time before the rest of the world sees you for who you really are."

"We're leaving. Now," Brock announced sharply, jump-ing up and helping Evelyn to her feet a little too roughly. "Let's go, Blaine," he said over his shoulder, already walking toward the door.

"I'll meet you outside. I want to take Paul's records and scans with us."

"Yes, good idea," his father said on his way out, slamming the door so hard that one of the large, framed diplomas fell off the wall, shattering the glass.

"I'm sorry, doctor," he said quietly. "My father is . . . he's just . . ."

"He's an asshole," the man said. "And I'm sorry to say it, but your mother doesn't seem to be especially . . . shall we say . . . independent."

There was a time not long ago that a comment like that would have enraged Blaine. But everything changed the sec-ond he'd cradled his broken brother in his arms. Something broke in *him* that day, too. But maybe that wasn't such a bad thing. Sometimes things needed to be broken in order to heal correctly.

"Yeah, that's fair," he agreed.

Epstein came out from around the desk and put both of his hands firmly on both of Blaine's shoulders, forcing him to look directly into his eyes.

"Listen to me, son, Paul needs someone in his corner, and I'm sorry to say I don't think it's going to be your parents. I can't say what your brother's prognosis is—and any doctor who tells you they can is a liar. But I have a hunch that with consistent therapy—speech, cognitive, occupational, physical—Paul could make some measurable progress. But it could take years, and one huge factor is going to be interaction."

"Interaction? With who?"

"Well, that's a good question. I feel strongly that if Paul doesn't have any contact with someone who actually cares about him . . . who engages with him on a personal level . . . well, then he has no chance at all. None."

"I don't understand what it is you're trying to tell me," Blaine said softly as he shook his head.

"I'm trying to tell you that Paul's condition is deteriorating by the day. If someone doesn't step up and commit to getting him the physical and emotional support he needs, I don't think he'll last a year."

Once they were in the air, Evelyn promptly curled up on the leather couch and fell asleep. Blaine felt sorry for his mother. She had taken the news so badly, and with each doctor's verdict, a little more of the hope had been crushed out of her. They'd all been elated when he'd finally found his brother, but as the reality of Paul's condition crystallized in all of their minds, that joy just crumbled away.

Brock, who had never had trouble buying whatever he wanted, was more frustrated than anything else. The man had led a charmed life and simply could not accept that he was powerless in this—or any other—situation. Right now, he was sitting at his usual spot at the table so he could spread out with his newspaper or read through the sheaf of paperwork he'd brought with him from the office. They would be back in Texas in a few hours.

Blaine took the seat across from his father and fastened his seat belt.

"So, what's next, Dad?" he asked.

His father glanced up at him over the top of his reading glasses.

"What's next is I'm done consulting doctors about this . . ."—Brock made a dismissive gesture with his hand—"this debacle."

He nodded slowly.

"And that means what, exactly? For Paul, I mean?"

Brock put the paper down and set his forearms flat on the table.

"Son, no one wanted to hear there was hope more than I did. But we have to be realistic now. We have to move past this and regroup."

"Regroup . . . ?" Blaine echoed.

His father nodded.

"Yes. I've been looking at facilities that handle cases like this, and I've found some very promising options abroad."

"What kind of options, Dad?" he asked cautiously.

"Well, Paul would be well cared for, with topnotch therapists around him around the clock. We could even fly out and visit him for his birthday. You know how your mother loves to ski. No reason we can't make a regular family trip of it . . . spend a few days . . ."

"Skiing where?" he asked, even though he already knew the answer. He just needed to hear it from his father.

"Switzerland, son. It has some of the best skiing *and* medical care in the world! And as you get more active in your role at WinCo, you'll do more traveling in Europe, too . . . you could always stop in and visit him when you're in the area."

Blaine thought about what the doctor had just told him. Somehow he didn't think seeing family a few times a year was going to cut it. But he had to tread carefully here—get his father to change his mind about anything took a good deal of finesse.

"Why do we need to send him so far away? We have the space and the money to give him full-time care at home, don't we?"

Brock's jaw tightened slightly, and when he spoke again, his voice was softer—presumably so Evelyn wouldn't over-hear what he was about to say.

"I'm going to tell you what I told your mother. We are simply not equipped for the level of care Paul is going to need going forward."

"I don't know, sounds risky to me."

This got his father's attention.

"Risky how?"

Blaine shrugged. "Don't you think maybe it's better to keep him close? You know, in case she turns up again?"

Brock looked confused for a moment. "She?"

"Emilia, Dad—his *wife*? If we park him somewhere that far away, it'll be hard to keep a close eye on things. Think about it—if Emilia surfaces again and finds a way to prove she's his wife, then *she's* the one with the control. Not us. Suddenly she's making his medical decisions, she gets to determine who can and cannot see him, she's in charge of his money." He paused dramatically, saving the best—or worst—for last. "Dad, she could exercise control over Paul's share of the company."

His father seemed to consider this. "We took care of that marriage certificate. You really think there's a possibility she could convince a judge somewhere she's his next of kin?"

Blaine shrugged. "It's worth having a conversation with the lawyers about. But in the meantime, why don't we set him up in the St. Croix house? I could work from there as easily as anywhere else, just fly into Texas once or twice a week to be at the office? Mom's there every chance she gets anyway—and you could visit when it's convenient without it looking like anything more than a family getaway."

"It's a good idea, Brock."

They were both surprised when his mother weighed in from the couch.

She looked at Blaine.

"You really want to do this, son? Because it won't be easy, even with round-the-clock help."

He nodded. "Yeah, I think I do," he replied, then quickly added: "I know I'd sleep better at night, anyway."

"No. I don't think—" his father began but the look on his mother's faced stopped the man cold.

"Make it happen, Brock. Or I'll make it happen without you."

CHAPTER 28

EMILIA

Today

Her mother hadn't always been a grifter. From the time Emilia was a little girl, she had pleasant memories of the people who crossed the threshold of their modest home— visiting for an hour or two like old friends over *café con leche* and *mandecaditos*. Imelda Oliveras would pull out her tarot deck, giving personalized readings to help the lovelorn, the grieving, the desperate, the hopeful. She interpreted and related the meaning of each hand that unfolded at their kitchen table with care and concern, guiding every neighbor, friend, and stranger in the direction set forth by the cards.

Imelda had a knack for making people feel heard, and respected. And rather than charge a set fee for her services, she would put a large glass jar out on the counter with the understanding that people pay what they could. Some days that wasn't even cash, but a dozen fresh eggs from their own hens, or a *caldera* full of *arroz con pollo* that the two of them would enjoy for dinner later on. It wasn't an ideal business model, but it was enough to sustain their modest lifestyle— with some left over for Emilia's piano lessons with Señora Diaz down the street. They weren't rich, but they were happy.

Until *he* came into their lives.

Sergio Braga was a charming, attractive man more than

ten years Imelda's junior. He used his good looks and charisma to get his foot into several women's beds, including her mother's. Emilia was a shy fourteen-year-old at the time, and while she didn't have enough life experience to understand who or what this man was, she knew, beyond a doubt, that nothing good could come of his presence in their home.

He took to strutting around the house like a peacock, as if he owned the place and everything in it—including them. Inexplicably, Imelda deferred to him on virtually everything—including her only child. Sergio alone decided which of Emilia's needs were important enough to be met and whether or not she had earned them. Food? Sanitary products? School supplies? His decision alone. And once he'd become the overlord of their home lives, he moved on to her mother's business.

Casting himself in the role of de facto manager, he took responsibility for booking appointments, enforcing time limits on each session, and suggesting an exact amount that should be paid—regardless of whether or not the person was able to afford it. Emilia was often tasked with turning fifty-cent pillars into "spell candles," and stringing tiny pouches of potpourri onto strips of nylon to create amulets meant to ward off evil spirits. Despite the obscene mark-up, they sold out quickly.

There was no denying an uptick in business, but it was all from outside their tiny community. Imelda's longtime devotees slowly fell off—which was exactly what he hoped would happen. Now there was room for what he considered more suitable prospects—all carefully vetted by him. Because, in addition to being well-dressed and well-spoken, Sergio had an uncanny ability to read people—their body language, their expressions, their actions. Emilia often thought he should be the one doing the readings . . . and perhaps he would have, had it not been for the fact that he was already a well-established con man with an extensive list of shady activities. Sergio Braga was already on the radar of law enforcement and had been in need of a gig that would get him out of the major metropolitan areas like San Juan, provide a roof over his head, a home-cooked meal on the table, and a warm body in his bed. But most important was his need to run the scam from behind the scenes and out of the sight of anyone keeping an eye on his activities.

Later on, she would conclude that he must have searched long and hard to find someone like Imelda—a vulnerable woman he could seduce and manipulate into doing all the work while he reaped the profits. This setup gave him a degree of distance, not to mention deniability, from anything that could potentially constitute fraudulent behavior and land him back in jail. Her mother was only too happy to comply if it meant she could continue to enjoy the attentions of such a suave, smooth man.

Under Sergio's oversight, there were no more freebee "sob-story" readings and certainly no more pay-as-you-can arrangements. He had his sights set considerably higher than the modest income they'd been drawing up to that point. The kind of individuals he sought out—and he *did* seek them out—included insecure, suggestible, lonely women . . . the richer, the better. His charm would get them in the door, and Imelda's so-called abilities would keep them there—plopping down cash day after day, week after week.

Emilia did her best to make herself invisible. She had permission to use the school's piano to practice before and after school. She felt safe there, away from the creepy, overbearing Sergio. She dreaded weekends and school holidays most. Not only did she have to be at home, but she couldn't practice the piano—the only thing that made her life bearable. But practicing soon became the least of her concerns.

The year she turned fifteen, Sergio and Imelda were married, with her standing by as an unwilling bridesmaid at her mother's insistence. That was the year Emilia had filled out in all the places that made the boys at school stare and make comments to one another . . . and to her. It wasn't long before she caught her stepfather's attention, as well. He had this way of watching her with hooded eyes and dilated pupils that sent every genetically wired red flag and alarm bell in her body flashing, waving, and blaring. Her instincts proved to be spot-on when, more than once, he walked in on her as she was dressing or showering, having "forgetting" to knock.

She wouldn't have thought it possible, but as time passed, Imelda became even more beguiled by her younger husband. Suddenly it was as if Emilia didn't exist unless she was directly in Imelda's line of sight—which wasn't very often. Sergio, on the other hand, was always aware of her. And more and more, he took advantage of Imelda's total and utter infatuation to take advantage of Emilia. He grew bolder—and more menacing—as the weeks went on. That was the point where Emilia knew her mother would not be there to protect her. It was going to be up to her to find a way out of there. And fast. Unfortunately she didn't find it fast enough.

It would take more than a year of careful planning. But with the help of her beloved piano teacher Emilia secured a full scholarship to the Manhattan Conservatory. She didn't even leave a note the day that she left—just packed everything she cared about into the suitcase she bought at the Salvation Army for a dollar and walked the two miles to the bus stop bound for the airport in San Juan.

She was three months shy of her seventeenth birthday.

By then her mother had become a total stranger . . . and a complete fraud.

For so many years, Emilia had to keep the truth from her daughters—her beautiful, brilliant girls. She should have known there would come a day when they'd stumble upon the grave of her first life. And now here they were, staring down at the tombstone, trying to figure out who the hell Emilia Oliveras was. Paul's wife? Richard's ex-wife? Criminal? Fugitive? Mother?

It had been Hilda's suggestion that she take them down to Caña Gorda beach for a long walk and a little privacy while Miguel and David Raña worked their police connections to track down the Winsteads. And while the introductions between the Alvarezes and her daughters had kept the mood relatively pleasant back at the house—now that the three of them were alone, the tension was almost unbearable. She had screwed this up so badly and didn't have the slightest idea how to walk it back.

Right now, the soft lapping of the waves against the beach was the only sound between them as they padded down the crescent-shaped expanse of sand in their bare feet. Periodically the warm breeze would catch in the leaves of a palm tree, creating a rustle. The sound took her back to the days when she'd spread a blanket in the shadow of these trees and spend the afternoon reading or napping or listening to her classical music cassette tapes. Anything to help her pass the time anywhere other than under her own roof.

Meg was the one to finally break the ice that had formed between them.

"So how did you meet him? Paul, I mean?"

Emilia was grateful for an easy question to start.

"We met at the Manhattan Conservatory when we were both students. We fell in love and were together for three years when we eloped."

"And his parents thought you were a gold digger?" she followed up.

Emilia nodded. "They did."

"And were you?" Gracie asked.

She didn't bat an eye at her daughter's attempt to rile her. The girl had every right to be furious. She might decide not to forgive her, the same way that Emilia had decided not to forgive her own mother.

"No. I didn't want his money, and I didn't want anything to do with his family's company. I just wanted to be with Paul. And then he just . . . disappeared. And suddenly I found myself pregnant, sick, and alone with the weight of his family bearing down on me. So Miguel and Hilda helped me to start over. And that's when *our* life together began," she said, using her hands to gesture between the three of them.

"Why didn't you stay and fight?" Gracie wanted to know. "Running away just made you look guiltier."

She sighed heavily, trying to figure out the best way to convey just how different things had been at the time this all took place.

"Today your generation can just call out injustices where you find them—sexual harassment, racism, pay parity. All you need to do is throw it out on social media with a catchy hashtag and suddenly you've got a crowd of supporters all over the world. But at the time this happened, thirty years ago, bad people got away with a lot more because they could bury the evidence, frame you, or simply lock you up and throw away the key. I knew there was simply no way I could have gone up against them and gotten a fair shake, and losing you, Gracie, was not a risk I was willing to take. Under any circumstances." She paused a moment to let the intent behind those words sink in before resuming her explanation. "I don't regret that decision, but I *do* regret keeping it from you for so long. You had a right to know who your father was. And I'd planned to have this conversation with you before your eighteenth birthday, but then . . . you know . . . the accident. And I just couldn't put you through it. Not when you were grieving the loss of your dream like that."

Emilia didn't miss the way her youngest daughter veered off to the side slightly to where the surf just reached, its frothy, bubbling head tickling her toes before retreating. Something had shifted between her two girls since she left them in Oregon the day before. Something serious. But they were grown women now and they would have to figure it out because she had too many of her own demons to wrestle with at the moment.

"So you didn't give up on your big dream because you got pregnant," Gracie deduced. "You didn't do it to raise me. You did it because you were afraid someone would figure out who you were—*where* you were."

Emilia stopped and looked at her.

"Gracie, can't you see how they're the same thing? I was pregnant with a baby I wanted desperately. A baby I loved more than anything or anyone from the moment I knew she existed. It was the easiest decision I've ever made in my life, and I'd do it again and again and again, just so I could be your mom."

"But what about *your* mother?" Meg demanded, her tone filled with anger all of a sudden. "We had a grandmother all this time!"

"No," Emilia said firmly, shaking her head. "No, you did not. For all intents and purposes my mother *was* dead. There was no way I was going to allow her anywhere near the two of you under any circumstances. I'll apologize for keeping my life with Paul a secret from you, but I will *not* apologize for keeping Imelda out of our lives."

"Why? Because she's a murderer?" Gracie challenged. "You know, you could have come forward and testified at her trial. She killed the scumbag husband of hers when she found out what he'd been up to with those young girls. With you. Some people would call her a hero! You speaking up might have made a difference of decades in her sentence!"

Emilia stopped short there in the sand, and it took her daughters several feet to realize she was no longer with them.

When they turned back around they found her staring at them, fists clenched by her sides.

"You have no idea," she began in a chilling tone, "what it is to be utterly and totally abandoned by someone whose job it was to protect you. Not only did she not protect me from the predator, she invited him into our home! She *married* the predator! Every single day I prayed she'd help me, but every single day she chose him over me. This was week after week, month after month, until I knew I was going to either have to leave or kill myself, because I couldn't live like that another day. I look at the two of you and I know without a single doubt that I would lay down my own life before I'd let anyone hurt you. Any. One. So, yeah, she killed him. But not before he made my life a living hell. I wouldn't have testified against her but I sure as hell wasn't about to testify for her."

Meg closed the distance between them and took one of her hands.

"Mom, please don't cry. It's okay. We understand. I'm so sorry, you don't owe us or anyone else an explanation. We were just . . . stunned is all."

Emilia used the back of her free hand to wipe the tears from her cheeks. When had she started crying? She'd known this would be a difficult conversation to have, but she hadn't anticipated all the emotions that would come with it. Giving voice to Imelda's betrayal was like experiencing it all over again, just another cloud of debris rousted from the bottom of the swamp.

As the wind picked up, the waves began to pound the sand with more force, spraying them with salty mist from several feet away. That was when Gracie came to wrap her arms around Emilia—and Emilia finally let it all go.

"I'm so sorry, Mom," she said, rubbing her back through the sobs. "Meg's right, we were just so shocked. And, honestly, hurt. But here you've been carrying all this by yourself all these years. But don't you see? You didn't have to do that! Look how strong we are! You made us that way! And you could have trusted us with this. *All* of this. We could have helped you carry it the same way you've helped us carry all our fucked-up shit."

Smiling through her tears and nodding, Emilia lifted an arm so Meg could slip under it and join them.

"It's okay, Mom. We're here. Gracie and I are here now," her youngest daughter murmured into the wind. "We've got you now."

The three of them stood there, clinging to one another, as the tide started to come in and the sun started to go down.

CHAPTER 29

GRACIE

Today

"Okay, *mijas*, the remote for the air conditioner is there on the table on your side, Meg. You know where the bathroom is, and help yourself to anything in the kitchen if you wake up and need something to drink or a snack," Hilda tells us as she's bustling around the guest room, closing the shades.

It reminds me of when I got home—God, was that just a few nights ago?—and Mom did the same thing. In the span of about five days, I've won my big case, broken up with my fiancé, found out I have a father who's been MIA for three decades *and* a grandmother who was convicted of murder. Oh, and apparently, my mother has been living under an assumed identity my entire life so as to avoid having me be kidnapped by some pretty freaking despicable people. It's been a week, that's for sure.

"Thank you for everything, Hilda," I say as she bends down to pull the sheet up over my shoulders, tucking me in like I'm nine instead of twenty-nine. "I'm sorry we just showed up on your doorstep like that."

The woman sinks down so she's perching on the side of the double bed that Meg and I are sharing.

"I know how confusing all of this must be for you both," she says, looking between my sister and me. "And no one would blame you for being frustrated or angry with your mother. But I was there when Paul went missing—and when his family came after her. She was such a sweet, soft-spoken young woman. Oh, but she was very, very sick when she was with us—that was in our other house near San Juan. She didn't even know she was pregnant!"

"Really?" The single-word question comes out of me spontaneously.

Hilda nods adamantly, making the honey-blond bun atop her head bob up and down.

"She was totally surprised! And sadly, Paul never knew about you, Gracie. But perhaps . . ." The thought fades on her lips.

"Did you know our grandmother?" my sister asks. "Imelda?"

"No, sweetheart. She was in prison before I met your mother. I knew about the case because it was big news at the time. Miguel was still a patrolman back then, so he wasn't part of the investigation."

"So she really murdered her husband? Sergio?" Meg confirms.

Hilda sighs deeply. It's the kind of sad, wistful sigh I sometimes hear from my mother, as well.

"She told you what happened, yes? Your mother?"

I nod. "Yes. He was sexually abusing her, and Imelda didn't believe it."

"Ah, well, as I said, I don't know Imelda, but I believe she was blinded by her love for this man. He was very charming—he knew how to seduce a woman. *¿Entienden?* You understand what I'm saying?" she asks, looking from me to Meg and back again.

"Are you saying it was about sex?" I ask.

"Mmm, yes, but also about feeling pretty and loved. Imelda was a single mother. It had been a long time since she had a partner, and he was much younger. A con man too. He knew what he was doing. And when she realized what she had done—what she had allowed *him* to do—she was crazy with rage."

"I want to go see her."

As soon as Meg says the words, I know I feel exactly the same way.

"Yes, me too. Do you think we can do that? Visit her?"

Hilda considers this. "I don't see why not. She's not in the penitentiary anymore; they moved her to a hospice that is maybe forty-five minutes from here. I will call in the morning and find out about the visiting hours. And"—she begins, pausing for just a moment—"I can also talk to your mother if you like."

I feel a sudden swell of gratitude for this kind woman who once helped a stranger—a young girl in trouble. And, in doing so, helped me.

"Would you? I can do it, of course, but you have such a calm way about you, Hilda. I think if you suggest it, she's less likely to be upset."

She takes my hand and gives it a squeeze. "Yes, of course! Now, you girls get some sleep, and we will make a plan in the morning, okay?"

We both murmur our agreement, and she presses a kiss to first my forehead, then Meg's, as if we're little girls. Not that I'm complaining.

Once she's gone, Meg turns out the light without a word and rolls over onto her side so that her back is to me. She's still angry from our confrontation in the car. And I can't really blame her—I treated her like an opposing witness. I knew *exactly* where her weak spot was . . . and I went for it. With everything I had.

"I'm sorry for what I said, Meg," I tell the darkness.

"No, you're not," she replies flatly, not bothering to turn over.

"Yes, I am," I insist.

Now she looks at me over her shoulder.

"No, you're not. At least not for what you said. *Maybe* you're sorry that I'm upset . . . but that doesn't change the way you actually feel."

"You've been watching too much Dr. Phil," I mutter.

"I'm not doing this," she claps back. "It's been a long, emotional couple of days, and I'm exhausted. Once we get this genealogical shitshow sorted, we can go back to living our lives. Our very different, very separate lives."

"C'mon, don't be like that," I coax.

When she doesn't respond, I turn over, as well, so that we're back to back. I'm just starting to doze when my mother's words come back to me:

"If you really, truly didn't know what an exceptional pianist Meg is, then it's because you didn't want *to know."*

She was right. I didn't want to know. Because I was jealous of what Meg had. What Meg has.

Without warning, I elbow my sister in the back.

"Ouch! What are you doing?" she demands, angrily flipping over.

"Getting your attention," I tell her, turning onto my back.

"Okay, so what do you want?"

"I want to tell you something."

"What? Can't it wait till morning?"

"No. It's waited too long."

"Fine, I'm listening. Now what. Is. It?"

I blurt out the words before I can change my mind. "It's not your fault I didn't become a concert pianist."

My vision has adjusted to the darkness well enough now that I can see her rolling her eyes.

"Gracie, don't. You pretending it didn't matter is not helpful, alright? Not a day goes by that I don't think about what I took from you."

"But that's just it," I begin evenly, eyes now trained on the ceiling directly above me so I don't have to see her expression as I explain this. "You don't need to feel guilty."

"How can I *not*? Every time you hear me play, it's just a reminder of what you could have had, what you could have been. No wonder you hate me!"

Now I flip to face her. "Is that what you think? That I hate you?"

"Yes, of course," she replies matter-of-factly, as if I've just asked her if the Pope is Catholic.

I sigh with my own frustration.

"Meg, the doctor told me I probably had a fifty-fifty chance of making a comeback—that if I'd commit to physical therapy and rehab I could, possibly, play competitively again."

There's a pause as she tries to work out what this all means.

"But if that was an option, why didn't you take it?"

"Okay, so when Trey and I were fighting on the phone the other day, he said I have a pathological need to be the best. At first I thought he was just being an asshole, as usual. But now . . . now I realize there's something to that."

She's quiet again for a long beat, and I'm surprised when she breaks the silence with first a scoff, then a snort.

"Ya *think*? Jeez, Gracie, only took you about thirty years to figure that one out!"

"I'm being serious here!"

"Yes, I know you are. But I'm *still* not getting what it is you're trying to tell me."

"Ugh! Okay, so all this time I let you think it was because of what happened that I didn't play again. When really, it had nothing to do with you."

"Are you insane? I broke your hand in four places! You needed like three surgeries!"

"I did. But don't you understand? I could have maybe worked my way back. But I wasn't willing to take the chance that I wouldn't be as good as I had been—that I wouldn't be good enough to go the distance. If I had loved playing the way you do, nothing would have stopped me, Meg."

"Right," she murmurs, more to herself than to me.

"I'm so, so sorry I let you feel so awful for all this time . . ."

"Gracie," she interrupts me, "you're the lawyer. You know how this stuff works—the cause and consequences. Were it not for the fact that I slammed your hand in the car door, you wouldn't have had to make that decision. You had every right to weigh out your options. No one would have thought any less of you for deciding not to start over again—for whatever reason."

I'm struck by something.

"Did you hear what you just said?"

"Um, yeah . . ."

"The same goes for you. No one will think any less of you if you decide not to keep going, Meg. I hope you will, because *my God* you're amazing! But that's your call. Not mine, not Mom's. And I'll back you whatever you choose."

One of the slats in the blinds is a little askew, and it allows a thin little slice of moonlight to enter the room, paving a path across my sister's pillow. But now as she shifts slightly, it changes its course, falling over her eyes and illuminating her long, dark lashes and the tears that are glittering behind them.

"Thank you for that," she whispers.

"No," I reply in the same soft, reverent tone, "thank you, Meg."

The image I've created of Imelda in my mind over the last thirty-six hours is very different from the reality of Imelda now that I'm standing less than five feet away. Lying in a hospital bed, she resembles a newly hatched baby bird—weak and frail, unable to lift even the weight of its own featherless wings. A window on the opposite side of the room is open, allowing a warm breeze to spill in the room in accompaniment to the sunshine. Still, pleasant as it is, I'm struck by the absence of any personal items—no flowers, no cards. No crocheted blanket folded over the footboard or family picture on the nightstand. There's nothing that offers even the slightest glimpse into Imelda's life. But then again, maybe she'd prefer not to have any glimpses into her life.

I feel an unexpected swell of sadness for this woman I didn't even know existed just a short time ago. More than likely, she'll die here in this strange place amongst strange people. I almost have to wonder if she wouldn't have preferred to die in prison—her home for the last thirty years.

Meg and I are so transfixed, we don't even notice the nurse who's joined us.

"Are you her granddaughters?" she asks us quietly.

"Yes. I'm Gracie and this is my sister, Meg."

She nods at each of us. "I'm one of the nurses taking care of her; my name is Andrea. It's good to meet you at last."

"At last?" Meg echoes.

"Oh, yes, your grandmother has been talking about your visit for days now!"

My sister and I exchange confused glances.

"Um . . . I don't see how. She didn't know we were coming. *We* didn't even know we were coming until last night," I explain. "In fact, we didn't even know she existed!"

I was surprised when Mom didn't fight us on our request to come here and meet Imelda for ourselves—though she was adamant she didn't want to come. And I was okay with that. Except now that we're here, it's more than a little awkward.

"Ah, well, that's our Imelda! She's very special, you know? She's what they call an *espiritista* . . . sort of like a medium. She talks to the spirits, and they show her things. They must have showed her your visit!"

"I guess," I murmur, still not sure what to make of all the woo-woo talk surrounding this woman.

"Can we speak to her?" Meg asks. "I mean, can she hear us?"

"Oh, yes! Of course!" Andrea says. "Just a moment . . ."

She walks to the side of the bed and squats down so she's close to the woman's face and murmurs something in Spanish, giving her shoulder a slight shake. The old woman stirs, her heavily lidded eyes opening just a slit.

The nurse leans in closer, speaking so quietly I can't make out what she's saying and pointing at us every once in a while. I put my best nonthreatening smile on—the one I save for children and the elderly who sit in the witness chair in court. I see the moment she gets who we are. Her eyes open wider and she murmurs something to Andrea, who immediately raises up the head of the bed, nodding as she listens to what her patient is saying.

"She says you look like your mother. Both of you . . ." the nurse tells us.

My sister and I look at each other, not quite sure what to do next.

"*Ven, ven,*" the old woman says, beckoning us closer with a hand that's been gnarled by time and, I assume, arthritis.

"She's telling us to come," I tell Meg.

"Oh! You speak Spanish!" Andrea comments, surprised.

"Gracie does," Meg says, as we start to move cautiously toward the bed.

"Ah, well, then I will leave you to chat," the nurse tells us, making her way toward the door. "Just let me know if you need me."

"Thank you, Andrea," I say over my shoulder as I move around to stand opposite of Meg.

She looks a little scared so I catch her eye and give her a tiny smile and a nod, even though I'm feeling much the same.

Imelda pats either side of the bed, encouraging us to sit. We do so, each of us perching on the mattress gingerly as if we might break her. And she looks so fragile that I'm thinking it's a distinct possibility.

Now that I'm closer, I can see some of the fine features she and my mother share.

This first thing she does is take Meg's hand.

"*Ven aquí, mija,*" Imelda says, pulling her closer.

When their faces are only a foot apart, the old woman raises a hand, then stops just short, raising her brows as if to ask permission. Meg gives it with a single nod. I watch, entranced as our grandmother strokes my sister's cheek gently, paper-thin, wrinkled hands against a plump, dewy complexion.

"*Mi linda nieta,*" Imelda murmurs so softly, I have to strain to hear her.

"She's calling you her beautiful granddaughter," I translate.

My sister puts her own hand over the hand that's already on her face. We're both surprised when she begins to speak in English. We hang on every slow, deliberate word.

"So much time we lose," Imelda murmurs. "But I see you!" she says, pointing to her temple. "I see you in my mind and I *hear* you play piano. Like your mother. Oh, my Emilia! My girl, my girl . . ." She pauses here as tears start to slip down her cheeks. Meg reaches over to the box of tissues on the table, plucks one out, and gently wipes them away. "When she little," our grandmother continues, "we used to go to *la playa*—em . . . the beach? Yes, the beach. And we watch the sunset there. Sometimes I read her some of the poems I like." When she turns in my direction I hold my breath, afraid she might ask why my mother isn't there with us. But, thankfully, she doesn't.

"And you, my love, my other granddaughter," she says with a big, gummy smile. "You know you have my gift, yes?"

"What gift is that?" I ask, confused.

"*¡Los espiritos, mija!* The spirits come to you and tell you things."

Me? With the woo-woo? I think not.

I shake my head. "No, Imelda, I don't think so—"

She's nodding. "Oh, yes! Maybe you not know is them, but they are there. And they help you."

"She's a lawyer," Meg volunteers from the foot of the bed. The old woman looks to me. "*¿Qué quiere decir esto?*"

She has no idea what my sister is talking about, so I repeat it for her in Spanish.

"*Ella te estaba diciendo que soy abogada.*"

"*¡Una abogada! ¡Qué maravilloso!*" she exclaims, clapping her hands in delight.

"I guess she likes that you're a lawyer?" Meg guesses.

"So it would seem," I confirm.

Without warning, the frail wisp of a woman takes my wrists and pulls me to her until she can wrap her arms around me. Then she whispers in my ear.

"Do no be angry with your mama. All she do was so she can protect you—to keep you safe."

I pull back slightly so I can see her face. This time, I'm the one who's tearing up. I sniff and nod. "Yes. I understand."

She closes her eyes, and a pained expression crosses her face.

"You need to rest," I tell her quietly. "We'll come back soon, I promise."

Imelda offers a weak smile as she whispers.

"*Mi nietas.* My granddaughters."

Her eyes are full of tears, her voice is full of love.

CHAPTER 30

MIGUEL

Today

Miguel and Emilia rocked companionably on the front porch exactly where he and Raña had been the day before. As Gracie and Meg were inside helping Hilda prepare dinner; snippets of their conversation and laughter floated out through the open jalousie windows.

"I'm glad their visit went well," he said, with a nod in the direction of the kitchen.

He was rotating his wrist in small, tight circles, creating a mini vortex in his gin and tonic.

"Me, too," she agreed, sipping her own drink thoughtfully. It was her second, and he suspected she might be needing a third before the evening was done. "They want me to see her, but I can't, Miguel. I just . . . I can't."

"That's okay, you don't have to. In fact, you don't have to do anything you don't want to do."

Emilia looked at him, her eyes narrowing slightly. "Why, what have you found?"

Either she had gotten more observant over the years, or he had become more obvious. It was probably a combination of both.

"David Raña called. It took a little doing, but he was able to untangle a half dozen levels of red tape. Someone *really* didn't want the Winstead name associated with any property or business dealings here in Puerto Rico. But that man is like a dog with a bone when it comes to this kind of stuff. He was able to trace some property through a shell company and back to WinCo Oil. There are two of them—one is a larger home overlooking the beach in Rincón. The other is much smaller but also much more remote, and if Google Earth is to be believed, it has a substantial wall surrounding it."

"And you think Paul is there," she said, leaning forward in the rocker. "Oh, my God. So it's true! He's in Rincón!"

"There are still a lot of 'ifs' here, Emilia," Miguel said cautiously, feeling the need to slip in a disclaimer—just in case. "We can't forget that everything hinges on this one photo. But it does certainly seem to look like it."

"The property—does Detective Raña think it belongs to Brock and Evelyn?"

Miguel shook his head. Obviously she hadn't been keeping close tabs on her in-laws, which maybe wasn't such a bad thing.

"No, it seems Evelyn Winstead died about ten years ago—cancer. Then Brock had a stroke a few years back that he never quite came back from. He passed away the beginning of last year."

Taken aback, Emilia sat back hard, an involuntary whoosh of air passing her lips in the process.

"That's . . . wow," she began, her eyes moving out toward the yard as if she were expecting to find the couple there, a pair of ghosts standing next to the banana tree. "I suppose I shouldn't be so shocked considering how many years have gone by. It's just that they stayed the same in my mind, you know? They never got any older. But now that I think about it, when Paul went missing, they were probably a good six or seven years younger than I am *now*. So I guess that just leaves his brother, Blaine."

Miguel flashed on an image of the young man, tall and muscular, wearing his cowboy boots in Paul and Emilia's stateroom that fateful morning on the ship. In the ensuing years, he'd encountered very few people he disliked as much as that arrogant *pendejo.*

"How well did you know him when you and Paul were together?"

She shook her head. "Not very. We met a few times when Paul would bring me home—mostly for family holidays. It was mainly the parents I interacted with. Still, I'll never forget how he talked about me in the papers after Paul went missing. And on television. The bastard stopped just short of calling me a whore."

Miguel saw a shiver run down her body.

"Well, I don't think he'll try that again."

Her head jerked in his direction a single brow raised.

"Damn straight he won't. I'm not that sick, weak, terrified little girl anymore. I'd like to see that son-of-a-bitch come after me or one of my girls. He won't know what hit him!"

"Right," Miguel replied with a smile. "That's why we're going to let David speak with him tomorrow—"

"What? No. No, no. Miguel, assuming Paul is there, if you give Blaine *any* kind of warning, he might move him somewhere! We might never get this close again!"

He held up a reassuring hand. "Not to worry. You and I will already be on our way to the property where we think Paul lives. Once we're close, David will call and tell him to meet us there."

"Oh, my God. I might see him tomorrow . . ." she murmured, seemingly stunned as the possibility of it finally began to sink in. Then just as quickly, a look of alarm crossed her features. "What do I say to him?" she asked in a panicked whisper.

He shook his head. "My friend, you are asking the wrong

person. I think maybe you want the other Alvarez," he told her, tipping his head back in the direction of the kitchen and his wife.

Emilia shook her head as she reached out to put a hand on his arm.

"No, I think I'm asking exactly the *right* person."

Miguel looked down at the drink in his hand for a few seconds before giving her the answer she was waiting for.

"Tell him the truth."

"But which one?" she asked. "There are so many of them now."

"That you never stopped loving him."

CHAPTER 31

BLAINE

Today

Blaine was in the hammock when the first call came in.

"Don't get that," Claudia murmured groggily from next to him, still wrapped up in their decadent afternoon nap.

He reached down and plucked his cell from the grass, where it had landed earlier when they flipped the stupid thing trying to get in. He peered at the number.

"Sorry, baby, it might be important," he said, pushing the screen to accept the call. His voice was cool and cautious when he answered. "Hello?"

There was a pause on the other end, and he was about to hang up when a deep male voice filled his ear.

"Is this Mr. Winstead?"

Shit. He'd picked up on a telemarketer. What had he been thinking? He should have listened to Claudia.

"I'm sorry, but I'm not interested in any—"

"Please don't hang up, Mr. Winstead. My name is Detective David Raña, and I'm with the San Juan Police Department."

For a split second, Blaine froze in place, unable to move, unable to respond.

"Mr. Winstead?" the voice persisted. "Are you Brock Winstead Jr.?"

That snapped him out of it.

He got up so fast that the hammock flipped again, sending his wife to the grass with a hard thud and a string of expletives in Spanish. He waved his apologies as he began to pace the yard, phone glued to his ear.

"It's Blaine. Blaine Winstead. I don't use the name Brock or the junior anymore," he informed the man coolly.

"Right, sorry about that . . ."

"What is it that you need, detective?"

The man cleared his throat before speaking again.

"Mr. Winstead, I have reason to believe that your brother, Paul, who's been listed as missing for the last thirty years, is actually alive and well and living in Rincón."

This wasn't the first time he'd been contacted by the police investigating a report of a Paul-spotting, though it had been several years. He took the same approach he always did: incredulity.

"Excuse me? Is this some sort of a prank, because I don't think it's very funny."

"I think you know exactly what I'm talking about, Mr. Winstead, so please stop pretending to be clueless. I've pulled all your information—"

"How did you get this number?" Blaine demanded, doing his best imitation of Brock. "This is my private cell, and no one has this number but . . ."

"Mr. Winstead, I not only have your private phone number, I have your address. And, I believe, your brother's address."

He felt his blood run cold.

Blaine looked over his shoulder at Claudia, who was watching him with growing alarm—an exact mirror of his own emotions at that moment. There was a long beat of silence on the phone before he finally responded quietly.

"What is it that you want, detective?"

* * *

There had been weeks of preparing the house in St. Croix for his brother's arrival—putting everything that would be needed for his immediate care, hiring the nurses, physical therapists, and aides who would manage his day-to-day care while he continued to manage his father's expectations. But once Paul was there, under the same roof, Blaine knew he'd done the right thing by insisting on this arrangement. Being able to keep an eye on his brother's progress and monitor everyone who came into contact with him was a huge weight off his mind.

Six months later, a letter had arrived from the women's penitentiary in Puerto Rico, asking him to return. At first he had no intention of going, but there'd been something about the idea of seeing the interpreter—Claudia—again that he had found appealing. So he'd gone, finding Claudia and Imelda waiting for him in the same small interview room. The older woman smiled broadly.

"*Lo encontraste,*" Imelda said.

"You found him," Claudia translated.

"What makes you think that?" he replied, not willing to give anything away.

"*Los espíritus me lo dijeron.*"

Blaine had held up his hand before Claudia could speak.

"Let me guess, the spirits, right?"

"Yes! Imelda told me that you had found him where they said you would but that he was hurt very badly."

"I can't talk about this," he had told her flatly. "Any of it. I have no idea if she's going to call a TV station or write to a newspaper or something."

"And me?" Claudia asked.

"You what?"

"How do you know *I* won't do these things?"

"I—I guess I don't."

And he hadn't known—not for sure, anyway. But there was some irrational part of him that had trusted her from the very beginning.

"Well, we do not want to do this," she assured him. "Not me *or* Imelda."

"Then why am I here?"

Imelda had locked eyes with him then in a way that made him shift in his seat, uncomfortable.

"Now *you* do for me something," she'd said in her slow patchwork English.

That was how he'd come to see the two women several times a year.

Finding Emilia had been difficult, but not impossible, and once he'd located her, it was just a matter of hiring a P.I. to keep an eye on her. The arrangement worked well for both of them. Blaine could rest assured that Emilia had moved on, staying far away from anything having to do with his brother, while Imelda could have vicarious snapshots of a life she would never be a part of, lived by a daughter she would never know. And, of course, there was Claudia.

"Honey, slow down, please!" his wife pled from next to him now.

"I can't," he said, shaking his head resolutely.

"Blaine, no one is going to see him before you get there. No one is even going to let her through the gates without your say-so," his wife reminded him.

"What if she shows up with that detective? Or with the entire Rincón PD?"

She waved a dismissive hand. "Pfft. Unless they have a warrant, they can't come onto the property. It's that simple."

He glanced at her, then back at the road.

"Claudia, I'm not going to throw up another roadblock between them. Not now. Not after everything I did."

"How many times are we going to have this conversation? You are *not* responsible for your brother's—"

"Yes, I am!" he cut in loudly, then shook his head again. "Forget it," he muttered sullenly. "You couldn't possibly understand."

Claudia put a hand on his shoulder, and he felt the connection between them. It was that same undeniable magnetism that had kept him going back to that prison again, and again, year after year until she was finally released. And she was finally his.

Now he could scarcely remember a time before her.

"No? Okay, then just . . . just explain it to me," she suggested gently, making small circles on his arm with her thumb.

For a long time, Blaine had been able to tell himself any number of things to keep from accepting the responsibility— and feeling the guilt. He blamed his father for being a ruthless son of a bitch who valued his business over his children. He blamed his mother for falling prey to alcohol and pills and depression rather than standing up to Brock and fighting for her own children. He blamed Paul for being weak and naïve and a colossal pain in the ass who needed constant minding. He blamed Emilia for being a greedy interloper hoping to cash in on a rich husband. The only one Blaine hadn't blamed at the time was himself. But gradually that had changed. With every agonizing hurdle that Paul had had to endure, he'd seen the consequences of his own hubris.

"Paul wasn't like the rest of us," he started slowly, softly. "He was . . . special. He was wired differently, and he couldn't have cared less about the company or the money. He was just this happy guy, you know? He wanted to play his cello. He wanted to be with Emilia. But that wasn't good enough—and she wasn't good enough. Not for the high and mighty Winsteads!"

The last sentence came out as an overly dramatic declaration.

"Blaine—"

"No! Paul is the way he is because of me . . . and my parents. I mean, look at me! Look how happy you and I have been since we met. And by the same standards my parents applied to Emilia—that *I* applied to Emilia—you wouldn't have been good enough either. In fact, your . . . you know, your past would have made Emilia look like a Kennedy by comparison!"

"Gee, thanks," she muttered, irritated.

"Claudia, you know what I mean. I didn't get it at the time. How could I have? I'd never loved anybody. All I could see was what Brock put in front of me. The company, the job, the money. Especially the money. I actually convinced myself to keep my brother from the woman he loved because I was afraid she'd come after our money. Can you believe that? God, I was such an asshole!" he said, smacking the steering wheel in frustration. "I should have been looking for Paul . . . and all I did was look out for myself."

"And you've more than made up for that," she reminded him. "You've taken such good care of Paul for all this time! And your parents came around to me, didn't they? Okay, maybe not your father so much, but your mother . . ."

He couldn't hear any of this right now.

"All he ever wanted was her, Claudia. And music. I took both of those things from him. I ruined his life. And hers."

"Honey," Claudia said gently. "If you really felt that way then why didn't you just pick up the phone and call the woman? It's not like you didn't know how to reach her."

He shot his wife a sideways glance.

"And say what? 'I know you had my brother's baby, and, oh yeah, by the way, he's alive!' Then what? What if she didn't want him because he wasn't the way he'd been before? Besides, then she got married to that other guy and had another kid. There was never a good time to tell her."

"And then they got a divorce," Claudia reminded him.

"Look, please just trust me on this, I've got one chance to make this right, and that means I need to be the one to tell her about him before she sees him. I need for her to know how sorry I am."

"Okay, Blaine. Okay," she murmured, reaching out to touch his shoulder.

They rode the last several minutes in silence. Using the remote clipped to his sun visor, they drove through the gate, and he pulled around to the side entrance of the house.

"No police," she said. "No cars at all."

He shifted to face her.

"I appreciate it. I appreciate you—and how you're always trying to convince me that I'm not a total and complete douche. But I know the truth and . . ."

"And what?" she asked when he didn't finish the thought. "What, Blaine?"

"And . . . I'm sorry, sweetheart, but Emilia Oliveras is the only person on this planet who can offer me the redemption I need."

Claudia offered him a sympathetic smile.

"Oh, honey, you don't need redemption, because you've *already* redeemed yourself a hundred times over." She paused and sighed deeply. "But you do whatever it takes so you can *finally* sleep through the night."

He didn't even dare to dream about that possibility.

CHAPTER 32

GRACIE

Today

"Are you sure this is it?" my mother asks as Miguel signals our turn onto a narrow, unmarked road. "Shouldn't there be a street sign somewhere or something? This doesn't look like it leads anywhere."

Her anxiety has been building since leaving the Alvarez's house nearly an hour ago, and now that we're in the final mile, I'm wondering if she's just going to implode right there in the front seat.

"I think that's the idea," he explains gently. "No signs anywhere, an unwelcoming, unmarked dirt road, high up a hill in the middle of nowhere—whatever it takes to keep people from wandering up here uninvited, right?" Miguel says, jerking the steering wheel from side to side in an attempt to navigate the craggy, pocked stretch of road.

"It's going to be okay, Mom," my sister says, anchoring herself against the rear passenger armrest as we bounce around in the back seat.

Mom looks back at us, smiling weakly. "Thanks, sweetie." Her eyes catch mine. "How about you, honey? You okay?"

I shrug. "You mean considering I'm about to meet the father I didn't know existed until about five minutes ago? Yeah, bring it on!" I declare with faux enthusiasm.

The truth is that I'm as freaked out as I've ever been—and I don't get freaked out very easily. Not that I'm about to admit that to my mother, who's barely holding her shit together as it is. Somehow Meg seems to sense it, though. With eyes glued outside of her window, she nudges my foot with hers—a quiet, lowkey gesture of support.

Without warning, the rocky road gives way to a steep incline of smooth pavement, the car interior growing markedly quieter. No one says anything as we continue to climb another five hundred feet until, finally, the drive levels out and we see a massive concrete wall ahead of us, broken up only by a large panel on wheels, which must be a sliding gate.

Miguel stops several feet short of the small entry kiosk set in concrete outside the wall. He shifts in his seat so that he can see all of us.

"Okay, this is it. Are you *sure* you don't want me to go in ahead and check it out?"

My mother shakes her head.

"No," I agree.

Miguel looks at Meg.

"I'm just here for moral support. This is totally their show," she tells him with a nod toward Mom and me. "I'm down for whatever."

It's true. My sister—in this case, I should really say my *half*-sister—doesn't have a dog in this race. She's always had a father who loves her. Come to think of it, so have I. But this is something entirely different, and we all know it.

"Right, then," Miguel says with a nod. "Let's do this."

We pull up the rest of the way until his side is even with the intercom and the lens of the camera embedded in the panel is trained squarely on him. He rolls down the window and leans out, using his hand as a visor against the sun beating directly down on us. He looks like one of those old people trying to navigate the drive-up ATM or, worse, the Starbucks drive-thru. I have to stifle my urge to giggle. A few seconds later, there is a tinny voice coming out at them.

"Yes?"

"Uh, yes, hello. My name is Miguel Alvarez. I'm a retired detective with the San Juan Police Department—"

"Yes, detective. We've been expecting you. Please come in and park in front of the house. Someone will come out and meet you."

Miguel and my mother exchange looks—his curious, hers concerned. I know she's afraid that, after all this, he won't be there. That it will be the wrong person, or he will have picked up and left before we managed to get here.

The gate starts to slide open, revealing a modest house painted in a fresh teal color accented by terra-cotta room tiles. The lawn surrounding it is all lush green Bermuda grass and palm trees. I can just make out some bright pops of color several hundred feet back that must be a garden.

"This is beautiful," Meg comments, looking around as we all get out of the car.

"It is," Miguel agrees. "And you'd never know it was up here."

When I glance at Mom, she's just standing there, wringing her hands in front of her. I go to stand next to her.

"We've got this. Whatever it is," I say.

She just nods, still fretting silently.

Before we can make our way to the path leading to the front of the house, the large, arched wood door swings open, and a man comes out to greet us. I recognize him immediately as an older version of the guy I saw in the newspaper articles. The asshole who trashed my mother to anyone who'd listen. And he has absolutely no idea what's about to hit him.

"Who *is* that?" Meg whispers.

I hadn't even realized she'd come to stand next to me.

"That's the brother, Blaine Winstead."

Miguel starts toward the man but suddenly Mom is moving in that direction, too. Quickly.

"Oh, shiiiiit," I hiss, starting toward them. "Here we go."

She overtakes Miguel before he even realizes she's following him. For his part, Blaine simply stops where he is, transfixed as my mother strides right up to him.

I try to reach her even as she's pulling her arm back, but I'm too late and she slaps him with a loud, sharp crack.

Miguel and I reach them at the same time, both of us crying out.

"Mom!"

"Emilia!"

He puts himself squarely between the two of them, while I attach myself to my mother's side. I don't know this man, I don't know what he's capable of. He'll have to go through me to get to her.

But he doesn't budge. His only movement is to press a palm to his face where she's just struck him.

"Hello, Emilia," the man says quietly. "I'm glad you're here. I've been waiting a long time to tell you just how sorry I am—"

But my mother isn't having any of it.

"Apologize for which part?" she spits, without waiting for an answer. "Trying to destroy me? Keeping the fact that Paul was alive a secret? Forcing me to live the last three decades waiting for the other shoe to drop—for your family to resurface and try to do it all over again? Is that what you want to apologize for, Brock?"

"Emilia, calm down," Miguel says firmly when she makes a move to get closer.

"Please, *please* don't call me that," the man implores her. "I haven't been that person—I haven't been Brock Jr. for a very long time now. I'm just . . . I'm Blaine . . ."

"How nice for you," Mom replies caustically. I'm surprised when she turns to me. "Gracie, this is your uncle, Blaine Winstead."

He looks at me now, as if noticing me for the first time. That's when I see the light of recognition in his expression, as if he's known me forever but just hasn't seen me in a while.

"Gracie . . ."

I'm not sure he even realizes he's murmured my name. And I don't care.

"Well, hey there, Uncle Blaine," I say, my own voice dripping with sarcasm. "So nice to meet you in person! I've been reading up on you, and I have to say, you seem to be right at home in front of the reporters and the cameras. The way you managed to call my mother a gold-digging whore without actually saying those words was just *brilliant*!"

He flinches. "I can't tell you how much I regret that."

When my mother lunges toward him again, Miguel has to actually wrap his arms around her, engulfing her small body in a bear hug to keep her from gouging his eyes out. And that's when things get exponentially worse.

The front door flies open, and a woman comes running out, arms waving, yelling the whole way.

"Are you out of your *mind*?" she demands, her face flush with anger. "That's assault! I don't care who you are or what's happened to you, I'm not going to stand here and let you assault my husband!"

"Oh, hell," I hear Miguel mutter.

Blaine Winstead manages to grab his wife by the forearm before she can rush Miguel from the back in an attempt to reach my mother. This has the potential to turn into a melee, and fast.

"Oh, a wife!" Mom sneers, struggling to extricate herself from around his grip. "How wonderful for you! I'm so glad at least one of the Winstead brothers got his 'happily ever after.'"

I have never seen her like this—she's like a wild animal.

Out of the corner of my eye, I catch sight of Meg, who's looking more alarmed by the second.

"Okay!" I'm shocked when she yells loud enough to get everyone's attention. "Just stop! Everyone *stop!*"

We do. All of us. Mom, panting and red-faced, stands upright again, and Miguel relaxes his hold on her, stepping to the side slightly. Blaine's wife takes a begrudging step back. Meg looks to me and nods. She wants me to take it from here.

"Okay, will you please just tell us what the hell's happening here?" I ask, eyes pinned to my newfound uncle.

He looks down at the ground, then up again to my mother.

"Look, Emilia, there's so much. I *swear to God* I'll give you all the details about what happened *later*. But for right now, there are some things you need to know. About my brother. Before you see him . . ."

It's as if my mother has turned to stone. For several long moments, she doesn't move, she doesn't blink, and she doesn't breathe. When she speaks again, there isn't a trace of the fury that had engulfed her not thirty seconds ago.

"So it's true?" she asks softly. "Paul *is* alive? And . . . he's here?"

Blaine nods.

"Yes. But before you see him, you just need to know that Paul isn't the same. He was . . . he was hurt and he had a brain injury . . ."

She lets out a terrifying combination of choke, gasp, and sob.

"Oh, my God! How—how bad?"

"He doesn't always recognize faces. He probably won't remember yours—just because it's been so long. It has something to do with the way he processes the information around him. His speaking can be very slow sometimes and a little halting—but he *does* understand and he *can* communicate." Blaine lets out a long breath, as if he's relieved to be doing this at last.

"You should know he has virtually no memory of the time around or before the accident. All we know for certain is that he fell from a ship—"

The wail my mother lets out is absolutely shattering, and it terrifies me.

"So he *did* fall overboard!"

"No! No, no—it wasn't the cruise ship, Emilia," Blaine says quickly, shaking his head and waving his hands. "He never got back on that boat in San Juan. It's a long story and, again, I swear I'll tell you. Just . . . please let me get through this so you can see him."

Mom nods, tears streaming down her face.

"So his physical injuries have mostly resolved over the years. It took a lot of time and therapy. He learned how to walk again. He had to rebuild the strength in all his muscles. Though there's some weakness in his right arm. Not that it stops him from playing . . ."

"He still plays?" she asks incredulously.

"Every day. Mostly the same piece though—a cello sonata. I've tried to bring in pianists to play with him, but he won't do it. He only plays alone."

No sooner has he uttered the words than a soft strain of Bach floats out of the house from someplace we can't see.

"This is our piece," she says to no one in particular. "That's why he won't play it with anyone else. Because he's waiting for me."

And then she turns . . . and she runs.

CHAPTER 33

EMILIA

Today

For a long time after moving to Oregon and "becoming" Emily, Emilia was plagued by dreams about Paul. Always she'd be standing in a long hallway lined with doors on either side—like a hotel. In the distance, she could just make out the music—a cello—and she knew it was Paul immediately. So she ran from door to door, throwing them open, growing more desperate with every empty room she encountered. As the music grew louder, she knew she was drawing closer to its source. Or so it seemed. Because every time she finally reached the last door, she'd reach for the doorknob only to have it open onto another hallway. And another. And another.

She had no idea how long those dreams lasted, but they certainly felt endless. And she always woke up the same way—breathing hard and sweating, as if she'd really been running. Her heart would be pounding so hard, she was certain she'd be able to see it pulsing against the wall of her chest if she just looked down. It took years to finally rid herself of the nightmares. Except now here she was, standing in one. Or, actually, running in one.

Through the huge, arched front doorway, across a marble foyer, and down a hallway that seemed to go on forever. She was vaguely aware of someone behind her calling out, asking her to stop and wait. It was Meg. Then a man's voice—Blaine? Tells the woman that it's okay, to just let Emilia go. As if they could stop her!

In this incarnation of the dream, she didn't pull doors open, because she didn't have to. They were all open already as she ran through each of the airy, sunlit rooms. A gentle breeze blew through windows with their slats cranked all the way open. She didn't know what she was expecting to find in this place, but this certainly wasn't it. Not something so bright and open.

Emilia followed the music all the way through the house along a corridor that finally bent into an elbow ending at one last dark-paneled door. There were small glass panels embedded in it, so you could see who was inside and what they were doing. But she didn't peek, because she didn't have to. She'd have known the sound of Paul's playing anywhere. It, too, had featured regularly in her dreams.

"Emilia! Emilia, hold on, let me go in with you . . ." She heard Blaine call out behind her now.

She didn't wait.

She *wouldn't* wait.

When Emilia threw open the door—the Bach came spilling, tumbling, falling out—cresting over her like a rogue wave in the ocean and nearly knocking her back to the floor. Somehow she managed to push forward across the threshold of the large, bright room with its floor-to-ceiling windows and a baby grand piano in the middle. Less than six feet away sat a man with his back to her, looking out one of the huge windows onto the vast tropical garden running along the back side of the property.

It was during freshman year at the conservatory that the blond cellist from Texas and the brunette pianist from Puerto Rico were randomly paired together to learn one of the Bach sonatas for cello and piano for a student showcase. The instant they began to play together, the entire world around them just fell away. It wasn't exactly love at first sight—but it was the first indication their lives would never be the same for having met one another.

Those were the same notes he was playing right now. There was an ebb and flow in his tempo and volume. It appeared as if the man was accompanied by a piano part that only he could hear as he counted out beats of silence in his head, nodding in time to a nonexistent melody. When he judged it was time to come back in, he and his cello rejoined, continuing through the last measures of the piece.

Emilia found herself walking slowly and silently to the piano. Then she slipped onto the bench, her eyes glued to the man with the silvery blond hair rocking from side to side as he played. When the piece ended and he set himself up to play again, she watched and she waited, focusing closely on his pace as he drew in a breath, lifted his bow, and began to play.

She drew in a breath, she lifted her hands, and she began to play, too.

His shoulders tensed with a quick inhalation, and then he stopped for a moment that lasted no longer than a heartbeat. She kept going until he joined in again, his cello drawing a single delicate line—a gossamer thread of sound pulled gently from his instrument as she picked out a sparse melody beneath.

If she stopped to think about it, she'd have been dumbfounded by the fact that her fingers remembered each and every note, leap, and trill. They walked up and down the keyboard, spelling out the melody the same way someone might spell out a sentence in sign language. Above the piano, the cello floated along, in no particular hurry. They were two distinct voices carrying on two distinct conversations at the same time. You heard them separately, then together. It should have been cacophony, but it wasn't. It shouldn't have been beautiful, but it was.

She found herself stretching the notes across the keys—lingering as her fingers executed the tiny grace notes and turns, picking out chords note by note. It was a melody that moved horizontally—sprawling across the measures rather than forming bold vertical blocks of sound. Under Bach's pen, the music unfurled and expanded. It grew and spread and slowly revealed itself. The cello was full and lush above, the piano providing the structure—the framework underneath.

He was the flesh, she was the bone. And together, they were complete.

CHAPTER 34

GRACIE

Today

I'm not ready. And that's saying a lot. Because I'm *always* ready—for whatever comes my way. Whatever crazy testimony a witness gives, whatever unreasonable ruling a judge makes—whatever curveball, monkey wrench, or crazy-ass thing that comes out of nowhere for no good reason at no particular time.

I'm the one who's ready for it.

Except not today.

Mom is following the music, and we're following Mom. Not that she has any idea where she's going, having left the two people who do in the dust when she took off. She hardly seems perturbed as she winds her way through the unfamiliar hallways of someone else's home. Some part of me is taking mental inventory as we pass an impressive array of amenities including a home gym, an indoor pool with jacuzzi and massage table, a movie screening room, and a gourmet kitchen that would make Julia Child envious. Near as I can tell, it's all laid out on the single floor in one sprawling floorplan. I don't think the place quite qualifies as a mansion, but it's pretty damn close—and it's pretty damn posh.

Along our route, we encounter a few people—two women and a man in scrubs, and another woman in an apron. They're all forced to flatten themselves against the walls as we fly by. I can only imagine what we must look like to them with Mom leading the pack, Meg and I about fifteen seconds behind in hot pursuit. Newly minted Uncle Blaine and Aunt Claudia are on our heels, while Miguel is bringing up the rear.

When Mom disappears around a sharp corner, I think it's just the start of another segment of hallway. But it's not. She's standing, frozen, in the doorway of the room where the music is being played. It takes every bit of traction my shoes can grab just to keep myself from plowing into her. Meg, unfortunately, is not quite able to manage the same, so she slams into me with such force that the two of us go tumbling to the carpet. Our mother, standing only about six inches away, doesn't even notice.

"Oh, my God! I'm so sorry, Gracie!" Meg gasps. "Are you okay?"

"Yeah, I'm fine," I say, nodding before I get up onto my knees.

From there, I grab the wall for support and pull myself up. Once I'm vertical again, I offer a hand down to my sister. She takes it. By the time we turn back to the doorway, Mom is already on the other side of the threshold, walking across the parquet floor slowly in the direction of the man. He's facing the window, his back to her as he plays his cello. I think she's going to go straight to him, but she doesn't, making her way to the piano instead.

In less time than it takes to blink, she has slipped onto the bench, put her hands to the keyboard, and her feet to the pedals. Her head is tipped back, her eyes closed, and she's playing Bach from memory. Clearly she knows him or, at least, she knows his playing, because she seems to anticipate his every push and pull, piano and forte and silence. At one point, they play a trill in unison, and I'm reminded of a pair of figure skaters doing side-by-side axels—executed with perfect precision, landed in perfect symmetry.

And then my eyes are glued to him—what I can see of him, anyway. His hair is a mixture of blond and gray that catches the sunlight, with broad shoulders and long legs. As he plays, the muscles in his arms contract and relax with every smooth pass of bow across strings. Suddenly I want desperately for him to turn around so I can look at his face. I need to know if I'll see myself reflected there in his features. I need to know if, against all reason, he'll know who I am without ever having met me. It's a ridiculous thought, I know, but somehow I just can't help myself.

Everyone in the room seems to feel it, too, as they all stare along with me and Meg. We all know we're bearing witness to something extraordinary. To a miracle.

CHAPTER 35

EMILIA

Today

She couldn't say how many times they played through the same movement of the sonata over, and over, and over again. But at some point, Emilia sensed he was ready to let the last note be the last note.

It struck her as funny how you could want something for so long—yearn for it, pray for it, beg for it—but then, when it was finally close enough to touch, you were terrified to go anywhere near it. Be careful what you wish for, you might just get it, right? Well, Emilia had wished and wished and wished.

She pushed back from the keyboard, stood, and put her right hand on the sleek, smooth wood of the piano. Then she moved forward slowly, the fingers of one hand trailing along the instrument as if in need of grounding, which she supposed, in a way, she was. But eventually she ran out of piano, forced to step out into the cavernous breach between the end of her space and the beginning of his. It took less than ten seconds to cross the floor to him, though it felt more like ten minutes.

When she was finally standing in front of him, this man she had been married to for the briefest of moments, Emilia took the cello from his hands and set it aside carefully, stopping just long enough to run a finger along the gouge that occurred so many years ago. How had it happened again?

Time had a way of fading scars and, with them, the memory of how they came to be. But there were some scars that you never wanted to heal over for *exactly* that reason. Because, in those endlessly dark days when the past felt so distant as to have been a dream, the scar was proof that it had been real. It was the thing that kept you tethered to the memories surrounding them, no matter how long ago or how far away.

Without the instrument between them, she slid down onto her knees in front of the man. Still she couldn't bring herself to look up at him. So she sat like that, suddenly overcome by the tears that had been waiting three decades to come. The happy tears. They spilled past her lashes, streamed down her face, and landed in fat droplets on his shoes.

She startled at the feel of his hand on her cheek, noting the slight tremor in his fingers as he wiped away the dampness. She put her hand over his and looked up, into his face. Into his eyes.

For three decades, Emilia conjured Paul over and over again, reconstructing him in her mind line by line, curve by curve. She couldn't risk forgetting a single inch of his body, because to forget *them* was to forget *him*. And now she saw exactly how well she'd done—how faithful a transcription she had created. Somehow, inexplicably, she was completely blind to the effects of time on his features. All she saw was the young man with the clear blue eyes and blond hair. The strong, chiseled jawline. The lips tipped upward ever-so-slightly, making him appear to be perpetually amused.

"Hello, Paul. I'm Emilia," she said.

These were the most special of tears—the ones reserved for welcoming a child into the world, fulfilling a lifelong dream or pledging before God and the ocean to love someone for all of your days in sickness and in health.

"I-I know," he replied slowly.

She wanted to ask if he remembered her—remembered them or any fraction of the life they shared, but she didn't. Partially because she didn't want to pressure him, and partially because she didn't want to hear the answer. She already knew what it was . . . but that was okay. They fell in love once before . . . she thought there was an excellent chance they might manage it again. Either way, she would never again let go of him.

An entirely foreign sound bubbled up and out past her lips—a combination of sob and gasp and wail.

"P-please don't c-cry, Emilia," he said softly, reaching out to wipe her damp face with his thumb once more.

She grasped his hand and held it there to her cheek.

"I'm just happy," she told him, smiling through tears. "I . . . I know you don't remember me—remember *us*, but I've been looking for you a very long time. Not that I expect . . ." She stopped, taking a second to slow the torrent of thoughts and emotions that were flowing from her heart to her head to her mouth. "Paul, I'd really like it if we could spend some time getting to know one another. I don't expect anything . . . I mean, you don't know me—"

"I w-want to know y-you," he said, this time with a smile of his own. "D-do you h-have to go h-home soon?"

Did she?

Emilia shook her head slowly.

"No," she told him quietly. "This is the only place I need to be."

CHAPTER 36

GRACIE

Today

Most everyone slips out after the music ends, and I'm glad for that. Even I feel like some sort of creepy voyeur standing around and watching this long-awaited reunion. It's too intimate. Too raw. So I hang back, awkwardly looking on, not sure how I fit into this moment. Or even *if* I fit into this moment. But then I'm joined by the person who fits even *less* than I do.

"It's amazing, isn't it?" Blaine marvels, staring across the room at my mother and his brother. "After all this time . . ."

"After all this time what? She never stopped loving him? Does that surprise you, *Uncle Blaine*?" I ask with a disdainful accent on his name.

He looks at me now. "I was thinking more about how he held onto her through the music. I don't think *he* ever stopped loving *her*—even if he couldn't exactly remember her."

Okay, sure, I can see that, too. Not that I'm willing to give this asshole an inch. So I do what I do best—I disarm my opponent by pivoting faster than he can.

"I'm a lawyer, you know, and a damn good one."

"Yes, I'm aware."

So much for disarming him. I move right on to strategic attack.

"If this had happened today, you can be damn sure I'd have exposed you and your vicious, vindictive family for the bullies you are—"

"*Were*," he corrects me, then gestures for me to continue. "But go on, please."

He's really starting to piss me off with this shit.

"Go ahead, just stand there all smug and amused. You have no idea what she gave up. What she went through for all those years."

"Actually, I do," he replies simply.

I scoff.

"Yeah, I doubt that, buddy."

He shrugs.

"Believe what you want, Gracie, but I've kept an eye on you."

"On *me?*" I ask incredulously, pointing to myself.

"Well, you and your family. I mean, you are, after all, my niece."

I open my mouth to rail at him—to deliver one of my soul-crushing, testicle-shrinking, pronouncements . . . but I don't get the chance. Blaine Winstead snatches my hand and begins to tug me across the room.

"Paul?" he calls out as we approach the spot where my mother is having what looks to be a very private moment. "Paul, there's someone here who wants to meet you."

I'm just thinking about extricating myself from his grip when Paul Winstead looks up.

And then I see the truth of it written right there on his face.

His eyes are my eyes. His chin is my chin. His nose is my nose.

My God! How did she look into my face every single day? She must have seen him over and over again. And she could never say a word.

"Hey, Paul?" Blaine addresses his brother again as we approach. "Do you know who this is?"

My mom stands up and steps back a little, wiping at the tears on her face. She's smiling at me as I approach him, and she gives me a little nod of encouragement.

"I love you," she mouths silently.

"You too," I mouth back as the man from the picture stands up so that we're face-to-face.

I smile at him a little.

He smiles at me a little.

"Hi, Paul," I say, just quietly enough for him to hear me. "I'm Gracie. I'm . . . your daughter. And I'm so happy to finally meet you."

There are so many things to discuss. Are the police obligated to do anything about this newly found long-missing person? Has any crime been committed? Any fraud perpetrated? Does my mother want to stay in Puerto Rico for a while and get to know the man who was once her husband? Does Paul even want this major upheaval in the life he's built over these years with the help of his brother? So many questions, not all with immediate answers. And way too many people "taking my temperature"—Mom and Meg slipping me hugs and hand squeezes, Miguel cornering me with his concerned look, even the Winsteads keep asking me how I'm holding up. I tell them all I'm fine, because that's easier than telling them the truth—that I have no idea how to feel.

I have to get away. I need to find someplace quiet to just sit and think and feel. For just a little while. I find my way back to the now-empty music room and take a seat on the piano bench, staring down at the keys as I force myself to take long, deep breaths.

I really thought I had this all under control, but I'm starting to think I have seriously overestimated my own capacity to manage emotions. And there are a lot of them. They're coming fast now—faster than I can absorb them. Suddenly I have the uneasy feeling that I'm about to be caught in something akin to a flash flood, and if I can't find a way to redirect the water, I'll be swept away. I might even drown.

I don't make the conscious decision to put my hands on the keyboard, they just sort of land there as if my fingers have a mind of their own. Next thing I know, Beethoven's *Moonlight Sonata* is a conduit, drawing out the churning, swirling feelings and siphoning them off into notes that I have no business remembering after all this time. I close my eyes the way my mother sometimes does when she plays, and I just let it all come . . . and let it all go. The fear, anger, hope, love, joy, and sadness are a torrent feeding the music that's been there, just under the surface, all this time. When the last note has finally faded away into the air around me, I find myself shaken— and shaking. That's when I feel his hand on my shoulder.

Paul—my father—is looking down at me.

"Can I . . . sit with you?" he asks.

"Um . . . yeah, sure," I murmur, using my hands to wipe the dampness from my face.

I can't tell if it's sweat or tears. Or both.

"Y-you're good," he tells me.

"I used to be."

He looks confused. Shit, have I done something wrong already?

"No." The word just hangs there for an awkward beat until the rest of the sentence joins it slowly. "You're g-good now."

"I mean I used to be really good. Like professional-level good. But I hurt my hand, and that was that."

He stares at me for so long that I'm considering repeating myself—or maybe moving on to an entirely new topic—when he finally forms a response.

"You can't tell."

"*I* can tell," I say, maybe a little harsher than I intended. "I can't enjoy it anymore. Meg, she's the one who's going to go all the way."

"She looks like . . . your . . . mother. Emilia."

I don't know why, but his observation produces an icy stab of jealousy. Even this man who supposedly "made" me is struck by how much more Meg and my mother share— physically and musically.

"Y-you look l-like my . . . mother. Ev-Evelyn."

In the time it takes him to communicate the second part of his thought, the jealousy breaks down and rearranges its particles to produce a sensation I can't immediately recognize. It's something along the lines of gratitude dipped in pride and edged with joy. He's telling me that I am part of *him*. At least, I think that's what he's telling me.

"Thank you," I say softly. "Maybe you can show me pictures sometime?"

This makes him smile, and it's a glorious sight. I don't think my mother has even experienced this from him yet today. It feels special, like it's just for me.

"I'd like that," he tells me.

Then, in an unexpected move, he takes my hand in his. I think he's going to hold it, but he places it on the piano keys instead.

"I used t-to . . ." This is the longest pause yet, but he tries to find the words to accompany the thought. "I used to be g-good, too," he says. "B-before . . . *my* . . . accident."

For a second, I'm not sure if he's talking about being a good cellist—or being a perfectly healthy twenty-two-year-old man. It dawns on me then, the astounding lack of gratitude I have had for the last thirteen years of my life. Maybe longer. Definitely longer.

This man was at the top of his game—newly married, soon to be a father (not that he knew that), and a fast-rising star in the classical music world. He had this brilliant, wonderful life ahead of him until a profoundly tragic accident took that all—and so much more—away from him.

I was very talented, super-promising, and everyone said

I was destined for greatness, including me. In reality, I was just a stupid, spoiled kid who had no idea just how lucky she was—for whom being "the best that you can be" wasn't nearly enough. And if I couldn't be perfect, I didn't even want to try. It wasn't fate, or luck, or Meg who took the piano from me. It was *me*. I did this to myself.

"I don't know," I tell him. "I heard you and Mom play, and I'd say you're pretty spectacular right now."

He shrugs. "I'm w-working on it. It's a little b-better every day."

I follow his eyes as they glance out the window. He's looking for her.

"Do you . . . Paul, do you remember her? Or anything about that time?"

He moves one of his hands to rest on his temple. "It's f-fuzzy. Sometimes a part of a p-picture. B-but things s-sometimes f-feel familiar. S-she feels f-familiar. You?"

I don't know why I'm surprised by the question.

"Me what?"

"D-do you have s-someone?"

Oh, that.

"Not right now. I'm afraid I'm not so good at relationships. It's always something—one dud guy after another."

Paul nods. "N-nobody is perfect, G-gracie."

I can't tell if it's a commentary on me or him. Maybe both. Definitely both.

When I glance down, I notice my hands are still on the keys where he put them.

"You wanna hear some more Beethoven?" I ask.

He smiles. I smile. And I play.

CHAPTER 37

EMILIA

Today

Emilia couldn't shake the feeling that she was in the company of her enemy as they walked across the huge back lawn. Hibiscus bloomed all around them in spectacular shades that mimicked the sunset, set against the canvas of the ocean view from this height.

It was clear they didn't know how to speak to each other, but she had to force herself to get past her deep-rooted hatred for Blaine Winstead and all he represented. Because one thing was certain, he was the only person on the planet who could provide her with the answers she needed.

"Please tell me what happened," she requested softly.

He didn't need for her to clarify. So he laid it all out—his plan to bring Paul home for some sort of twisted intervention, all meant to placate Brock and force his brother to own his share of the family misery. He explained how he had bribed Stenhammer to make it look as if his brother had reboarded the ship and, later, to direct suspicion onto Emilia. Then of course, Paul's kidnapping and subsequent disappearance—for real.

"But how did you *find* him?" she asked, breathless with rage and disbelief—and even a little vindication.

She'd always known she had been set up, she just hadn't realized to what extent.

"It was your mother. Imelda."

She stopped again, this time in a full-on, unapologetic gape.

"I'm sorry . . . what?"

Blaine nodded soberly. "I went to see her, hoping she could help me find you. I figured you were the only person who might have a clue where he would go."

"I—I didn't . . ." she whispered, shaking her head slowly from side to side.

"I know that now, of course. So I went to see Imelda and she directed me to Vieques, where I found him in a small hospital. She's . . ." He paused and looked down, a little embarrassed. "She's also the reason I met my wife. Claudia was another inmate, and she was our interpreter."

Emilia blinked hard at the confession.

"Are you telling me *you* . . . married an ex-con? Is *that* what killed your parents?"

He rolled his eyes. "Believe me when I tell you I am not unaware of the irony there. I thought you weren't good enough for my brother. I called you . . . those things."

"A whore? A gold digger? A murderer?" she supplied in rapid succession.

He sighed sadly, nodding.

"Yeah. I'm sorry, and I'm ashamed. So I'd go visit your mother, really just to see Claudia—who translated for us. And little by little, I fell in love with her. I didn't give a damn where she came from or what she'd done. I just knew I didn't want to live without her. That was when I *really* felt the weight of what I'd done to Paul. That's when I realized what I'd taken away from him."

"I don't even know where to start unpacking all that," she admitted dazedly.

"It'll take time, I'm sure. I know a good therapist if you need one," he said, testing a small smile out on her.

She scowled, but she didn't rebuke him. And then, out of nowhere, there was Beethoven.

"Is that Meg?" Blaine asked.

Emilia felt the corners of her mouth turn up slightly as she shook her head.

"No, that's my Gracie. And she hasn't played like that in years."

"That'd be Paul then," he informed her. "He's got a way of making people do things they never thought they'd do." He paused, clearly reluctant to say something.

"What is it?" she coaxed.

"Please don't be offended by this, but there's something about Gracie that reminds me of my mother. I mean, I told you they look alike, but it's more than that. She has this natural elegance . . . this ease. I know you never got to see the best of Evelyn. That came later, after . . . Paul. After she got off the pills and stopped drinking—and left my father. You know she actually moved here? She bought a small place down here and split her time between Puerto Rico and Texas. In fact, it's the house that Claudia and I live in now. I'm just grateful she lived long enough to see my brother here leading at least a somewhat independent life."

"I'm glad your mom found her way. I'm sure being married to Brock would have driven anyone to self-medicate. Though I have to admit . . . God, I don't know if I can say this out loud." She muttered the last line to herself.

"What is it?" he prompted, obviously intrigued.

Emilia rolled her eyes. "Ugh, I *hate* to even go there, but I've been thinking for years now there's definitely some of Brock in her. There's no denying it."

He smiled. "Yeah, I kinda thought so maybe. It's her drive."

"The drive!" she echoed, pointing at him and nodding enthusiastically. "You have no idea! That child came out of the womb *spoiling* for a fight. She's ready to debate anyone about anything anytime—whether or not she's right—and she almost always wins! Mainly though, it's that she works tirelessly, and she plays to win."

"Yup. Sounds about right," he agreed with a chuckle, but then got serious again. "You know they'd have loved to have had a granddaughter. Even my bastard of a father."

She glanced at him sharply, wiping out all traces of the goodwill they'd just been building.

"I'm sure they would have. Which is why I ran. Why I changed my name and started over. I couldn't let them—or anyone—know I was pregnant. Your family had too much sway, too much money. I knew they'd take my baby and leave me locked up somewhere."

Blaine dropped his head for a second, as if he'd just noticed his shoelaces were untied. When he looked up again, his expression was full of regret.

"I knew where you were, Emilia."

The words stopped her dead in her tracks.

"You . . . you *knew*? For how long?" she demanded.

"A long time."

"Sweet Jesus. Why didn't you . . . ?" She let the question hang out there, unfinished.

But he knew.

"Get in touch? I didn't want to disrupt your life—or hers."

The anger was back in a flash, laying waste to the incredulity and shock.

"Bullshit!"

"No, really, I swear. In the beginning *we* were hiding from *you*!" She saw the shame creep into his expression, and when he spoke again, she heard it in his tone. "I was certain you'd come after the money, the company, control over Paul and his care . . ." Her fingers twitched with the desire to slap him again. He must have sensed it. "What do you want me to say? Yes. That's what we believed. Like I said before, I was young and stupid. Plus, my asshole father didn't want anyone to know he had a son who was 'damaged goods.' So Paul went missing, and he stayed missing—as far as the rest of the world was concerned. I'm just so, so sorry you had to live your life waiting for the other shoe to drop."

"So much wasted time," she muttered, slowly resuming their walk of the property perimeter. "If you'd have found me, I would have come, you know. I'd have *helped* you. Despite everything."

She watched his expression in her peripheral vision.

"You know, first there was just too much with the day-to-day. Would he survive? Would he walk? Both of his legs and one of his arms were broken. And of course, the brain injury. Would he speak? How much could he process? We just didn't know at that point. But then . . ."

"But then what?"

"But then I started to tell him little things—like stories. I'd show him pictures of himself with the family—with you. At school, at home, and even a few of him performing in New York. There came a point when he understood. He didn't remember you—but he understood that you had been someone very important in his life."

Emilia stopped once more, waiting till he did the same—and she was looking him in the eye.

"I—I appreciate you doing that. I know you could have lied or even pretended I never existed."

He offered a rueful smile.

"It took a while, Emilia, but I changed. A lot. I had to because I knew if I didn't, I'd be a miserable, soulless bastard like my father. Over the years—with the help of my beautiful, brave, and totally unpredictable wife, all the nonsense went out the window. The ego, the attitude, the pretentious, entitled bullshit."

As much as she wanted to hang onto the rage that had been her constant companion for so long, Blaine's words rang true in her ears and in her heart. This was not the same man she knew thirty years ago. The truth of the matter was that, were it not for the events of that day, Blaine Rockwell Winstead Jr. would have been well on the road to following in his father's footsteps.

"So, back to my mother," she began, following him to a bench in the shade. "She really told you where Paul was?"

He nodded.

"She did. I mean, she didn't exactly draw me a map, but those spirits of hers gave me enough clues to get me there." He paused for a few seconds. "I uhhh . . . I was really sorry to hear how sick she is. Do you have plans to go visit her?"

"No."

Blaine bent forward so that his forearms were resting atop his thighs, hands clasped in front of him. When he spoke again, he was looking out toward the ocean.

"All I'm going to say about that, Emilia, is that you don't get this time back. You talk about the wasted time away from Paul. All those years you spent terrified that someone would try to take your child from you. I'm afraid you'll feel the same way years from now, when you look back and realize you could have seen her one more time—you could have had one more conversation with her—even if it was just to tell her how you feel." He turned to her. "I know you haven't asked for my opinion, but I think you should go and see her. She's not the monster you think she is. She's just a frail old woman on the verge of death. And I'm sure it would mean the world to her if you came."

She wanted desperately to change the subject.

"Let me ask you something, Blaine. If you finally had this great epiphany—if you finally understood what Paul and I had, and what we lost, then why did you let me go on thinking he was dead? You must have known that I wasn't after your money. And by then, Gracie was a young woman; I didn't have to worry about anyone trying to snatch her away from me."

Her unexpected question caused him to sit up straight once more, staring at her. He blinked hard, pulled his brows into a deep V.

"I, uhhh, I *wanted* to reach out . . ."

"Riiiiight." And just like that, she was back to the disdain and disbelief.

"No, really, I did. It was Paul."

"What? You were afraid I'd do something to hurt him? Did you think I'd reject him because of his injuries?"

"No," he objected quickly, holding his palms up and shaking his head adamantly. "No, nothing like that. I'm saying it was *Paul's* decision, Emilia. *He* didn't want me to tell you he was alive."

"W-what?" she stammered. "I don't understand . . ."

Blaine looked more than a little miserable.

"My brother may not remember everything, and he may seem very deliberate at times, but he's still wicked smart and so damn stubborn! Believe me, we've talked about you a lot over the years. I actually thought seeing you might help jar something loose in that brain of his—that he might start to remember. But he was absolutely adamant. He didn't want you to feel obligated to come back to a man who didn't remember you."

She propped her elbows on her knees and dropped her head into her hands.

"I can't believe it. You didn't want me to know because it might have hurt your family. He didn't want me to know because it might have hurt mine." She looked to Blaine. "I never stopped loving him, you know. It's what ended my second marriage, in fact."

"Yeah, about that," Blaine said, reaching an arm behind his back, producing an envelope from his pocket. "So . . . um . . . I have something that belongs to you," he told her as he handed it over. "To you and my brother."

She took it from him, flipping it over and running her finger under the piece of tape holding the flap down. Then she pulled out the single page of creamy paper, folded neatly into thirds.

It was their marriage certificate—a little yellowed but perfectly preserved.

"Oh, my God," she gasped softly from behind the paper.

There it was in black and white, witnessed and certified by a clerk in Miami, Florida. At last the proof that she was—and always had been—Mrs. Emilia Winstead.

"I'm sorry. Again," Blaine was saying quietly from next to her. "Brock wanted me to destroy it, and I just couldn't bring myself to do it. So I lied to him. I, uh, I realize that doesn't make me a hero or anything."

Emilia took a long beat to consider everything he'd just told her . . . and how much better her life would have been if . . . if what? If she hadn't met Richard and had Meg? If she hadn't been forced to become a strong, independent woman? If she hadn't had the years she did with her girls and Richard? What part of it would she give back if she had to?

None of it, she realized for the first time. Not a single second.

"Well," she began with a sigh, "you might not have recognized it at the time, but I think it was a sign that you weren't the same as your father—that you had a conscience. Somewhere deep inside of you was the man you were destined to be." She gestured to him with her hand. "This man. And look what happened in the end? You came through. You sent Miguel that picture that got me here."

He turned to look at her, a confused expression on his face. "What picture?" he asked.

"You know, the picture," she said with a half-smile, wondering why he thought this was a good time to be silly. "The one in the email you sent to Miguel. The birthday picture with those two women in scrubs and Paul in the background?"

Blaine's eyes went wide at the same time that the color drained from his face.

"No . . . I don't know," he said in a soft, slow voice that she found vaguely unnerving.

Now she shifted in her seat on the bench, her own smile fading even as her concentration sharpened. Something was off here. Very, very off. But she didn't know what it was.

"Blaine, the picture you sent to Miguel Alvarez," she repeated with emphasis, as if he might suddenly remember. "The one of Paul playing cello in the background. Here . . ." she said, gesturing toward the building behind them.

"*Here* here?" he confirmed, pointing to the ground.

"Yes! Hang on . . ." She flipped through her phone until she found the picture Miguel had forwarded to her. "This one."

He looked down at the image, then back up at her. That's when she knew somehow. She knew exactly what he was about to say, and she felt the hair on the back of her neck stand on end a second before he uttered the words.

"Emilia, it wasn't me," he whispered, dead serious. "I swear. I did *not* send you that picture."

CHAPTER 38

CÉSAR

Today

For years the *turista*'s face had haunted César's dreams—the man slipping through his fingers over and over again, night after night. Only, in his nightmares, the man had been swallowed up by the gaping black abyss of the sea. The reality had been very different. Miraculously, when he went over the side, he didn't hit the water, but managed to catch the suspended rigging and platform that supported a huge, enclosed lifeboat. It had been clear from his twisted limbs and the pool of blood forming under his head that the man was seriously injured. He didn't know if the man would live, even if he did get him to a hospital. But there was no doubt in his mind that the *turista* would die if César just left him there. With some difficulty, he was able to retrieve the broken, bloody man and get him back to the car, laying him out across the back seat and wrapping his head in a shirt to stanch the flow of blood.

Rather than taking the cargo ferry all the way to St. Croix, as planned, he took advantage of their docking at Vieques, the small island off the southeast coast of Puerto Rico. From there, he drove to the island's only hospital. He carried the man, already half-dead, into the waiting room, called out for help, and was five miles away before anyone even thought to ask about the man who'd brought in the *turista*. César ditched the car, caught the next passenger ferry back to the main island, and he never looked back. Until the day he almost lost everything—the day his own son was fighting for his life.

Javier was fifteen when his mother allowed her drunk boyfriend to drive them home from a baseball game. The *pendejo* flipped the SUV into a ravine, killing himself and César's ex-wife, and leaving his boy in a coma. He'd kept vigil by his son's bedside in the ICU, watching the respirator breathe for him, listening to the monitors count every weak beat of his heart. The doctors had not been optimistic, but he would not give up on Javier. Then, late one night, he went to the deserted hospital chapel and dropped to his knees before the great gold cross hanging against the wall. He lowered his head and prayed, begging God to bring him a miracle. He sobbed. He pleaded. He bargained. César swore that if God would only spare his Javier, he would spend the rest of his days making amends for his greatest sin. Because, clearly, God held him responsible for the death of the *turista*.

An eye for an eye. A son for a son.

Even now, he sometimes dreamed of those long nights in that frigid hospital room where his child lay under the blankets, watching the artificially generated rise and fall of his chest. And of that morning when he awoke to find Javi conscious and alert—looking straight at him. The news was promising—the boy would live, though it would be a very long road to recovery, and there were no guarantees that he'd be the same young man he was before the accident. Not that César cared. He was just grateful for this gift and determined to honor the promise he'd made. He only had to figure how to go about doing that—hoping God would show him the way. And He did—but it took a good long while.

In the meantime, Javier healed, grew, and thrived with the help of his cello, and by the time he graduated university with his degree in music therapy, the horrific accident was nothing more than a distant memory. César's heart swelled with pride to see his son travel all over the island helping others who had suffered injuries like his to heal, to express themselves, and to find joy through music. It didn't take long for his reputation to spread and the job offers to come. Javier had received offers for positions in New York City and Los Angeles but didn't want to leave his beloved Puerto Rico.

The perfect opportunity came in the form of a full-time, live-in position in Rincón, only a half hour from where César had settled. They offered an excellent salary and the use of a little *casita* on the property. Javier loved working with Señor Paul, a very affluent middle-aged man who also played the cello. He was excited for his father to meet his new client, and arrangements were made for César to visit the beautiful hilltop property. When he arrived, he was told they were still working together in the music room and would meet him in the back gardens shortly. So he had strolled the stunning grounds, admiring the view of Sandy Beach, and circling the back of the sprawling home. He was immediately drawn to the windows that spanned what must have been floor-to-ceiling. Taking a peek inside, he found Javier and another man playing.

Had his son looked up at that moment, he'd have seen the huge smile on his father's face—followed in quick succession by shock, horror, and fear. César was not the sort of man who believed in ghosts, and yet there was one sitting right on the other side of the paned glass. He staggered backward before either of them spotted him, then dropped to his knees.

The *turista*.

But . . . how had he survived such severe injuries?

Not that it mattered.

The odds that such an extraordinary confluence of events should occur to bring the two of them back together after all these years was simply inconceivable. The whole thing was astronomical to the point that it could have only been orchestrated by the Almighty Himself.

César knew in that instant that God was now calling his debt. It was time for him to atone for his part in the destruction of a man's life—especially when it became clear that he was no longer the easygoing, easy-moving, carefree man who had stepped off the boat in San Juan nearly three decades earlier.

He knew from Javier that the man had suffered a severe injury many years ago and that a significant portion of his memory had been affected. So he held his breath when they were finally introduced, watching for the slightest hint of recognition, but to his great relief, there was none. Still, he couldn't shake the fear that the man would recognize him at any moment, leveling an accusing finger at him as his would-be murderer. But never once did he catch the light of recognition in the *turista*'s eyes, then or in the subsequent weeks when he came to visit and observe.

A large part of the man's days were spent working with physical and occupational therapists who ensured he stayed physically strong and moved as efficiently and safely as possible. It was the music that seemed to bring him the most joy, and he and Javier often spent hours on end together playing and listening. Aside from a housekeeper who oversaw the day-to-day operations of the house and a chef who prepared meals, the man was largely independent. Had it not been for the irregular gait, no one would have guessed he suffered from any sort of physical challenge. And memory loss aside, the man seemed to speak and process information very well, if a bit slowly and tentatively at times.

So César visited whenever possible, waiting and watching for the opportunity to make good on the bargain he'd struck in the hospital chapel that night. But what could he possibly do for this man? He couldn't turn back the clock and make him whole again. He had no money—and even if he did, money was one thing the man *didn't* need. Even the brother, Señor Blaine and his wife, were there often, ensuring the man had plenty of companionship.

Still there was something just below the surface that César found worrisome—a sadness so deep that it had simply became a part of who the man was. It was so subtle that the people who surrounded him daily didn't seem to notice. He recognized it because he had experienced this kind of profound loneliness that embedded itself into your very soul.

That's when it came to him. It was the *woman*. His wife. The one who had been meant to be with the man that day in San Juan. Ultimately it was she who had been blamed for her husband's disappearance. She was the woman this man had loved.

Of course! But how to find her? How to bring them both together again? He spent hours on end searching the internet for traces of Emilia Oliveras, but there was nothing. Wherever she was, she'd made certain to cover her tracks well. And who could blame her? César now knew that despite the great care he took with his brother, Señor Blaine had been the one to set in motion the events of that tragic afternoon.

Again and again, he came up short in his search—until the day he saw the story in the newspaper. The one about the special detective who worked on the very old cases that no one else had been able to solve—Detective David Raña. César knew that if anyone could find the woman, *he* could.

And he hadn't been wrong.

CHAPTER 39

RAÑA

Today

Technically speaking, there was no official Cold Cases department, but ever since that profile piece had run in the paper a couple of weeks earlier, David had been receiving calls and letters from people from all over the Caribbean, asking for his help in the cases of their own lost or dead loved one.

He'd been irritated by the romanticized portrayal of him as some after-hours Sherlock Holmesian hero who, tortured by the unsolved cases in his district, spent his every spare hour investigating events that were born and died before he arrived at the San Juan PD. But at least it had garnered some attention for the cold cases on which he did, in fact, spend several of his own hours. He found he had a knack for spotting things that only a fresh pair of eyes could catch. As a result, he'd been instrumental pulling several unresolved cases from their purgatorial status and heating them up until something or someone popped out at him.

Whoever sent the message had obviously seen the story and, like dozens of others, reached out to him. He'd been about to head out for the weekend when it landed in his inbox, a single picture with two simple sentences:

Por favor encuéntrala. Por favor dile.

Please find her. Please tell her.

At first he thought the *her* was one of the two women in scrubs. But when he looked closer, he spotted someone else there in the background. When he magnified the image, he found himself looking at the figure of a blond man playing a cello.

Already late for pizza night at home, David made a mental note to forward it to the forensic tech team on Monday for a closer look. It was two in morning when he sat bolt upright in bed, staring through the pitch-black darkness of their bedroom, his wife breathing deeply beside him. Something had woken him—as it often did. He waited there in the dark for several long seconds as it wended its way up from his sleeping subconscious to his waking conscious. When it finally arrived, it hit him like a car impacting a brick wall at a hundred miles an hour. Less than a thirty minutes later, he was walking through the doors of the precinct.

The large space shared by the detectives was dark, silent— a stark contrast to the perpetually humming squad room down the hall. He dropped his jacket and car keys in his office, then made his way down to the archives. It only took him a few minutes to find what he was looking for. Tucking the folder under his arm, he returned to his office and closed the door behind him.

He'd been a teenager when the story of the missing son of the oil tycoon had broken. But it only lasted a few days before being knocked out of the public eye by the breaking news of a baby kidnapped from La Perla neighborhood of San Juan. When little Marianna Ruíz became the lead on every television and radio news show, and the front page headline of every newspaper, the story of a *turista* who'd spent less than a day on Puerto Rican soil had just faded away.

It had been the detail of the cello that stuck with David— and triggered the association of the case with the photo. He suspected whoever sent him the photo had been counting on that. And, sure enough, there was enough of a resemblance with an old file photo of Paul Winstead to confirm his suspicions. From there, figuring out who the "she" was hadn't been very difficult—Emilia Oliveras's name was all over the file. She'd claimed they were married right before boarding the cruise ship, though no documentation or witnesses to that effect had ever surfaced. There was a brief report from the detective who'd been sent to interview Emilia and do a preliminary assessment of the events. This struck David as strange. The ship had been out in international waters and much closer to St. Barts than Puerto Rico. And surely, even back then, this would have been the purview of the FBI rather than local police.

As he read the notes, it became clear to him that the detective believed strongly that Emilia had nothing to do with the young man's disappearance. And, in fact, seemed to imply that someone higher up in rank was orchestrating how the whole thing was being handled. This had also caught his attention. Based on what he knew from the "old timers" on the force, it would have been quite unusual for an officer to implicate one of their own in the rank-and-file, let alone a high-ranking superior, of wrongdoing. That was when he'd flipped to the last page to find the signature of Detective Miguel Alvarez.

He'd been the one to go out to the ship and interview Emilia. He'd been the one to defend her in the report. And he'd been the last one to see her before she simply disappeared off the ship—and off the face of the earth, never to be heard from again. Coincidence? Knowing Miguel as he did, David doubted it. But for as long as they'd known each other—and for all the secrets they shared between them—his oldest friend had never entrusted him with any of this. His first impulse was to call Miguel right then, but he stopped himself.

The person who sent him the email wanted Emilia Oliveras—wherever she was—to know that Paul Winstead was alive and well and . . . *where*, exactly? Rincón, according to the metadate attached to the image.

He couldn't be certain that Miguel had something to do with getting the woman out of Puerto Rico, but the odds were pretty damn good. The timing fit perfectly, he had access to and knowledge of the creation of false documents, and it would be just like him to risk everything to help someone in danger. The more he thought about it, the more certain David became that this message had been meant for Miguel. So he'd made certain that it found its way to him. And he didn't have to wait long to see if his hunch had been right. Not twenty-four hours later the daughters of a woman named Emily Oliver, stumbled into his station with an extraordinary story.

In the end, Miguel had asked for his help when he needed it, and David had been only too happy to help him track down the properties owned by Blaine Winstead. But he would not pursue the matter any further, nor would he make any amendments to this particular file, because no one else needed to know anything about the whereabouts of Paul Winstead or Emilia Oliveras. Or about the involvement of the detective assigned to the case back then.

David Raña owed Miguel Alvarez his life, and he'd spend the rest of it repaying him with his unquestioning loyalty.

CHAPTER 40

EMILIA

Today

When she arrived, Emilia saw them sitting side by side in beach chairs. This was a quiet spot, a little too rocky for the tourists, a little too tame for the locals. Today Meg, Gracie, and Imelda were the only three souls watching the brilliant skyscape unfolding against the canvas of the blue Caribbean Sea—a shifting watercolor ombre of orange, yellow, pink, and red.

The girls had set them up just at the edge, where the cool water met the warm sand so that it would lap at their feet and swirl around their ankles briefly before being inhaled back amongst the white-capped waves. Meg had a book in her hands and appeared to be reading aloud. It wasn't until Emilia drew closer that she could make out the words. She knew them immediately.

She felt compelled to move forward as if in a trance, walking around to the side of Imelda's chair and sinking down onto her knees in the sand next to it. She chanced a quick glance, wondering if Imelda's eyes would catch hers— if she'd even know her mother's eyes after all this time. But her lids were closed as she listened to the words and to the water. Emilia was more than a little startled by the woman she found.

This was not the Imelda she left behind when she was still a teenager. That woman was strong, vibrant, three-dimensional. The one sitting there on the beach was pale and gaunt, eyes sunken, cheeks hollow—her skin nearly translucent. She had *never* looked frail like this—like a tiny baby bird. Even at the height of her beguilement with Sergio, she had a quiet strength. But now this shell was all that remained, just enough echo of Imelda for her to be recognizable to her only child.

"*Stay with me here, in the quiet hush of fleeting time,*" Meg read. "*Stay with me.*"

Emilia knew this poem. It was one of several that Imelda used to read her when she was a little girl. Before him. Because that was how their relationship had been divided historically—before him and after him.

"*Should you drift away, even for a moment's breath, the emptiness will seep into me.*"

Emilia caught Meg's eye and tapped her own chest. She wanted to take over the recitation. When Meg tried to hand her the small, leather-bound volume, she shook her head. She already knew this one by heart. So she sat like they were sitting, facing forward, bathed in the golden reflection of the sky, and she became the little girl she used to be, speaking to the mother she used to have.

She couldn't see Imelda, but a small gasp told her she was aware of Emilia's presence. Without looking, she extend her left arm out so that her hand rested on Imelda's thigh, palm upward toward the clouds. Her mother's grasp was weightless in her own. She was all bones and no flesh.

Emilia continued to the next stanza of the poem.

"*For in that fleeting instant you will journey beyond reach, leaving me adrift in life's vast expanse. Lost amidst the echoes of your absence, longing for the gentle brush of your words against my skin, Anxious in the silence.*" She paused, finally feeling able to turn slightly and look up at her mother.

Imelda was watching her with tears in her eyes, the barest smile touching her lips. *"Will you return to me?"* the poet asked in Emilia's voice. *"Or will you leave me here to suffer the ache of my loss and the darkness of my longing, alone in the fading shadows of the sun."*

At the sound of the last words, Imelda pulled slightly on Emilia's hand, a request to come closer. No words passed between them as she lay her head in the old woman's lap, allowing her to stroke her hair. Once more they were mother and child.

There were some things that time simply could not erase. But if you were very lucky, it *would* hide them for a little while. Those were the moments Emilia chose to haunt for now.

For as long as she was able.

They sat like that, the four of them, watching the horizon until every fiery plume had been extinguished from the sky and they were left with only the moon and the stars for comfort.

CHAPTER 41

GRACIE

Today

"Gracie, are you sure about this?" Meg asks me, looking more concerned than surprised by my sudden change in plans.

I nod and smile.

"I have never been more sure about anything in my life. I'm going back to L.A. to pack up my stuff and arrange a leave from work. Hopefully I'll be back here by this time next month."

"Any idea how long you'll stay?"

I consider this, then shake my head. "No. I just want to spend some time down here getting to know my father . . . and my mother."

Her brows draw together in confusion.

"What do you mean? You know your mother very well."

"I don't know, Meg, do I? I mean *really*? When I was younger, I used to tell myself I'd never be anything like her. That I could do so much better than just be a wife and mother. I was gonna have a big, fancy career, and a big fancy condo, and big, fancy life."

"You do have all those things," she points out.

"Yeah, I suppose I do," I agree a little sheepishly, then continue. "Now I see how much more of her there was below the surface of that 'PTA mom' exterior. She had dreams, she had love. And she had more baggage than any one person should ever have to carry on their own. So, yeah, I think I'd kinda like to be in her orbit for a while, too. What about you? What have you decided about that gold medal you snagged last week? Are you gonna give it back and drop out of the tour? Maybe go back to school for something else?"

As I ask the question, it occurs to me that I've been so wrapped up in the bizarre turn my life has taken that I haven't checked in with her. She's been grappling with her own identity crisis all by herself, and I'm sorry that it's only now coming as we sit out front of the departure terminal.

"Actually," she starts slowly, "I'm thinking I'll keep that first prize—and the tour that goes along with it."

"Really!" I can't keep the surprised delight out of my voice.

She smiles a little sheepishly. "It's like you just said, Mom had dreams once, too. Only she never even got the chance to make them come true. Then here I am worrying about something that hasn't even happened yet. So I'll try living my dream for a year, and if it doesn't make me happy, then I'll call it quits and find something else that does. But at least I'll be able to live the rest of my life knowing I gave it a shot."

I look at Meg long and hard, searching for some trace of the eight-year-old little girl. But there's none. Sitting across from me is a woman.

"Well, I think that's an excellent decision," I say softly, irritated by the tears I can feel building behind my lashes and the lump that is already forming in my throat. "I, uh, I want you to know something."

"Gracie, what is it?" she asks, suddenly concerned.

"I know I haven't always been there for you, but I love you. I *always* have. And never once have I *ever* thought of you as a *half*-sister. You're not a half *anything*. Um, yeah . . . there've been times when I was a little envious of you . . . okay, a lot envious of you," I admit, rolling my eyes at myself. "But mostly I'm just so damn proud of you. And I really like the woman you've become. I guess what I'm trying to say is that I would have picked you. I may be shit at picking men, but not friends. And if I had been given the chance, I'd have picked you as my sister *and* as my friend."

"Oh, God, now I'm going to start crying!" She fishes around in her purse, producing a couple of crumpled Subway napkins.

Someone raps on the window next to me, and I just about jump out of my skin.

"*¡Sigue moviendote!*" says the not-so-happy-looking traffic cop as he does a shooing gesture.

"Well, I guess I'd better—*oof!*"

Meg throws herself over the console between our seats and pulls me so close and so tight, that I can't breathe for a moment. And I don't mind a bit.

"I pick you, too," she whispers in my ear.

As soon as she releases me, I get out of the car without another word, grabbing my bag out of the back seat and walking toward the terminal. When I get to the sliding glass doors, I turn, look back, and our eyes meet. Then my sister smiles and nods slightly an instant before she pulls out into traffic and disappears. For now.

I manage to get a direct flight from San Juan to Los Angeles. And while I find myself missing Meg's company, I'm also grateful for a little time to think. I've already been in touch with Trey. The car was shipped back to him earlier in the week, and I apologized for taking it in the first place. He is, as everyone has pointed out, an asshole, but he apologized for ruining our relationship—not to mention the best yoga class I've ever had. Low bar, I know, but it still made me feel marginally better.

His mother the realtor will list our condo, and we'll split the proceeds. In the meantime, I have found a lovely Airbnb close to the beach and a short distance to work. I'll stay there for a month, maybe six weeks—just long enough to put a few projects to bed and convince the partners that they should allow me to have that leave of absence. After all, I do have a new father to get to know. I've wasted one opportunity too many, and I don't intend to make that mistake again. Not now that I've found the family I never knew I'd lost.

Meeting Paul has been a profound experience. I see so much of myself reflected back when I look at him—both physical traits and personality traits. It would seem I'm very much a product of my Winstead DNA. My insane work ethic, ruthlessness in the courtroom, and acerbic wit are all well-documented traits on my father's side. Even my love for shoes can be traced back to my paternal grandmother who, Blaine tells me, had a shoe collection that would have made Imelda Marcos green with envy.

And speaking of Imeldas, I was able to see *our* Imelda a few more times before I left. I promised to come back and see her soon . . . and she promised to still be there. I'm hoping that she's got a little "inside intel" from the spirit world on that one and that we'll have just a bit more time—if not for me, then for my mother.

I spend the first hour of the flight pulling photos off the cloud and dumping them into a folder on my desktop. At Meg's suggestion, I'm making a giant digital album of some of the big moments of my life so I can share them with Paul. Birthdays and graduations, proms—even the revolving door of exes. I'm just looking back through my high school graduation pictures when something catches my eye. It's a picture of me, Mom, Dad, and Meg. I'm standing in the middle in my cap and gown, smiling. I can't recall who took this picture, but they manage to capture some of the people in the background.

And *that's* what strikes me.

Leaning against a tree several yards behind us, a man appears to be watching us from the back. He has a familiar tall frame with broad shoulders and hair that's dirty blond. He's wearing sunglasses and a leather jacket. He looks just a little bit like . . .

Wait . . . is that . . . Blaine Winstead?

No. No way. I convince myself it's just someone who looks like him.

But when I open up the folder with law school graduation pictures, there he is again, caught in the background and off to one side. And he looks as if he's taking video of me as I pose with a professor, holding up my diploma for the camera. I make the picture bigger so I can be sure. And I am sure.

"Oh, I've kept tabs on you all over the years . . ."

I'll be damned. Blaine Winstead wasn't just blowing smoke.

Well, I can't accuse him of being a coward. My mother would have flayed the skin from his flesh if she'd caught him anywhere near me. Looking back with new perspective, I see that she spent my entire life trying to protect me from what was, in her mind, the most dangerous threat of all: the truth.

On impulse, I close the laptop, pull out my phone, and begin examining all the pictures I've taken over the past week up at Paul's home. There's one in particular that catches my eye—a shot of him and Mom playing together one afternoon. They don't know I've captured them in the frame of my lens—nor does the man standing just outside the window, peering in. I hadn't noticed him until now, but there he is. A smallish Puerto Rican man around my mom's age.

He's just standing there watching them. And he's smiling.

EPILOGUE

PAUL

Tomorrow

Paul is climbing.

His ascent out of the fog is so slow that sometimes he can barely tell he's moving at all. Still, each day he's a little closer.

Each day he is gifted with just a little more of the life he had—the before. It comes to him in the form of a frame, a flash, or a snippet that plays out in his head like a tiny movie. Each one a single piece of a huge, complex puzzle. He has to remind himself often that he must be patient. Puzzles aren't meant to be assembled in a matter of hours or even days. Not by him, at least.

As each new piece is added to his slowly growing collection, he moves them around, aligning edges, matching colors, building out corners, and looking for the patterns he knows will eventually emerge there. Sometimes it feels as if a long time has passed before he has enough contiguous pieces to form a section resembling anything he can recognize.

But he keeps trying. And trying. And trying.

There is no rush.

The very instant she entered his orbit, a switch was tripped somewhere deep inside of him—churning up debris that had long been mired at the murky bottom of his memory. It can be disconcerting at times, as he can't control which pieces float up to the surface or when. Like the lightning-fast flashes of a man who looks a lot like Javier's father, César. Not that Paul can trust what his mind is showing him. Not yet, anyway. So he waits as his brain gradually reroutes its conduits to bypass the injured sections, creating new routes along which the impulses can travel.

It is all just confirmation of what he's known all along—that the endless longing for something he couldn't name had been real and not some figment of a warped or broken mind. She had been real. She *is* real.

Yesterday he remembered the sound of her voice, even though she wasn't speaking. Today he remembers what it feels like to touch her. He hopes that tomorrow, there will be yet another piece that he can snap into place.

And the day after tomorrow, and the day after that.

Until then, he will wait patiently, looking at her face, listening to her voice, feeling her touch. He knows that someday, there will be more pieces in the puzzle than there are blank spaces. Someday he will have enough words to tell her what is in his heart. Someday they will be what they were meant to be all along.

And until that day comes, his heart will speak in the language of love and his soul in the language of music.

AUTHOR'S NOTE

In writing the character of Paul, I pored over countless articles, interviews, and first-hand accounts from and about people who have suffered traumatic brain injuries. I lurked in forums and read blog posts. I spoke with friends-of-friends about their individual experiences. What is clear to me is that, even after so many years of intense research by so many brilliant people around the globe, we still have so much to learn about this extraordinary organ. There were simply no hard and fast rules or expectations or outcomes that I could reference in the creation of a character facing this uniquely devastating condition.

So I looked closer to home for my inspiration.

About two years ago, I reconnected with a family member whom I hadn't seen for more than a decade. And while I knew she'd suffered a devastating event which led to permanent, irreparable brain damage, I didn't know what to expect exactly. Thankfully, her memory is sharp—as is her sense of humor. But, while she used to be a flirty, sassy, energetic whirlwind, my loved one now moves through each day with painstaking thought and effort. She moves, processes, and articulates much slower than she used to but that hasn't stopped her from getting up every single day and working hard to live a full—and fulfilling—life on her own terms.

That was what I wanted for Paul.

Also central to this story was the response of the people around him to his condition—both in the immediate aftermath and decades later. For that I drew upon my personal experience with a degenerative neurological condition that has plagued my family for generations. I realize this is very different from a TBI, but I mention it because it helped me to flesh-out the emotional reactions of Paul's family and, later Emilia. Because watching someone you love fight so hard just to hold on to who they are—or to recover pieces of who they once were—is an emotional soup of heartbreak, humility, frustration, and pride.

All of this is to say that my depiction of an individual living with the effects of a traumatic brain injury is not meant to be a definitive one. There are as many outcomes and experiences as there are individuals. But I will add this—the one theme I came across again and again as I researched is the extraordinary capacity of people to reclaim, rebuild, and redefine their lives in the wake of the most traumatic events—and the extraordinary faith of the people who love them.

ACKNOWLEDGMENTS

There are so many people who go into the writing of a book—not just the author. These are just a few of the ones who helped with *After the Ocean* . . .

My amazing agent, Jill Marsal. As always, I'm so appreciative of your time, your attention, and your guidance.

The folks at Kensington Books Publishing, especially my editor, Liz May, and the entire editorial team. And to Michelle Addo and Matt Johnson, who have been such huge champions of me and my books.

My husband, Tom, who I think has worried about me more in the last few months than he has during the entirety of our eighteen-year marriage. I'm okay, honey—until the next one, anyway! And I love you so very much.

Quote of the year: "Honey, why does the computer say you spent three hundred dollars at Starbucks last month?"

And in case you read the acknowledgments for *Familia*, yes, I did get the house cleaner!

My family including my grandparents, Mike and Crucita, my sister Vanessa, and aunt/uncle combos Janet and Kwaku, Karen and Michael, David and Kim, Bonnie and David. And all those cousins!! Laura, Michelle, Jessica, Cheryl, Jeremiah, Nathan, Josh, Hannah, Michelle, Angel, Noah, and now baby Emmett!

To my sweetest Ursula and Frankie—Auntie Lauren loves you so much!

I am so blessed to have the most amazing friends! Thanks for talking me off the ledge more times than I can count. I love you so much Jannet, Patti, Nika, Patty, Jen, and Jeannie.

Kathy and Melissa who occupy a space that overlaps between friendship and family.

And to the best book club a writer girl could ever ask for—Mary Beth, Sue, Pam, Rosalie, Gaby, and Kathy. And especially Laura, one of the strongest, bravest women I've ever known. We love you so much and are so glad to have you back with us—where you belong.

After the Ocean Book Club
Discussion Questions

1. Gracie and Meg are entangled in a web of expectations—their own and other people's.

   a. Have you ever done something because it was what someone else wanted or expected for you?
   b. What—if any—regrets do you have surrounding that decision?
   c. Have you ever worked toward a dream or goal for a long time, only to realize that, somewhere along the way, you stopped wanting it? What did you do? How did other people react?
   d. Have you ever gone on to find success where a friend or loved one failed? How did that change your relationship with that person? What, if anything, do you wish you'd done differently?

2. Emilia gave up a lot to keep her daughter safe from her perceived threat of the Winsteads.

   a. Were you ever surprised to learn about a life-changing sacrifice someone had made for you?
   b. If so, how did it change the way you looked at them?
   c. What would you have done had you been in their situation?
   d. To what extent would you give up your own dreams to support a loved one?

3. Emilia never stopped loving Paul, even to the detriment of her marriage to Richard.

   a. Have you ever had a long-lost love that you never totally got over?
   b. How has that affected your life?
   c. Looking back, knowing what you know now, is there anything you'd do differently if you had it to do again?

4. Neither Meg nor Gracie had any idea about their mother's past.

    a. Did you ever uncover a family secret that totally shocked you?

    a. Looking back now what clues were there that you never picked up on?

    b. How did it change the way you think about that person?

5. At the heart of Emilia and Paul's difficulties was his family's belief that she wasn't good enough for him.

    a. How important do you think it is for a family to approve of a relationship?

    b. Have you ever found yourself on the receiving end of that kind of judgment?

    c. How did it affect you?

    d. Have you ever been with someone your family disapproved of?

    e. How did it turn out?

6. It is only with time and perspective that Blaine comes to realize what he took from his brother.

    a. What, if anything, do you regret about the way you treated a sibling?

    b. What life experiences changed your feelings about them or something they did?

    c. What would you do differently if you could?

7. At the end of *After the Ocean,* everyone is reassessing their lives and trying to figure out how best to proceed.

    a. What do you think happens to Emilia and Paul in the end?

    b. Should Emilia forgive Blaine?

Visit our website at
KensingtonBooks.com
to sign up for our newsletters, read
more from your favorite authors, see
books by series, view reading group
guides, and more!

Become a Part of Our
Between the Chapters Book Club
Community and Join the Conversation

Submit your book review for a chance to win exclusive
Between the Chapters swag you can't get anywhere else!
https://www.kensingtonbooks.com/pages/review/